The
New
Forest
Murders

The New Forest Murders

MATTHEW SWEET

**SIMON &
SCHUSTER**

London · New York · Amsterdam/Antwerp · Sydney/Melbourne · Toronto · New Delhi

First published in Great Britain by Simon & Schuster UK Ltd, 2025

Copyright © THE WRITERS' ROOM PUBLISHING LIMITED, 2025

The right of Matthew Sweet to be identified as author of this work has been asserted in accordance with the Copyright, Designs and Patents Act, 1988.

1 3 5 7 9 10 8 6 4 2

Simon & Schuster UK Ltd
1st Floor
222 Gray's Inn Road
London WC1X 8HB

Simon & Schuster Australia,
Sydney

Simon & Schuster India,
New Delhi

www.simonandschuster.co.uk
www.simonandschuster.com.au
www.simonandschuster.co.in

The authorised representative in the EEA is Simon & Schuster Netherlands BV, Herculesplein 96, 3584 AA Utrecht, Netherlands. info@simonandschuster.nl

Simon & Schuster strongly believes in freedom of expression and stands against censorship in all its forms. For more information, visit BooksBelong.com.

A CIP catalogue record for this book is available from the British Library

Hardback ISBN: 978-1-3985-3087-4
eBook ISBN: 978-1-3985-3089-8
Audio ISBN: 978-1-3985-4606-6

This book is a work of fiction. Names, characters, places and incidents are either a product of the author's imagination or are used fictiously. Any resemblance to actual people living or dead, events or locales is entirely coincidental.

Typeset in the UK by Palimpsest Book Production Limited, Falkirk, Stirlingshire

Printed and Bound in the UK using 100% Renewable Electricity at CPI Group (UK) Ltd

For Connie

Part One

Chapter 1

Henry Metcalfe is a little ruined around the eyes. But that's how war marks you, as it robs you of your sleep and your scruples. Henry is exhausted, because killing people is exhausting. Particularly if you do it as he does. Soundlessly, as your victim's lover lies in the next room, waiting for him to come back to bed. Coldly, for King and Country, to save the world from darkness.

Henry could sleep if he let himself. He is in the passenger seat of a dairy van, and the warmth of the evening and the steady growl of the engine seem to argue for it. If he drifted off, nothing would happen. Nobody would get hurt. The headlamps are dipped. The road ahead is straight. He trusts the man at the wheel beside him.

'Do it if you like,' says Karl.

'No fear,' says Henry. 'I can sleep when I'm in the clouds.'

'There are no clouds tonight.'

'Well,' says Henry. 'As long as we have the moon-light.'

The ground is rising. Karl changes gear.

They were lucky at the apartment in Brussels. The lover in the next room noticed nothing. Perhaps she preferred to stay in bed alone. Henry stepped over the body, slipped quietly out of the block with a confident nod to the concierge and found Karl waiting for him in the next street. He was wearing a pair of round wire-rimmed spectacles.

'They're a disguise. I'm a short-sighted Dutch dairy farmer.'

'Not a Communist intellectual?'

'It's a double bluff. Now get in.'

They were just as lucky at the checkpoint. When the young patrolman ordered them to open the back of the van, Henry could sense his nerves. He was like a spear carrier at Covent Garden, not quite sure of the part. His comrade in the roadside hut didn't even get to his feet – and lost interest completely when it became clear that the milk churns in the back were empty. Henry took comfort from this. Two men, somewhere near the end of their tether, somewhere near the end of the war, already calculating how to survive the peace. Maybe they had even decided where to bury their boots and badges.

'Why don't you take your coat off?' asks Karl. 'If

you don't want to fall asleep.' The air is still giving up its heat.

'I might forget it,' says Henry. 'It gets pretty cold up there, you know.'

Henry puts a hand to his chest. He can feel a fat envelope slipped into the lining of his coat. This is the prize for the night's killing. Ten typed pages of official Abwehr documents, as thin as you'd expect in an occupied nation as starved of ink and wood pulp as food. There's something else here, too. A roll of microfilm. One frame, Henry suspects, bears an image of his own face. This is the product of an accident. In the Brussels apartment, there were too many documents to steal. Henry had been hunkered over an attaché case of confidential papers, snapping away with his miniature camera, when their owner made an unexpected return from the bedroom. Sturmbannführer Von Reck gaped in surprise. He was wearing a silk dressing gown embroidered with a pair of dragons – presumably the property of the woman in the room next door. When Henry reached for his garotte, he fumbled the camera. The lens was pointing in his direction.

Click.

The long sleeves of the silk dressing gown made the man clumsy. Henry threw the wire around the German's throat and pulled hard on the garotte's brass handles. Von Reck slumped to the floor.

Perhaps, Henry thinks, when this mission is done, he can snip this shot from the film and give it to his sister. Jill is always complaining about his dislike of being photographed. At home, he avoids it by being the person with his finger on the shutter button.

Jill is two years younger than Henry. She is often in his thoughts. She might be the reason he volunteered for dangerous work in occupied territory: saving your sister is a less abstract idea than saving your country. He is anxious about returning home to her. Jill has always read him like a newspaper, and his story has acquired some new and brutal paragraphs. He thinks of her clear, bright gaze, which always seems to be urging him to get to the point. He can see her walking briskly along a woodland path, her favourite red scarf tied at her neck, the light shifting as she moves beneath the trees. At a certain moment, she sees him. She turns to him. She can see the blood on his hands.

And when the van goes over a bump in the road – the fault of an old root that has burrowed beneath the surface – Henry finds, with a jolt, that he has been asleep for some time. The air is cooler. The trees are thicker and overhang the road.

His hand goes to the envelope. Still there. He turns to Karl, who is looking steadfastly ahead. No harm done.

Henry realizes that he has never dreamed of Jill before.

'This is it,' says Karl. He brings the van to a halt. The silence that follows the death of the engine shocks them both.

And now there is the waiting, at the grassy margin of a field. They share the last of Karl's cigarettes. Listen for the distant rumble of the Lysander.

Henry flicks his stub to the ground. The tobacco is cheap and bitter.

'The next smoke I'll have will be—'

'Don't say it,' Karl says, sighing.

'What?'

'A Lucky Strike,' says Karl, rolling his eyes. 'Some Yank will be offering you one as soon you step off the aeroplane.'

'Will there be cigarettes in the Communist utopia?' asks Henry, raising one of Karl's favourite subjects.

'We'll smoke all day long,' says Karl.

'Will they be good ones?'

'Of course. That's what utopia means.'

'What about the beer?'

'It'll be cold.'

'What about the girls?'

'The opposite, of course.'

Karl tosses his own cigarette into the grass.

'I'd be dead without you, old man,' says Henry. 'If you hadn't been there outside Von Reck's apartment, I'd be in some Nazi basement now. Getting the third degree.'

'Having your final cigarette,' says Karl, nodding.

'You'll get a medal for this, you know, after the war.'

'A big one?'

'The biggest. A proper smasher. Truly, chum. You don't know what you've done, getting me here. The lives you'll have saved.'

From somewhere in the sky above them comes the low drone of the Lysander. Henry and Karl separate, crossing the field like a pair of duellists. When they stop, they shine their torches into the air to guide the pilot down. The Lysander is not a big plane but, barrelling across the pasture, it seems dangerous and powerful, like a charging metal bull. Henry holds his torch steadily. The beam cuts through the darkness. He is on his way home.

These are the events that should happen. The pilot juddering to a halt on the pasture, sliding open the glass panel of the cockpit, waving his passenger forward. Henry running to Karl, clasping his shoulder in a gesture of gratitude, then scaling the access ladder bolted to the matte-black body of the plane. The pilot, with Henry safe inside the rear cockpit, pressing the boost-coil and start buttons, bringing the propellor back to life. The Lysander riding the bumps until it is liberated from the ground and finding that perfect spot above the treetops and below the radar. Henry watching Belgian fields give way to the English Channel.

But this does not happen. Instead, the pilot waits. And waits. He sees a torch lying in the grass. He cuts the engine and peers into the gloom. And against his better judgement, he climbs down from the cockpit to investigate. He finds Henry Metcalfe, coatless on the ground, blood spreading across the cotton of his shirt, his eyes wild.

From the road beyond the field comes the snarl of a starting engine. The dairy van roars off into the night.

'Jack,' breathes Henry. He has the voice of a man who knows he is dying. 'Jack.'

Chapter 2

If you knew Larkwhistle in peacetime, perhaps from a camping holiday or a charabanc trip from Bournemouth or Southampton, you would remember St Cedd's, with its stubby eighteenth-century belltower rising over a nave constructed before the Conqueror. You might also recall the black timbers of the Fleur-de-Lys pub, at the edge of the green where the road turns to meet the forded river. The Post Office, too, beside the tearoom and the butcher's in the Victorian arcade built as an extension of the red-brick railway station. Maybe you would also remember that strange quirk of the New Forest – the horses sauntering between the streets and the thistled fields, oblivious to human boundaries. Not wild, but free to roam under an ancient body of rules that few of its beneficiaries could have quoted in any detail.

But if you visited after 1939 – harder, admittedly, thanks to the radar stations and landing strips that have sprouted here in the last few years – you would notice some absences. No oranges or bananas in the greengrocer. The missing fingerposts, uprooted from the grass during the invasion scare as a precaution against German spies and saboteurs. And the bleakest absence of all – the young men, gone from the cricket team, the congregation of St Cedd's, the public bar of the Fleur-de-Lys. Only the presence of Peter Brock, the vicar's son, ruled out of service by a weak heart, would remind you that Larkwhistle was once a place that could support male inhabitants above the age of sixteen and below the age of fifty. It was a village of women, some hoping for the restoration of the old world, some hoping for a better one.

Mrs Brunton was thinking of that lost place. She often did, as she stood in the kitchen of the Metcalfe family cottage, performing some paid duty that gave her mind the space to wander. For her, as for several families in Larkwhistle, the world divided into before Dunkirk and after. Her son, Michael, had been in the first wave of the British Expeditionary Force. He had gone missing during the week of the evacuation. In Mrs Brunton's daydreams, Michael was in a Prisoner of War camp somewhere in Europe, under a false name, plotting a daring escape. In her nightmares, he was beneath the waves.

'She's good,' said Mrs Brunton, allowing a strip of potato peel to drift to the counter. 'She saw the war coming.'

Jill Metcalfe had walked into the kitchen. This conversation had been going on all morning. 'I'm not sure whether anyone needed a crystal ball for that,' she said.

If you had known Jill's brother, Henry, you would have seen the resemblance straight away. Eyes that were large and brown without a trace of docility. Quizzical eyebrows that Jill's science instructor at the teacher-training college in Southampton had learned to respect. A strong jaw; stronger, perhaps, that she might have liked. Jenny Spode, a girl from the village school who smelled of milk, had once told Jill she could use it to open a sardine tin, and the insult came to her mind whenever she picked one up and turned its key.

'She doesn't use a crystal ball,' said Mrs Brunton, defensively. 'She's a cut above that stuff. Not one of those pier or fairground types. It's a science to her.'

With anyone else, Jill would have relished an argument on this ground. When philosophers wrestled with bishops on the radio, she never took the side of the bishops. But Mrs Brunton was a special case. The kind that develops if you lose your mother at an early age and your father's housekeeper has enough generosity and bodily warmth to comfort you when you graze your knee or find yourself raging at a world that has not played fair, and to share your hope that a boy with whom you once climbed into orchards is hungry, somewhere, behind barbed wire, and not drowned in the English Channel.

'Do you believe in it?' asked Jill, gently. 'A spirit world?'

'I'm not sure,' said Mrs Brunton.

'A place where the dead go about their lives, waiting for us to get in touch with them. What do they do all day, do you think?'

'What do the living do all day?' asked Mrs Brunton, putting the last clean potato in a pan of cold water.

Jill's dog, Wimsey – Henry's dog, Wimsey – bustled into the kitchen, his claws clattering on the linoleum. He looked up at her hopefully.

Jill looked seriously at Mrs Brunton. 'All right. But not a word to Dad. We're just going into Southampton to do some shopping.'

Harold Metcalfe was in the bathroom, combing his hair, of which he had little. Last night's *Portsmouth Evening News* was propped up against the mirror. The door was ajar. Jill stood beside it, neat in her navy-blue jacket and slacks, checking her coupons. 'Curtain rings,' she said. 'And whatever seems fresh at the fishmonger. Anything you want?'

'Belgian chocs?'

'Are you all right, Dad?'

14

'Only a matter of time.'

'Have you concussed yourself in there? I didn't hear the bang.'

'Front page,' he said, putting down his comb. 'Blimey, it's wonderful!'

'What is?'

Jill watched last night's *Portsmouth Evening News* slide through the gap in the door. 'Read it to me,' said Harold. 'It makes me cheerful. And it's being so cheerful that keeps me going.'

She found the story. 'A British Tommy summed up the reaction in Normandy to the new landings in the south of France by saying, "We've been punching Jerry in the face and now we're kicking him in the trousers. Blimey, it's wonderful."'

Harold was brushing his teeth. 'We'll be in Paris by the end of the week, I reckon. After that, the Low Countries. Where the chocolate-covered nuts come from.'

'I bet he didn't say trousers.'

'Eh?' He was spitting into the plughole.

'That Tommy. I bet he didn't say trousers.' Jill pushed open the door and placed the newspaper on the side of the sink.

'Before the First War,' said Harold, 'you could get these boxes of chocs at the pictures. Came with a free gift inside. I had one with razor blades in it. Seemed ridiculous then.'

'And hazardous,' said Jill.

Harold rubbed a hand across his face. 'Imagine it now. Soft centres and a free shave. Paradise.'

Jill kissed him on his cheek. Felt the mild prickle of his stubble. 'I'll do my best, Dad,' she said.

Jill and Mrs Brunton took the shortcut to the railway station across the green. Wimsey raced ahead to gaze, ambitiously, through the door of the butcher's. This desire produced a small disaster when Wimsey's small scruffy body became entangled with the feet of a customer leaving the shop – Captain Patrick Deever, a thin-faced man whose reddish hair was fighting its own war with the green tweed of his jacket. The Captain was not celebrated in the village for his gay sense of humour. He had returned from France in a state of disrepair, his left eye replaced by a glass sphere and his left forearm by a prosthesis retained inside a flesh-coloured glove. Charitable people used this to excuse his habit of asserting blimpish authority over his neighbours, despite having barely reached forty.

The collision with the dog sent his waxed paper package tumbling to the pavement. Jill dipped to her knees and scooped up the item before Wimsey could impose himself upon it.

'I'm so sorry, Patrick,' said Jill. 'He gets under my feet, too.'

Captain Deever blushed. He was a vain man who considered himself a sophisticate, and the incident had embarrassed him. To be knocked off balance, however briefly, by an animal as cheerful and harmless as Wimsey was an affront to his dignity. That Jill had bent down on his behalf to retrieve a small parcel of sausages from the street did not reduce his discomfort.

'It's nothing,' he said. But it *was* something.

'How's Mary Rose?' Jill said, smiling, bringing Wimsey to heel.

Jill did not really listen to the answer: together, she and the Captain produced a small cloud of pleasantries that carried them over the awkward territory in which they had landed. Patrick Deever said his wife was well, that she was busy, and that she was always on the lookout for fresh supplies of typewriter ribbon. If any came Jill's way, he would be glad to know. Though there were moments, he said, when Woodlander House – their bright, clean, modern villa on the road out of Larkwhistle – might benefit from the silence that would follow if she gave up her Remington and switched to longhand.

Jill noticed the gates of the level crossing sinking downward. Their train was about to arrive. She and Patrick Deever made polite gestures of farewell – a tipped hat, a shrug, a nod in the direction of the station. Three minutes later, Jill and Mrs Brunton were settling into a Southern Railways carriage, watching gouts of steam rise from the engine.

As they passed the level crossing, Jill looked out of the window. A jeep was waiting for the train to pass. Nothing unusual about that. The New Forest was a militarized zone. In the past four years, heath and mire had gained new chain-link borders. Huts and hangars had risen like mushrooms. Children had been instructed to jump from their bicycles into roadside ditches at the first sound of an approaching tank. D-Day and the Allied invasion of Normandy had thinned them out in recent weeks, but it was still a common sight to see platoons of soldiers moving down the B roads at dusk.

It was the man behind the wheel who drew Jill's attention. American, obviously. The teeth gave that away, as telegraphically as the cut of his service jacket. Something else, however, compelled her to keep her eyes on him. The faraway expression on his face. One that changed the moment he returned her gaze and made eye contact across the barrier. Changed to what, Jill could not quite say. But she thought about it all the way to Southampton.

Chapter 3

Lodge Road had been a pleasant place before it was undone by the Luftwaffe. Now, tarpaulins flapped on untiled roofs and clouds of willow herb gathered in gaping basements. Number eight, their destination, had been robbed of its railings and gateposts. The knocker was also missing. Mrs Brunton was obliged to use her duck-handled umbrella.

The door was opened by a desiccated housemaid who, despite being visibly undelighted by the presence of Wimsey, stood aside to let them enter.

'Madame Rachel will see you shortly,' she intoned, before disappearing into a back room.

'You didn't say she was French,' said Jill.

'She isn't,' hissed Mrs Brunton. 'She's from Cardiff.'

'"Madame", though?'

'It's an honorific.'

'Oh.'

Other clients sat in the hallway on a row of mismatched chairs. Four women with nothing in common but the faint, sick air of bereavement, or the dread of those who fear its arrival. An old lady in a shopkeeper's apron. Two pale sisters in their twenties, with sleepless, downcast eyes. One sister, Jill noticed, kept the palm of her hand pressed against her belly. The fourth client, a middle-aged matron in an unfashionable cloche hat, seemed faintly familiar to Jill. Perhaps they'd been in a queue together somewhere. Jill watched her fuss with the clasp of her purse and hoped the sense of recognition was not mutual.

The clock ticked. Wimsey went to sleep under a chair.

After a few minutes the maid returned to usher them into the parlour where the séance was to take place. Blackout curtains kept the room dim. Jill registered an old gramophone, a dusty arrangement of artificial flowers, a cabinet of curiosities collected on the travels of some absent seafaring person – and Madame Rachel herself, a mild and smiling figure in a patternless grey tea dress. She was seated at a baize-topped card table, above which was suspended an oil lamp, the only source of light.

The ladies settled themselves around the table. 'All are welcome,' said Madame Rachel, in a forceless and unmusical voice. 'Old friends and newcomers.'

Jill had expected more melodrama, more costume jewellery. Madame Rachel, however, was an unsensational being, and her preamble – a speech about the thinness of the veil between worlds, the organization of life on the Other Side – was entirely matter of fact. She made the spirit world sound municipal, as if it were a branch of local government that could be contacted with the correct telephone extension number.

'Hands on the table,' she instructed. 'The thumbs touching like this. And the little fingers touching those of your neighbours.' Her clients obeyed. Both sisters, Jill noticed, bit their nails.

'It's very important not to break the circle, whoever may come through to us,' warned Madame Rachel. 'If the spirits do come, they come only to help. They can do us no harm.'

The preliminaries over, Madame Rachel nodded to the maid, who set the gramophone running. The needle bumped and crackled, after which a Schubert impromptu underscored Madame Rachel's words. 'Are there any spirits present here today?' she asked the air. 'Does any spirit wish to convey a message to the circle? If so, we are ready to receive it.' She raised her eyes upwards, then closed them in concentration.

Schubert occupied the space of the parlour.

'Your Bill is here again,' said Madame Rachel.

One of the sisters caught her breath.

'Yes?' she replied, in a small, querulous voice.

Madame Rachel smiled, as if responding to a voice audible only to her. 'He's asking about the baby,' she reported. 'Oh. He hopes it's a boy. But he doesn't mind, really.'

The sister with the small voice shifted in her chair. Jill sensed her desire to touch her full belly in conflict with the necessity of keeping the circle unbroken.

'He says you mustn't neglect yourself, Margaret,' said Madame Rachel. 'He's talking about an allotment. Who has an allotment?'

The sister, clearly the Margaret being addressed, looked like a schoolgirl eager to supply the teacher with the correct answer.

'Oh, that's Francis,' she said. 'Bill's cousin Francis. It's on Bunny's Hill.'

Madame Rachel nodded. 'Spinach and French beans will be good for the baby, he says. And stout too, Margaret, he says. Milk stout.'

She opened her eyes. 'You may ask a question.'

For a moment Margaret was silent. Embarrassed, perhaps, to address the spirit of her husband directly.

'Is it cold, Bill?' she stammered. 'On the submarine. Is it cold?'

Madame Rachel's brow furrowed. 'He says it was at first. When the torpedo hit. And the ship went down. But then you feel yourself passing over to the other side. Across the barrier, we call it. And that

22

feels so warm and comforting. Like an eiderdown, he says. Like duck down. Eat the spinach, he says. The baby should be good and strong.'

Margaret let out a great sob of gratitude. 'I will, Bill,' she said. 'I promise.' Tears pooled in her eyes.

Madame Rachel smiled complacently, congratulating herself on her own good work. She bowed her head, as if bidding goodbye to Bill and encouraging some other unseen being to come forward. After a few moments she opened her eyes and turned to Jill and Mrs Brunton.

'The one you seek is not here. He is yet to cross the barrier.'

Mrs Brunton's hand tightened.

'My Michael?' she asked.

'No,' rapped Madame Rachel. She was looking directly at Jill.

'Henry?' asked Mrs Brunton, eagerly.

'So the guides tell me,' confirmed Madame Rachel. She closed her eyes again.

Jill bit her tongue. Mrs Brunton had fed her brother's name to Madame Rachel. Now she would have to endure the sound of it in this woman's mouth. She prepared herself to conceal further discomfort. Madame Rachel was in full flow.

'You will have news of him soon. Perhaps this week. And it will be brought by . . .' She broke off. Her face crumpled into a bashful smile. 'Oh, surely not,' she said, as if in protest about the quality of information relayed by her spirit guides. Opening her eyes, she shrugged apologetically. 'It will be brought by a tall dark stranger.'

The record sputtered to an end. The maid returned the gramophone arm to its cradle. The séance was over.

'We thank the spirits,' said Madame Rachel. 'You are free to break the circle.' The company obeyed. Madame Rachel pressed a consoling hand on the arm of the lady in the unfashionable hat.

'Nothing for you this week, I'm afraid, Muriel.'

Muriel nodded solemnly. Then stopped. A low, insistent scratching sound penetrated the room. Muriel looked upwards, as if she expected to see some demon monkey squatting on the ceiling.

Jill turned to the parlour door.

'That's just my dog,' she said. 'I do apologize.'

As Jill and Mrs Brunton walked back towards the station, a wind was coming in from the sea.

'They're not called ships,' said Jill.

Mrs Brunton looked puzzled.

'Submarines,' said Jill. 'The crews call them boats. Not ships.'

Wimsey darted along the street ahead of them, barking at nothing.

There were no curtain rings to be found that day.

The fishmonger yielded only a coley that Jill might once have thought adequate for a cat.

She and Mrs Brunton parted at Larkwhistle station. Jill urged Wimsey out of the flower bed in front of St Cedd's and turned towards home. Perhaps she could disguise the shortcomings of the fish by adding some French mustard to the poaching milk. She sighed and thought of a filet of sole she had eaten in Quaglino's before the war. Breadcrumbs and butter and a man impressed by her command of menu French. Maybe there would be more nights like that, when the war was over and the lights went up in London. With Henry and his friends, perhaps. Or with someone she had yet to meet. It would be delicious not to have to make do. At mealtimes or with men.

Jill noticed the jeep from the other side of the green. The same US military vehicle she had seen waiting at the level crossing was now parked outside the cottage. She did not give herself time to speculate. As she raced Wimsey to the door, however, she could not quite stop herself recalling Madame Rachel's words about the tall dark stranger.

Seconds later, there he was – an American Air Force captain, rising to his feet in her own living room. His uniform was superbly crisp, his tie precise, his hair glossy, his teeth as white and even as a film star in an advert. There was a tea tray on the table bearing two freshly poured cups. Something, though, was wrong with the picture. Why was he clutching his hat so awkwardly? Why was he not smiling? Why was he looking with consternation from Jill to her father? Jill had no answer. Then she saw the ashen colour of Harold Metcalfe's face.

'Jill,' her father began.

There was no need to say it. She knew in an instant that Henry was dead, and that this American officer with the straight white teeth had brought the news. Something buckled beneath her. It might have been the world.

Chapter 4

There was tea. There was always tea. Now there was also brandy, from a bottle that had been gathering dust in the kitchen since Christmas. Jill had a glass in her hand and could feel the warmth of the alcohol in her throat. She was sitting in the horsehair armchair usually occupied by her father as he filled his pipe and read his PG Wodehouse. The upholstery held the tang of Gold Flake tobacco. It occurred to Jill that this smell would outlive him.

The handsome American was at her knee, almost as if he were proposing.

'We all loved Henry,' he was saying. 'The bravest man I've ever known.' Jill watched his mouth move. She had the impression that he had been speaking for a while. The sound of his voice was pleasant. If only, she thought, it wasn't telling her the worst news in the world.

'Did I faint?' asked Jill. 'I never faint.'

'It's a dreadful shock,' said Harold Metcalfe. 'We feared it, of course. We feared it every day. But you can't prepare for it.'

The kneeling American shook his head.

'I'm so sorry,' said Jill. 'Who are you?'

The American rose to his feet.

'This is Captain Jack Strafford, Jill,' said Harold. 'He was with Henry at the end. Out in the field.'

Jill noticed the pistol in his belt. 'What field?' she asked.

'A joint Allied operation,' said the American. 'Your brother was killed in action. Somewhere in Europe.'

'You sound like the nine o'clock news.'

'I'm sorry, I can't give you any more details.'

'Careless talk,' said Jill, numbly. The phrase tasted sour to her. It meant those foolish ladies in the propaganda posters, gassing indiscreetly as a Nazi waiter served afternoon tea. No talk of Henry could be careless.

'How did it happen?' she asked. 'Was he shot? What can you tell me? Was he captured?'

'He completed his mission,' answered the American. 'I'd like you to know that he was a man of exceptional courage.'

'Would you?' said Jill. She fixed him with a look that her brother would have recognized. 'I think these are just words, Captain Strafford. And they're fine

28

for dispatches or a letter from the Head of the Regiment—'

'I mean them,' said the Captain.

'I'm sure you do,' returned Jill. She was surprised by her own reproachful tone. 'Forgive me. I'd just much rather have the facts.'

'There's nothing to forgive, Miss Metcalfe.'

Jill's questions came more easily than she had expected. The answers, too. Henry's body, Captain Strafford explained, was at RAF Stoney Cross. It would be released to the family after the completion of some simple paperwork. If she wished to view the body at the base before the casket was closed, that would also be possible. If the Captain did not share Jill's natural dislike for euphemism and throat clearing, then he was, at least, respectful enough to defer to it. He spoke with a simple and unaffected clarity, and for Jill, this was enough. This stranger was listening to her; he understood exactly what she required. She was grateful to him for it.

'I can drive you there and back,' said the Captain. 'And help with any other things you might need.' His eyes fell. 'It's why I came, you see. I didn't want to leave it to anyone else.'

Harold sank down on the arm of the chair and curled an arm around his daughter. Jill rested her head against his chest.

'This war,' she breathed. 'This bloody war.'

For a few moments, they sat in silence. Jill thought of her brother running in from the garden, disconsolate over a broken toy. She saw him doing his prep at the dining table, attempting to draw a stickleback kept in a marmalade jar full of pond water. She imagined him lying in front of a winter fire, reading a detective story with a green cover. She remembered him saying goodbye, his uniform and his smile in order.

'We could drink to him,' she said, indicating the brandy bottle on the tea table. Captain Strafford took the hint. He found more glasses and poured out three measures. They raised a toast. A little ritual to help them navigate a conversation that none of them knew how to conduct.

Wimsey scuttered in from the kitchen, where he had gone to drink from his bowl. The dog took an immediate liking to the American officer, nuzzling at the man's leg with his woolly grey head.

'Wimsey!' he exclaimed. 'I've been hoping to meet you.' The feeling seemed to be mutual. Here was proof of a friendship: Captain Jack Strafford knew all the canonical Wimsey stories, from the mysterious affair of the missing lamb chops to the curious incident of the hedgehog in the pantry. He had heard about Larkwhistle, too. He knew about Pam Sharp in the Copper Kettle, the church pew cut from a Spanish galleon, the chequered history of the first eleven. 'I recognized it all as soon as I arrived,' he said. 'The church, the pub, this cottage. Like I'd been here before. He talked about it all so much. I always felt a little envious.'

Jill listened to the cadences of the Captain's voice, trying to place his accent. Polite, well educated, a little strait-laced. Bostonian, perhaps? It was easy to picture him in a college refectory singing 'Ten Thousand Men of Harvard' under a pair of crossed oars. And to imagine Henry mocking him for it.

'Where are you from, Captain Strafford?' she asked. 'You know so much about us. We know nothing about you.'

'Philadelphia. The Mainline.'

He said it like a question, convinced they would not know it. Jill, though, had seen Katharine Hepburn in *The Philadelphia Story* – horsey and smart and haughty and discovering, to her surprise, that she'd loved Cary Grant all along.

'Heavens,' she said. 'Do you have a swimming pool? A butler? A south parlour? A silver omelette dish?'

'Oh, we have two of those,' he said, scratching Wimsey under his chin, and clearly understanding the joke.

Jill smiled sadly. Partly because Henry, whom this man clearly loved, was not in the room, and never would be again. Partly because Captain Jack Strafford was sitting in his place, and Wimsey was so profoundly at ease with him, as Captain Strafford seemed at ease with the world around him. She wondered what it would be like to be part of that world.

In the weeks to come, Jill would often look back on this moment. Not as one of shock and agony, but as a precious hour in which the death of her brother had received proper and undivided attention. The three most important people in Henry's world were thinking of him, and nothing but him. In retrospect, it seemed almost a period of grace. One that ended when Jill looked out through the window and saw a girl running out of the trees.

It took her a few seconds to process the sight. A fast-moving blur of white moving over the grass of the village green resolved itself into the figure of Maggie Speed, daughter of the couple who ran the Fleur-de-Lys. Maggie was eighteen, but childishly slight: visitors to the pub were often surprised to see her serving behind the bar. For four days a week she was a maid-of-all-work at Woodlander House, the home of Patrick and Mary Rose Deever. Jill had known Maggie all her life. Now she watched her running, arms flailing, looking over her shoulder, as if something was pursuing her out of the forest. She was shouting for help.

Jill knocked over the brandy bottle as she rose to her feet. Her father picked it up while she and Jack bolted out of the front door, Wimsey at their heels. Others from the village came running too, including Maggie's father, Wally Speed, the pub landlord – a bar towel still on his shoulder, his customary grin wiped from his face – and Maggie's mother, Effie, her apron flapping, arms outstretched to intercept her child. The Reverend Guy Brock, vicar of St Cedd's – a Good Samaritan in a dog collar and black short-sleeved summer shirt – galloped out of the churchyard with a paperback volume of poetry in his hand.

Effie Speed gathered her daughter in her arms. Wally Speed hovered, asking questions, wanting to know who had hurt her. He was breathless, red-faced, ready for a fight with some unknown assailant. Maggie shook her head and sobbed. She seemed about to begin an explanation.

Then she noticed the Reverend Brock, and a new wave of dread broke over her.

'Peter's in the forest,' she said.

The vicar stared at her.

'He's in the forest,' she repeated. 'Under the fir tree.'

Chapter 5

—

This would be the most contested hour in the history of Larkwhistle. What was said, how they said it, the fitful human traffic. Jill would write it down as a list of points, draw it as a diagram, dream about it in the small hours. When the inquest came, she would describe it to the coroner and listen carefully to the accounts of others, trying to make meaning from the inconsistencies. Events in the world were slippery. They weren't experiments in a laboratory.

One point was fixed in Jill's memory. The sudden change in Guy Brock. With the confidence of someone used to mopping people up or dusting them down, he had run to help a neighbour in need, then discovered the need was his own. The Speeds, meanwhile, executed the opposite manoeuvre. Jill saw it on Wally's face – a father revising his assumption that his daughter had been attacked by some wolf in the woods and losing his anticipation of a hunt. Effie undergoing the same reversal, holding her daughter close, but turning her face to the vicar, knowing that he was now the person who required help. Jill also registered another interaction: the Larkwhistle villagers casting glances towards Jack, the odd one out in a situation too urgent for explanations or introductions.

It was Jack, however, who asked the necessary question first.

'Which fir tree?' he demanded.

'At the fork. Where the path goes to Brockenhurst,' said Maggie.

'The tree in the book?' asked the vicar.

Maggie nodded. And began to weep again. The tree in the book. Everybody but Jack understood the answer, but when Guy Brock launched himself across the green, he followed and kept pace easily.

Jill hesitated, thinking of the inevitable shadow of Wimsey. But here was her father, clipping the lead around the dog's neck, and Mrs Brunton, telling the Speeds to come into the parlour.

Wally Speed had other ideas.

'You go,' he told his wife, and belted for the forest. He was not a fit man, but he knew the way. As Effie raised their daughter to her feet, she watched her husband stumble, panting, over the stile that led to the woods. She imagined herself a widow.

'Should we be calling an ambulance?' asked Harold.

'The police,' said Maggie. 'Nobody can wake him now.'

When Guy and Jack arrived at the fork in the path, they saw a body sprawled among the roots of the fir tree. Something white was wrapped around its head; tightly, like the mask of an Egyptian mummy. A piece of cotton fabric, half of it as bright as it if had just been taken down from the clothesline, the other half wet and scarlet. Perhaps, Guy hoped, this wasn't Peter. Just some other young man in his boots and moleskin trousers.

A figure was hunched at the foot of the fir. He wore flannel trousers and a green tweed jacket. He had two fingers pressed gently on the dead boy's neck.

'I can't find a pulse,' said Patrick Deever. He was soldierly and unexcited, turning to Guy and Jack as if they were all comrades and the forest was a battle-field where casualties were to be expected.

Jack nodded. 'I did my best with the wound,' said Patrick. 'But . . .'

Guy was having none of this. He dropped to his knees and pulled the cotton wrapper from his son's face. His jaw dropped at the sight of what it concealed. He wondered whether to try the mouth-to-mouth resuscitation he'd been taught by the St John's Ambulance. The moment for first aid, however, had passed. The boy was dead: his blue eyes, sightless; his fair hair, somehow still neatly parted, darkened by blood as well as brilliantine. The left side of his face was open like a burst bag of flour.

The Reverend Brock fell upon the broken body of his child and drew it close. Blood was transferred to his skin like a potato print. He closed his eyes and gave out a low animal moan. It hit the trees. It was *addressed* to the trees. This was a primal scene of death and violence, and the forest had heard it a thousand times before.

Jill heard it, too, as she arrived. When Jack saw her, he moved in her direction; partly, she realized, to block her view of the corpse. Whether this was to spare her distress or the Reverend Brock's dignity, she could not tell.

'There's no hope,' said Jack.

Patrick placed his good hand on Guy's shoulder. 'I'm so sorry, old man,' he said. 'It's a damned tragedy. A damned waste.' He caught Jill's eye. He looked at her as if he felt he owed her an explanation.

'I heard the shot,' he said. 'I heard the shot and came running.'

Jill noticed that Patrick wore no shirt beneath his green tweed jacket. A bloodied cotton object lay in the grass nearby. He must, she surmised, have used it to staunch the wound.

Guy Brock stayed locked in an embrace with his

son. He was muttering. Apologizing, Jill thought. His eyes were glassy, as if he too had shifted out of the world. He paid no attention as Wally Speed came to a halt nearby and stood with his hands pressed to his hips, making a noisy attempt to catch his breath. The landlord looked as if he were about to be sick. Jill willed him to keep his lunchtime pint in his stomach.

Jack's eyes were darting over the ground. 'Where's the gun?' he said. 'This is a gunshot wound. There must be one here somewhere.'

'If he did it himself,' breathed Jill. 'Otherwise . . .'

She began pushing at the tangle of ferns beside the path, hoping to spot something metallic. She looked to Wally for help, but saw, instantly, that this was pointless. The publican stood, wheezing, made useless by the horror of the spectacle and his own weak lungs.

And here a new dancer entered the ballet. A compact, wiry man with a face that had acquired its wrinkles from the sun rather than the years. He moved easily and quietly through the trees. Another serviceman, Jack surmised.

'Ambulance is coming from Ashurst,' said the new arrival. 'And police. Ivy put the call through.' Patrick nodded in acknowledgement.

'Can you help us, Sam?' asked Jill. 'We're looking for a gun.'

Sam Hill squinted at the body on the ground; then he noticed the uniformed American. For a moment Jack thought he was going to salute. Instead, Sam picked up a stick and prodded at the undergrowth. He did it carefully, diligently; turning ferns, peering beneath them. Jack watched him carefully: he seemed the kind of man who might move over fields and woodland without leaving a trace.

Guy brought the search to an end. He removed Patrick's hand from his shoulder and rose to his feet, then bent down again and pushed both arms beneath the body of his son. It was difficult and awkward, but grief gave him strength.

'Guy,' said Jill. 'It's probably best to wait. Until the police get here.' She knew it was useless to protest. It was hard to say whether the Reverend Brock could hear her. He was rising to his feet, cradling Peter's corpse in his arms.

'Sir,' said Jack, in a calm and steady tone, 'if he's going to be moved, then let me help you.'

The voice of a stranger cut through. Guy looked at Jack and shook his head. 'He's my son,' he said. 'I'm taking him home.'

He began to walk, with a slow, Frankenstein trudge, down the path that led back to the village.

'His wife's at home,' said Jill. 'She can't see this. Just turning up on the doorstep. It'll kill her.'

'Run ahead then,' said Jack. 'Soften the blow.'

Jill obeyed. She ducked around the vicar and his cargo and raced on through the forest. Jack turned back to the tree. Its roots broke the ground into a network of little canyons and ravines. There, on the patch of ground that had been hidden by Peter Brock's body, was a standard-issue Army service revolver.

Sam Hill was staring at it.

'That's my bloody gun,' he said. And picked it up.

Chapter 6

It was like a dread pageant. May Day with a dead boy rather than a cheerful, garlanded girl. When the procession passed by, the mothers of Larkwhistle drew their children close. Others simply stared. Harold watched through the leaded windows of the cottage, and hoped that Maggie and Effie Speed would not turn to follow his gaze.

First came the Reverend Guy Brock and his awful burden, each step like one to Calvary. He did not look at the other villagers but kept his gaze on the spire of St Cedd's: the one fixed point in a changing age. Next, at a respectful distance, came Jack, his American stripes and brass buttons increasing the sense of ceremony. Behind him, Wally, sickly and colourless, his gut grateful for the funereal pace. At the rear, Sam Hill and Patrick Deever, straight-backed like the infantrymen they were. Sam carried a bundle in his hands. This was his revolver, bagged up in Patrick's bloodied shirt like a pudding wrapped in muslin.

They crossed the green and moved towards the Brocks' home; the Platonic ideal of an English vicarage, with a bed of hollyhocks in front of the kitchen window and wisteria drooping over the door.

As they neared the gate, the front door burst open and Helena Brock reeled out. She narrowed her eyes like someone looking out to sea, expecting a shipwreck. Helena was not well liked in the village. She was considered difficult; too clever by half; insufficiently deferent to her husband. Being a university graduate was thought to be the cause. Her predecessor had been wholly uneducated and, some thought, seemed all the more content for it. It was she who had planted the hollyhocks.

Jill was standing behind Helena, just inside the hallway, her bad news already communicated. The vicar's wife reached back towards her, using Jill to steady herself but also pushing her out of the way. Helena took a deep breath and ran down the crazy-paving path to meet her husband.

They did not embrace. The body of their child was between them. There were obstacles of feeling, too. Helena flinched at the sight of her son; his bloody incompleteness. She shook her head; put her hand to her mouth; looked at Guy as if she believed that he had fired the gun.

Unspoken protocols took over. Guy carried the body across the threshold as a bridegroom might carry a bride. Helena moved ahead of him, ushering her husband into the dining room, indicating that she required Jill's help to clear the table. The two women moved the candlesticks and the gingham cloth and the empty glass fruit bowl. They lifted Peter's crystal wireless set from one of the dining chairs and set it in the corner of the room. Guy brought the boy in, settling his body on the table as gently as he could.

In the plain domestic space of the vicarage, the sight of Peter's wounded face seemed even more terrible. This was his home. His nature books were on the shelf. His fishing rod was propped beside the window, half-repaired.

Helena took the gingham cloth and settled it over the body, turning the table into a catafalque, the room into a chapel. It was an old building. It was an old table. Both had performed the service before.

'It should be white,' said Helena. 'Not checks. I've no clean linen.' Her fist was at her temple, her breathing quick and shallow.

'We've got some,' said Jill. 'I'll bring it over.' War had reduced everything to cheerless practicalities. It gave you no space to scream or be sad.

'Right,' said Helena, blankly. She noticed Jack

standing in the hall like a pallbearer. 'Who are you?' she asked.

'Captain Jack Strafford, ma'am.' He offered his condolences in the way that strangers do.

'You one of those boys from Stoney Cross?' she asked. Jack made a noncommittal sound. More careless talk.

'The Captain was here to bring some news about Henry,' said Jill, quietly. 'It's bad, I'm afraid. Killed in action.' The news added more weight to the air. 'Still,' she continued, filling the silence, 'he came to tell me in person. I suppose that's better than one of those awful War Office telegrams. I've always dreaded them.'

Jill and Helena were standing close together. For a moment it seemed as if they would embrace. It might have happened, had Guy not torn his eyes from the shape beneath the tablecloth and broken his silence.

'We'll bury them together,' he said. 'Peter and Henry.'

Something in this remark angered Helena. Possibly because he had said it in his pulpit voice; possibly because he had spoken at all. She began to usher Jack and Jill back out into the hallway. She did so quickly and irritably, as if repelling a bee that had flown in through the window. Then she returned to the little dining room and pulled her husband away from Peter's body. He held up his hands in a gesture of surrender and allowed himself to be bundled through the door.

'I think I need to clear the house,' said Guy. Jack and Jill accepted his wishes. The vicar showed them out, muttering thanks and apologies. When he opened the front door, he saw Patrick and Sam standing at the vicarage gate like sentries. Patrick was absurdly shirtless. Guy registered other people from the village hovering on the green, not wanting to come closer, not wanting to leave. The butcher called out his condolences over the hedge, blushed and shuffled away. As he went, a new arrival broke through the knot of onlookers and approached the gate; a woman just shy of thirty, wearing a tight grey sweater and lipstick too red for a weekday afternoon. She held a mildly unhappy ten-month-old baby at her shoulder. Ivy Hill, the postmistress, had something to say to her husband.

'They should be here in ten minutes,' she told Sam. 'The police.' Postmistresses spoke to each other over the lines: easy for them to track a siren's progress from village to village.

It was at this moment that Ivy noticed the shape of Helena Brock. The dining room windows were open. She was staring in panic and bafflement at the small crowd of people who had gathered outside her home.

'Mrs Brock,' said Ivy Hill. 'I'm so very sorry.'

Helena returned her gaze, with an expression of ice-cold anger.

'Are you?' she asked. Jack was surprised by the hostility in her voice. More village history, he assumed, unreadable to strangers. Helena seemed about to challenge Ivy further, but the moment passed. She closed the windows, snapped down the brass latches and pulled the curtains tight shut.

The Reverend Brock was dazed. He opened his mouth as if to make a speech to thank everybody for coming.

'I . . .' he began, but the words did not arrive. He moved back inside the vicarage and closed the door gently behind him.

Patrick Deever shifted awkwardly in his tweed jacket. 'Tell the police I'm going home to get a shirt,' he said. 'I imagine they'll want to take statements. But I can hardly do that half-dressed, can I?'

He eyed the bloody bundle in Sam's hands. 'What are you going to do with that?' he asked.

Sam shrugged. 'Give it to the coppers. I don't want it.' He was frowning and agitated. 'That boy must have nicked it, the bloody fool.'

'Here,' said Patrick, removing the bundle from Sam and pressing it upon Jack. 'You take it. You're the senior officer here.'

It was now in Jack's hands.

'Why not let everyone in the village touch it?' said Jill, testily.

Jack took the point, but it was too late.

'Wouldn't make much of a detective, would I?' he said.

'Don't worry,' she said. 'You're an airman, aren't you?'

The baby on Ivy Hill's shoulder began to cry.

'Shh, Martin,' said Ivy.

Martin flailed a fat little arm across his mother's mouth, smearing her lipstick and leaving a streak of carmine across his hand. Sam sometimes winced at the sound of his son's cries. Often they stirred as much anger in him as love, and he wished that this was not so. Not at this moment. He took the little boy from the arms of his wife and held him close and wept.

Chapter 7

Larkwhistle held its breath that day. The butcher pulled his shutters down early. The Fleur-de-Lys was quiet. The sight of Wally Speed behind the bar, contemplating the middle distance, did not encourage customers to linger. The book club ladies rang round to cancel that week's meeting. Helena Brock was the secretary. Her friends in the village, of which there were few, had little appetite for sitting without her, trying to think of interesting things to say about Dostoevsky. Mary Rose Deever approached the vicarage door, intending to offer her condolences, but found her knock unanswered. Most people returned to their homes, like chess pieces removed to their starting positions on the board. Two more were missing now.

Henry Metcalfe had been gone from Larkwhistle for over a year. To most of its inhabitants, his absence was a kind of abstraction. When men leave their village to fight, death has them on approval and sometimes chooses to keep them. No arrangement had been made for Peter. That he had been torn from them without leaving home was beyond the rules of the game.

Jill gazed at the black Wolseley police car parked outside the vicarage. She had not seen the officers emerge, but a uniformed constable now stood on guard at the gate, blinking into the sun.

Jack finished his call and put down the receiver. 'Obliged for the use of your telephone, sir,' he said. 'Wouldn't want my CO to think I'd gone to the pub. Though I suppose I'd better go and see if he has a room free tonight. What was his name, the landlord?'

'Wally Speed,' said Harold, from the kitchen. 'But you should stay with us tonight. In Henry's room. If that's all right?'

Jill looked back from the window. Neither she nor Jack was sure whose consent was being sought.

'Of course,' said Jack. He looked at Jill, hoping he had said the right thing. He had, but Jill could not help but wish her father had made the offer with her agreement, or, at the least, while they were both in the same room.

Harold emerged from the kitchen with a fresh pot of tea. His eye was drawn by movement on the other side of the green. A man in his mid-thirties was on his way towards them. He had a sandy moustache, grown to make himself look older, a smart fawn raincoat that was too hot for the day and the inevitable fedora of a plain clothes policeman. A constable walked with him.

'It's Len Creech,' said Jill. 'I had no idea he'd been promoted.'

'Came to me for a reference,' said Harold. 'Looks so like his dad, doesn't he?'

Harold let Len in. The visitor had already taken his hat off. He stepped inside and left his constable at the door.

'Mr Metcalfe,' he said, smiling effortfully. 'Miss Metcalfe. I'm really very sorry to burden you with this. On today of all days.'

'Ah,' said Jill. 'You've heard, have you?'

'Captain Strafford brought us the bad news,' explained Harold. 'I'm afraid the village has given him some trouble in return.'

'How are they over there?' asked Jack. 'At the vicarage.'

'A direct hit, I'd say, sir,' Len sniffed. 'I'm bringing the pathologist over from Southampton to examine the body. Get it over and done with. The lad should be at the undertakers. Not on the dining room table.'

'I should be offering you some of this tea,' said Jill.

'There's no need,' said Len.

'I dare say. But it always seems the thing to do,

doesn't it? When you want to yell at the world and give God a piece of your mind.' She let out a bitter sigh. 'There I was thinking that after D-Day everything would be peaches. But Death's not done with us yet, is he?' She nodded across the green. 'That marriage won't survive it.'

Len felt ill-equipped to answer. He had always thought Jill a good-looking girl who scared him with her cleverness. His feelings had not changed.

'I'm told you have some evidence for me?' he said.

Jill ushered the policeman into the kitchen. Wimsey, lying in his basket, remained unexcited by the presence of a stranger. Even he was done with the day. Above him, on the kitchen table, was a glass bell jar used for the storage of cake. The object inside the jar made Len Creech think of a kind of pink meringue he had liked as a child. It was Patrick Deever's shirt, its bloodied mass enfolding the dark shape of Sam Hill's gun.

Len pulled a pencil from his jacket pocket, lifted the glass lid and teased at the bundle, exposing the revolver.

'I doubt you'll get many fingerprints off it,' said Jill. 'It was under the body, in the dirt, and then it was handed around like pass the parcel.'

Len grunted and replaced the lid. 'Let's just leave it here for a moment.'

They returned to the living room. 'The movement

of the body is a bit of a pill, isn't it?' said Jill. 'I'm afraid we couldn't stop him. Guy Brock was beyond reason, really, poor chap. The animal instincts take over, I think, in those circumstances. He had to gather up his boy. Bring him home.'

'Who else was at the scene?' asked Len.

'He got there before me,' said Jill, indicating Jack.

'I was fourth at least,' corrected Jack. 'The landlord's daughter was there before us. Have you interviewed her?'

'Well, I've had a go,' said Len, 'but she's pretty shaken. I may have to leave it until tomorrow.'

'She was sweet on Peter,' said Jill. 'Poor girl. She used to moon over him from the other side of the bar. They stepped out together once or twice. Village dances, that kind of thing. But the jitterbug wasn't really Peter's forte.'

'You think it was reciprocated, then?' asked Len.

'I think they may have kissed on the steps of the church hall, if that's what you're asking,' said Jill. 'But I didn't follow them home. If you want all the details, you'll have to ask Maggie.'

Len Creech fussed with his notepad. He was very chapel. Like his father, mentions of romance made him uneasy. 'So, of your party,' he asked, 'who reached the body first?'

'Guy Brock and then me,' said Jack. 'But Patrick Deever was there when we arrived.'

'What was he doing?' asked Len. 'Captain Deever?'

'He'd been trying to give first aid, I think,' said Jack. 'Using his shirt as a bandage or a tourniquet. But he gave up and used it to cover the boy's face. I've seen it in combat. Men do strange things around dead bodies. Rituals, I guess. You can't just leave a man how he fell. How the enemy has left him.'

'He looked frightful,' said Jill. 'I think there was wisdom in what Patrick did. Trying to spare others the sight.'

'Do you think he might have taken anything from the body?' asked Harold. 'Saw a lot of that in Flanders.'

'Robbery?' asked Len.

'You needn't call it that,' said Harold. 'The Captain's right about the battlefield. I carried a man's pocket diary for months. And a photograph. Took it round to his sweetheart when I came home on leave. Wasn't a picture of her, it turned out. It was Violet Hopson.'

'His mistress?' asked Len.

'Violet Hopson was quite popular before the talkies,' said Harold, mournfully. 'Felt a fool for not recognizing her. But I never was much of a one for the flicks, really. Especially anything with policemen. If you're not Sexton Blake you're an idiot.' He took a sad sip of tea.

Len turned to Jack and Jill.

'I think I'd like you to take me to the scene,' he said.

They got to their feet. Len pushed open the front door of the cottage, replaced his hat and tipped a wink to the constable standing dutifully outside. The afternoon was still bright and sunny. The kind of weather for lying in the grass and watching the clouds unfurl.

Jill was the first to see that something was amiss. The ground around the tree had been disturbed. The soil and moss around the roots had been dragged; the bracken was hacked and broken.

'Did you do this after I left?' asked Jill.

'I think I snapped a fern or two, looking for that gun. But not this.'

'What about Mr Hill?' asked Len.

Jack surveyed the damage. 'No. He went about it very delicately. Like he was going through his hand-kerchief drawer.'

'Where was the body?' asked Len.

Jack indicated the space. 'And the gun was beneath it.'

'Where it should have stayed,' said Jill.

'I agree,' said Len. 'How was the body lying? Did you sense there had been a struggle?'

'I think your pathologist will be the best judge of that, Len,' said Jill. 'If there was someone else here, you might find traces of them under his fingernails.'

'He was on his back,' said Jack. 'And the gun was

in a groove between the roots of the tree. If you're suggesting that he did it himself, I don't think we saw anything that would contradict you. He pulled the trigger, he dropped the gun on the ground, he fell backwards. So, nobody saw it until Guy Brock lifted up the body.'

'Who saw it first?' asked Len.

'Sam Hill, I think,' said Jack. 'He knew it was his straight away.'

'Yes,' Len confirmed. 'He reported it missing two weeks ago.'

'Missing or stolen?'

'Missing. That's what he told my desk sergeant, anyway.'

'So, for a fortnight that gun has been somewhere in Larkwhistle,' said Jack. 'In the hands of persons unknown. Until it ended up in the hands of Peter Brock. But did he pull the trigger?' He looked up into the branches of the tree, as if he thought they might whisper the answer.

'This was a service revolver, yes?' he asked. 'Where did Sam Hill serve?'

'With Patrick,' said Jill. 'They were in the BEF and evacuated at Dunkirk. Captain and Sergeant. Some of the last out, I'm told. Both came back wounded. Patrick more than Sam, though. Poor man. He gets frustrated with himself. He's adapted pretty well, but how do you tie a tourniquet with only one good hand?'

Jack examined the roots of the tree. The soil between them had been scored and scratched. 'Somebody's churned up the ground where he fell.'

'Don't jump to conclusions, Captain,' said Jill. 'An animal might have done this. The woods are full of crows and badgers. Foxes. Plenty of creatures appreciate a lick of blood on the forest floor.'

Len Creech went down on his haunches. 'There might have been something here for us to see. Footprints maybe. But whatever it might have been is gone now.'

Jill looked down. It was like a book that had once told a story, defaced and vandalized until nothing could be read.

'He'd have known,' said Jill. 'Animal tracks, broken twigs. Very much Peter's sort of thing. He was a proper forest boy. Much more so than Henry, really. Henry was born here. But he couldn't tell one bird from another. He just wanted to play cowboys and Indians.'

'When the girl from the pub was telling us where to find the body,' said Jack, 'the vicar said something about this tree. The tree in the book. What did he mean?'

'When we go back home,' said Jill, 'I'll show you.'

Chapter 8

The bell jar was gone from the Metcalfes' kitchen table. Len Creech had extracted Patrick's bloodied shirt for examination, after which Mrs Brunton had used her Jeyes Fluid without mercy and returned the glass to the back of the pantry. Now its place on the table had been taken by a fish pie – the morning's meagre catch of coley, bulked up with hard-boiled eggs and entombed below a layer of mashed potato. Fish and meat were scarce, but even in wartime the Metcalfes had never wanted for milk and eggs. It puzzled outsiders. New Forest people knew New Forest people.

'He'd never have eaten that,' said Mrs Brunton. 'He hated fish pie. I don't think I'll make it again.'

Jack watched her get up and clear the table. The Metcalfes employed Mrs Brunton to cook their meals and clean their house. However, every night she sat and ate with the family before washing the dishes and then leaving to go back to her own cottage. He thought of his mother in her house on the Mainline and tried to imagine Barrett, his mother's help, mixing her a highball and then sinking down next to her on the divan. Which of them would be more horrified? He found it impossible to say.

Larkwhistle had not rested that afternoon. From the cottage, Jack marked the movement of the policemen as they went from door to door. He watched the pathologist from Southampton enter the vicarage and emerge again. He saw the ambulance arrive and lowered his eyes as Peter's body was brought out beneath a blanket and borne away to the undertakers.

There had been visitors to the cottage, too. A constable, pulled unwillingly from retirement at the start of the war, asked them questions and filled his notebook with their descriptions of the day. The butcher delivered a note, written in the same swooping hand he used to paint up prices on his window. (There were several spelling mistakes: perhaps he only knew words for meat.) Effie Speed called and wept a little and talked about Henry and wondered whether she ought to follow her visit to the Metcalfes with a call to the vicarage. Jill advised against it.

Ivy Hill also arrived to express her sorrow; as did

her baby, in his own malcontented way. The postmistress had no intention of crossing the green to bring the same message to Helena and Guy. Everyone had already seen her try and fail.

'Is Mrs Hill not liked at the vicarage?' asked Jack, once she had gone.

'Or too well liked,' said Jill. 'By Guy. That's what Helena thinks, anyway. There was a time when Ivy was never out of church. Some women are awfully peculiar around vicars. Perhaps it's the incense.'

'She doesn't need to breathe anything in, that one,' said Harold. 'It's all smoking away inside her.'

'Don't be vulgar, Dad,' said Jill.

Harold was undiscouraged. 'She even does it with me sometimes. Making eyes. And she was doing it with *him*.' He jabbed his empty pipe in Jack's direction.

'Me?' said Jack.

'Of course, you,' said Harold, filling his pipe. 'Don't know how Sam Hill sticks it. Still, I'll say this for Ivy, there were an awful lot of GIs around here before D-Day. And she wasn't the sort to go riding in the back of a jeep, if you take my meaning. Not like that Pam Sharp from the Copper Kettle.'

'I do apologize for my father,' said Jill.

'He's in the forces,' said Harold, looking to Jack for support.

'He's from Philadelphia,' said Jill. 'And he's polite. Aren't you?'

'Impeccably,' said Jack. 'Unless I really want to know something.' He turned to Harold. 'So, Ivy and the vicar were an item?'

'So I always thought,' said Harold, warming to the subject. 'And Guy Brock was always going to be an object of interest in Larkwhistle because Helena is such a cold fish. Mind you, I always thought the vicar had his eye on Captain Deever's wife.'

Jill pursed her lips. 'When police officers retire, they have to acquire a new interest,' she said. 'With my father it seems to be rural adultery.'

'The Captain's wife is a writer, yes?' asked Jack.

'Oh yes,' said Jill. 'She's a bit older than Patrick. Though she tries to look younger, and he seems to be turning into Colonel Blimp, so you'd never know.'

'What does she write?'

Jill reached over to the shelf behind her father's chair and took down a sextodecimo volume in a bright green wrapper. 'There you go.'

Jack examined the book. The cover bore the idealized image of a boy about eight years old, with apple cheeks and a mop of yellow hair. The illustrator had given him a curiously feminine red mouth. He was wearing a dark green shooting jacket but carried no gun. Instead, he held a walking stick over one shoulder, from the end of which was suspended a bundle of the sort that Dick Whittington usually carried on his way to London. This boy, however, was heading into the forest. Above him spread the branches of an enormous fir. And above the fir, the title and the name of the author, in letters that appeared to grow from the branches. *The Boy Among the Trees*, by Mary Rose Deever.

'Maggie was right,' he said. 'This is the tree where Peter Brock was found.'

'And the boy is Peter Brock,' said Jill. 'When he was small.'

Jack gazed at the illustration. This little being, endowed with adventurous optimism, seeking his fortune, at the beginning of his story.

'It's a damned peculiar book,' said Harold. 'I always thought there was something devilish about it. But people seem to love it. Most of us in the village have a copy. I suppose it's something to be proud of.' He did not look convinced. 'Does she still stock it at the Post Office?'

'I've not noticed it for a while, Dad,' said Jill.

'It was always there,' said Harold. 'In the news-agent's too. Before the war, when we had more ramblers and day-trippers, people would sometimes turn up with a copy, hoping to get a dedication from herself, Mary Rose Deever. They used to ask where she lived.'

'And did you tell them?' asked Jack.

'The respectable-looking ones,' replied Harold. 'I think she liked strangers arriving at her gate in summer to tell her how brilliant she was. But if they asked about the boy, we never let on. Not good form. Our own Christopher Robin didn't like publicity. He didn't like attention.'

Someone knocked at the cottage door. It was an unwelcome sound.

'And neither do I,' Harold muttered, striking a match. 'I know they're doing it out of consideration, but I wish they'd show a bit more, well . . . consideration.'

As he struggled to find the word, Jack saw Harold's brave face fall. There was only so much sympathy a man could bear.

'Can we just thank this one on the step?' asked Harold, drawing air through his tobacco. But Jill had already opened the door. Guy Brock was standing on the threshold. He had changed his clothes and combed his hair, but his exhaustion was undisguisable. Jill noticed a scratch on his face. Unsurprising, as he had carried Peter's body through the trees. Jack put the picture book down on the table, face down next to a copy of the *Radio Times*.

'I wanted to offer my condolences,' said the vicar.

'Really, Guy,' said Jill, 'it's awfully good of you. But it's too good. There's no need. You must think of yourself and Helena.' She hoped that he would come no further.

'And I wanted to thank you, Jill,' he pressed on. 'And the Captain. I'm very grateful you were there.'

Jack was on his feet. 'As Miss Metcalfe says, there's no need.' Not for the first time that day, he felt unsure of English etiquette.

'Well, there is,' said Guy. 'I wanted to say something to Harold.' He moved forward into the living room and approached the old man in his chair. 'We have something in common, Harold. Something grave and terrible of which we were both quite ignorant when we woke up this morning.'

'It's true,' said Harold. His resistance had drained away. He motioned to Guy to sit.

'We're not unique in the village,' said Guy. 'Other fathers have lost other sons. But today, it was you and I. So, I just wanted to say that I would consider it an honour if you wished me to conduct the service.'

Harold would have replied, had Guy not raced on with his plans. 'I'm going to do the same for Peter,' he said. 'And I thought it might be fitting for the interments to take place on the same day. Saturday, perhaps? I know it's a bit unconventional, but Friday doesn't give much time for administration and, well, it's my church. And afterwards we might gather in the vicarage garden. We have the space. Many of the mourners will be the same people. Perhaps you might even consider a shared service.'

He faltered, realizing he had pushed too far. 'Just something for you to think about,' he said. 'The offer is there. So do chew it over. Let me know in the morning, perhaps, and I can set the wheels in motion. The diocesan stuff, you know.'

Guy was moved by thoughts he could not articulate. His own grief. His duty to salve the grief of his parishioners. The daily brutalities of the Problem of Evil. He put a hand on Harold Metcalfe's arm. Harold allowed him to keep it there, but more out of generosity than his own desire.

'When did you last see him, Reverend Brock?' asked Jack. 'Your son?'

The question sounded cold and professional. Hostile even, thought Jill. But she wanted to know the answer all the same.

'An hour or so before we found him,' said Guy Brock, withdrawing his hand from Harold's arm.

'And do you know why he went to the woods?' asked Jack.

'Because he went to the woods every day,' said Guy. 'He practically lived there.'

'Did you notice anything unusual about him that morning?' pressed Jack. 'Was he worried about anything? Was he pleasant? Did you argue?'

'We always argued,' said the Reverend, with a sad smile. 'There were times when we seemed to do very little else.'

'Argue about what, may I ask?' The words were polite for someone who clearly had no intention of taking no for an answer.

'Bombs,' said Guy. 'Economic warfare. But I came round to his way of thinking. He was a good teacher, my son. At first, you see, I was hoping against hope. I think a lot of us were. We wanted Chamberlain to be right. We wanted Munich to be the answer. Give Mr Hitler those little bits of land, and his appetite will be satisfied. And after that, well, there was a part of me that thought a German bomb hitting the church here was a less complicated moral problem than a British bomb landing on some family in Germany or Austria.'

Jack raised an eyebrow. 'That's a very honest answer,' he said.

'You were never a conchie, Guy,' said Harold. 'You don't have anything to apologize for.'

'Oh no,' said Guy Brock. 'It never came to that.'

'You did your bit bravely,' said Harold.

'How?' asked Jack.

'Because he met a Nazi, Captain Strafford,' said Harold. 'He met a Nazi in the forest.'

The vicar looked at Harold.

'Go on,' said the old man. 'Tell him the story. It'll show him who you are.'

Guy obeyed. 'He was pretending to be a hitchhiker who'd lost his way,' he said. 'But I'd already seen the parachute. He'd tried to hide it in the gorse. So I pretended I was convinced. Walked with him for a bit, along the edge of the mire by the shooting range.

Bringing him to Larkwhistle. It seemed the best thing. I could see he had a bit of a limp.'

'From the landing, I guess?' said Jack.

'Yes,' said Guy. 'He'd done his ankle in. And he saw that I'd noticed. He told me that was the reason why he wasn't in khaki. Something about childhood illness and the long jump team and an iron lung. Cock and bull story, really. So, I smiled and nodded.'

The tale put Guy Brock on a well-trodden path. But a new thought struck its teller. 'Do you know what I was worried about? I was worried about the moment when he stopped believing that I believed him. No, that's not quite right. The moment when he pretended to stop believing that I believed him. Because then he was going to have to do something about it. So, I decided to call his bluff. I told him I'd been listening to the wireless. And I'd heard a good joke about the ration. And I asked him if he preferred Gert and Daisy to Elsie and Doris Waters. And he said he thought that Gert and Daisy had the edge.'

'So, Gert and Daisy don't have the edge?' asked Jack.

'They're the same people,' explained Jill.

'Ah,' said Jack. 'And that was the moment? When he knew that you knew?'

'Yes,' said Guy. 'So, we walked a bit more. And then he went for his gun, and I threw myself at him.

Like I was on the rugger field, you see? And over he went. And . . .' He took a breath. 'And that's how I came to kill a German.'

'What happened?' asked Jack.

'I called out for help,' he said.

'Did any come?'

'Eventually.'

'We were coming anyway,' said Harold. 'We saw the chute come down. We were on our way with garden forks and spades. We must have looked a proper mob.'

'I hadn't been in a fight since school,' said Guy. 'Scrapping isn't considered the thing at theological college. Not in the C of E, anyway. And the gun went off. They make a tremendous noise, don't they, Captain Strafford? And I rather assumed it was me who was done for. Then I saw his eyes. The light going out of them. I've seen it on a hundred death-beds.' He gave a great sigh. 'All a bit of a mess, really. Nothing heroic about it. But try telling that to Peter. I was forgiven in a moment.'

Guy Brock's eye went to the clock on the mantel-piece. 'Well,' he said. 'Do come over when you've had a thought about hymns.'

Jill put a supportive hand on the vicar's shoulder. 'Guy's missed out an important part of that story,' she said. 'He went back and pulled the parachute out of the bushes. That silk went a long way that summer.

There'll be some ladies in Larkwhistle wearing it right now.'

'Well,' said Guy, 'it's good to know that a priest can make a material difference to the lives of his parishioners.'

As he got to his feet, he noticed the copy of *The Boy Among the Trees* lying open on the table. 'I see you've been doing some reading,' he said. Jill apologized and put the book back on the shelf.

'There's no need to hide it away,' said the vicar. 'There's no escaping that thing.'

'I suppose,' said Jill, 'it's given him a kind of immortality. People do love it so.'

Guy Brock snorted. 'I can't think of it that way, I'm afraid. It was a burden to Peter in life and it seems the same to me in death. A burden to the whole family. Helena hates the thing. Hates it. Won't have it in the house. She burned our copy.'

'I'd like to talk to Helena,' said Jill. 'Do you think she'd mind if I called tomorrow?'

'Of course,' said Guy. 'You're always welcome. At this time more than ever.'

Jack slept in Henry's bedroom that night. It was not a child's room, but the relics of childhood were plainly visible. A scuffed cricket bat was propped against the wall; the bedside table housed an illuminated globe that mapped the borders of the pre-war world; a shelf bore a box of ammonites and belemnites quarried on a seaside holiday. The only books in the room were a broken-backed run of Bulldog Drummond adventures.

Jack was tired, but he did not get straight into bed. First, he examined the globe. He shook it, held it up to the light, peered carefully at its surface. He opened the bedside drawer as quietly as he could, and lifted the wallpaper lining. An examination of the wardrobe revealed nothing of interest. Then he turned to the books, lifting them from the shelf like a concertina and setting them down on the bed. He produced a small green notebook from his jacket pocket and peered at the first few pages. His handwriting was neat and clear. He then took each novel in turn, looked carefully at the cover illustration and back blurb, fanned the pages to release any paper hidden inside and checked the text against his notes.

He recalled these stories from his own childhood reading – breathless intrigues involving artificial diamonds, a Communist takeover of Britain, a hunchbacked strangler on Romney Marsh. The one that had chimed with him most loudly was *The Final Count*, in which the villain – a Hun, naturally – held the world to ransom with an airship full of poison gas. Jack remembered the ghastly descriptions of its skin-blistering effects; how the hero despatched his opponent by feeding it to him in a liqueur glass.

He flipped to the last chapter.

'"Drink, you foul brute: drink." Thus, Carl Peterson did die on the eve of his biggest coup. As he had killed, so was he killed whilst, all unconscious of what had happened, the navigator still drove the airship full speed towards the west.'

'If only if it were that simple, Captain Drummond,' muttered Jack, closing the novel and his own notebook.

He slipped his shirt and jacket onto a hanger, placed his trousers under the mattress to keep the crease, put his cap on the bedstead. The eiderdown was pleasantly soft and dusty, but the warm night made it unnecessary. He opened the window to let in the night air. One of the buildings on the green, he noticed, was spilling light onto the ground. Someone had failed to draw one of the upstairs blackout blinds at the Post Office. Not a place for night owls, he thought, until he remembered the Hill baby.

Jack had been content to accept Harold Metcalfe's hospitality. The old man had made the offer out of kindness, but perhaps, Jack reasoned, he also wanted to keep his son close. Jill, he'd noticed, was less enthusiastic. As everyone got ready for bed, he thought he understood why. The cottage was small. Henry's room was next door to Jill's. When she turned off her bedside lamp, he heard the snap of the switch.

The day stayed with Jill, by the green glow of the clock dial. It held so much catastrophe that it seemed to require a special designation, like Dunkirk or D-Day. Two sons of Larkwhistle had been claimed by death. One far from home, one under familiar trees. And the figure that linked them together was now on the other side of her bedroom wall, lying in her brother's bed. A stranger who knew Henry's secrets and nursed a few of his own. A handsome and charming figure who, for a few minutes, had turned the living room of the cottage into an interrogation room.

She thought of Peter Brock's body, laid out on tiles at the police morgue in Southampton. She knew the place, its caged wall lights and the smell of carbolic soap from a visit to her father at work; unplanned – she had lost her latch key and locked herself out of the cottage. She thought of her brother's body at RAF Stoney Cross. The airbase was a mystery to her, but the scene was surely something similar. The needs of the dead were universal.

She did not weep. Had war, she wondered, robbed her of her tears? No. It had trained her into insouciance; made it her special virtue, like the convent made a nun proud of her chastity. Perhaps, she thought, when she saw Hitler on the front page of the *Daily Express*, sketched in a courtroom, or photographed on a gibbet, she might weep. It must come soon, she thought. The demobilization of the heart.

Chapter 9

Sleep was difficult, then waking up was difficult. When Jill came down from her bedroom, she saw her father was already in his chair. The sewing box was balanced on its arm and he was fixing a tear in a shirt.

'I've been meaning to pull that nail for ages,' he said.

Jill frowned and tightened the cord of her dressing gown.

'What nail?'

'In Henry's room. I think he used it to hang a calendar. This isn't so bad, though. I'll soon have it done.' The needle slipped easily through the cotton.

Jack emerged from the kitchen. He was not wearing a shirt because his shirt was in Harold's hands. Jill felt obliged to look away. She had seen plenty of bare male torsos in the past, some of them with similarly tight knots and bands of muscle. But these had belonged to men working in the fields or at the road-side, and were marked by uneven pink sunburn or dusted with chaff and grime. Their owners had not been clean and pristine and American and, perhaps most importantly, standing in her kitchen holding a cup of tea.

'I'm sorry about this,' he said. 'I would have fixed it myself upstairs but I'm hopeless at this sort of thing.'

'Dad's always been a wizard with the needle,' replied Jill. 'Thirty years in the force and never a button missing.'

'Would you like one?' asked Jack.

Jill found herself unable to comprehend the question.

'A cup of tea,' said Jack.

'Oh, yes please,' said Jill.

Jack seemed to notice her eyes, now on him. Something about this moment reminded Jill of Guy Brock's encounter with the German airman. She knew that he knew. They would now have to pretend otherwise.

'I used to be a coffee guy, but I've gone native in Blighty,' he said, clattering the cups and saucers. 'Or I'm turning into my mother. She drinks it too. When she's not drinking one of her corpse revivers. She likes it with lemon. Nobody does that here, right?'

'In a corpse reviver?' asked Jill, feeling her father's eyes upon her.

'In a cup of tea,' said Jack, returning to the kitchen.

'What a beastly notion,' said Jill. She regretted her decision to come down before dressing properly. She would not have chosen for Jack to see her in this state; nor for she to have seen him shirtless in the kitchen. Death, she thought, should have dominion over the day. And when she looked at Jack, it was not grief that stirred in her.

Harold cut the thread with his teeth and made good. Jack took the shirt and disappeared upstairs. Jill put a hand on her father's shoulder. 'What do you think about Guy's offer?'

'I think it's a good one, under the circumstances,' said Harold. 'Good for us and good for him. We shouldn't ask him to perform two services. It's too much.'

'Are you going to come with us?' asked Jill. 'To Stoney Cross?'

'No,' said Harold, quietly. 'You bring him home.'

'That's what Guy Brock said,' breathed Jill.

'Then Guy Brock was right,' said Harold.

The churchyard of St Cedd's was a record of Larkwhistle preserved in grass tussocks and monumental masonry. While Jill dressed, Jack wandered among its ranks of headstones – some pale, some mossy, some tilted drunkenly. If you had met him that morning, peering at the inscriptions, tugging at veils of ivy, you might have taken him to be a tourist researching his family history; looking for a sign of himself before the Mayflower landed at Plymouth Rock. A more careful observer, however, would have noticed the grim thin line of his mouth as he jotted down names and dates, and decided that the romantic past was not much on his mind.

Jill was a careful observer. She found Jack hunkered over a small limestone slab bearing a goggle-eyed death's head. In his hand was a slim green notebook with a marbled cover, which he slipped inside his jacket pocket as Jill approached.

'Do you know them well?' he asked. 'The residents?'

'Known them all my life. I'm related to some of them. No big family tomb though. The Metcalfes are not that grand.'

'How about the Whitechapels? Is that a local name?'

Jill shook her head.

'Or the Mays?'

'Ah, yes, I can help you there.'

Jill led Jack to a patch south of the belltower where the tomb of the May family rose from the ground. Children, grandchildren and great-grandchildren, named from the part of the Bible before Jesus turned up. Ezekiel May, taken to the Lord in 1844, received top billing. 'The line died out in the late nineteenth century,' she explained.

Jack bent down to examine the inscriptions. Gothic possibilities filled his mind. 'Ah. I've read *Fall of the House of Usher*. What happened to them?'

'I think they moved to Aldershot,' said Jill. 'Are they in your family tree?'

'No,' said Jack.

'So, what's your interest, Captain Strafford?'

'Just something Henry mentioned to me. I thought it might be important to him.'

The remark confounded Jill.

'Really? He didn't spend much time here. He wasn't one of those morbid boys. He liked adventure. The Wild West and spies. He told me he was an atheist when he was nine.' She stopped. Henry was suddenly so strong in her mind that she turned towards the lych-gate, expecting to see him running down the path towards her.

'You didn't just come here to tell us the bad news, did you?'

Jack got to his feet. 'It was very generous of your dad to put me up.'

'The base isn't so far away, though, is it? You could easily have driven back there last night.' She peered at him closely. 'What are you here for? You're not on leave, are you? You're doing some kind of war work.'

Jack cast a glance in the direction of the jeep.

'We could drive over there now, if you like,' he said. 'To Stoney Cross.'

Jill ran her fingers over a tombstone and picked off an emerald curl of lichen. 'You're a proper mystery, Captain Strafford. I thought you were just an ordinary GI at first. Sweet and upright and coming to do right by his fallen comrade – and then slightly out of your depth when the death of a stranger upended your day. You know about dead bodies – of course you do, you're fighting a war – but you don't know much about handling evidence. Or not handling it, I should say. Then, when you were talking to the vicar last night, I saw another side of you. The professional interrogator. And I didn't know whether to be shocked or to admire it, seeing you giving poor Guy Brock such a grilling.'

'You think that was a grilling?'

'I do. And it suddenly struck me how little we knew about Henry's work. We had a few suspicions, of course, because he would never answer a straight question about it.'

'Careless talk, Miss Metcalfe. Every ordinary Tommy has his letters censored.'

'But Henry wasn't an ordinary Tommy, and neither are you. The way you quizzed Guy about killing that parachutist; well, it convinced me that you were on some sort of mission. Here in Larkwhistle.' She looked at the grave beside her. 'And I was even more convinced when I heard you searching my brother's room.'

'Oh,' said Jack.

'Oh,' said Jill. Her voice had lost its steeliness. 'Look. You can pretend that we didn't have this conversation. And you can keep on pumping us for details about names on gravestones and whether the vicar is having an affair with the postmistress, and I'll answer as if I thought you were just a man with an eccentric taste in gossip. It's fine. Truly. But should you want my help, well, I'm here, Captain Strafford. I'm here.'

Jack nodded silently. 'Okay,' he said. 'When we get to Stoney Cross, I'm going to have a word with my CO. I'd like to take you into my confidence. If you're willing.'

Jack and Jill spoke little on the drive to the airbase. The gravity of the moment pulled at them both, and neither was inclined to shout questions or solemnities over the roar of the jeep. Around them, the New Forest made its daily offer of primordial beauty and drama. Larks hurtled towards the sun. A row of dead trees in a flooded ditch reached up from the duckweed. At Brockenhurst Jack slapped the horn to persuade an unimpressed pony to vacate the road.

'You must have more wild horses than Iowa,' said Jack.

'They're not wild,' said Jill. 'They're just free. Until the Drift.'

'The Drift?'

'When we gather them up. Check their health. Cut their manes and tails. Take the foals from their mothers to be weaned, if they're being sold.'

'I'd say this was all Greek to me,' said Jack. 'But my school was pretty hot on Greek.'

'You're in Deep England now, Captain Strafford,' said Jill. 'The laws are different here.'

Stoney Cross was prepared for their arrival. Even the sergeant on the gate was quiet and respectful. It was as if Henry's funeral had already begun. As Jack parked the jeep an officer emerged from a Nissen hut, a pipe clenched between his teeth. He offered Jill some words of condolence; commonplace but sincere remarks about bravery and fortitude. He also asked after Guy Brock. Jill could have predicted that news of Peter's death had travelled quickly, but the man's familiarity with the vicar of Larkwhistle took her by surprise – particularly when he mentioned that Guy and his curate Simon Pinn had sometimes been summoned to Stoney Cross to administer the last rites, or comfort men in their final moments. 'Not your brother, I'm afraid, Miss Metcalfe,' he said. 'I'm afraid we were too late for that.'

When Jill was asked if she wanted to view the body, she said yes, but not because she thought it would give her peace of mind or satisfaction. The coffin was plain and utilitarian, like all new things. Henry was in a dress uniform, pressed and neat. Someone had taken great care, as if to prepare him for a parade inspection. Who performed such duties in wartime, she wondered? Whoever it was, she was grateful to them. The sight of Peter's body had scarcely left her mind: it looked as if it had been pulled from the theatre of war. Henry, conversely, might have expired beside the mess room fire, having fallen asleep after dinner.

Once the coffin lid was closed, Jill expected to be driven straight back to Larkwhistle. Instead, Jack escorted her to a hut by the landing strip. As they arrived they were passed by a tea lady pushing an empty trolley. Jack tipped his cap to her.

'Afternoon, Violet,' he said. They had a brief conversation about her son. Jill was not introduced: Violet showed no curiosity about Jack's visitor.

The interior of Hut 22 was like a classroom, with rows of wooden desks and maps stuck with colour-coded pins supporting spidery lengths of string. Jill did not examine them. Careless sights preceded careless talk.

'I've passed the test then, have I?' she asked.

'Well, let's just say that the CO agrees with my decision, and the rest depends on you.' They sat down at what looked like the teacher's table, where the tea lady had left sandwiches from the NAAFI. Neither of them felt hungry or thirsty. Jack poured the tea anyway. Jill noticed that someone had left a black fountain pen lying on her side of the table.

'Before I say anything, Miss Metcalfe, I need to make sure that you want to hear this. There will be an inquest and a funeral – two funerals – in the next few days. Very shortly you and I are going to bring your brother's remains back to the village. So, you are under no obligation whatsoever.'

'Well,' said Jill, 'my obligation is to my brother. So that means I'm sure.'

'What about your father? What obligation do you have to him?'

Jill was puzzled by the question. But only for a moment.

'I can't discuss this with him?' she asked.

'No,' said Jack, flatly. 'You can't.'

He took an envelope from his jacket pocket and gave it to Jill. It contained an official form. Some of the details were already filled out. All it seemed to require was her signature. She considered reading through the whole text and asking questions, then picked up the pen. 'I'd always imagined the Official Secrets Act would look slightly more dramatic than a dog licence,' she said. 'Would you have to shoot me if I broke the terms?'

'It's all in the small print,' said Jack, stuffing the signed form back inside the envelope. 'We'd just stick you in Aylesbury jail for the duration. Which might be worse.'

Jill sipped the tea, which was somehow both stewed and tasteless.

'Were you working with him out there?' she asked. 'With Henry?'

'I was supposed to bring him home. I went out in a Lysander to pick him up at the agreed rendezvous point. A good, discreet one, we thought. He'd been taken there by a contact in the Resistance who's been helping us for years. A man we thought we could really trust. Well, we were wrong about that. I can't be certain, but I think this man killed your brother just before I landed the plane.'

Jill absorbed the information. Now she had a picture with some detail. A plane scudding over a field, her brother's body on the ground.

'Henry had some very important documents sewn into the lining of his coat,' said Jack. 'He'd risked his life to get them. He'd also disposed of their owner.'

Jill frowned. 'A bad Nazi type, I assume.'

'Oh,' said Jack. 'The very worst.'

'And what about your Resistance man?'

'I'm sorry to say that after he shot your brother, he took the coat. Then he fled in the truck he'd used to bring him to the rendezvous. I saw the lights moving as he made his escape.'

'Was he dead?' asked Jill. 'When you landed, was Henry already dead?'

'No,' said Jack. 'But he'd taken a bullet. I got him on board, but we both knew he didn't have much time. They're loud, those Lysanders. And he was weak. He couldn't tell me anything over the noise of the plane. So, just as we became airborne, he started scribbling on the back of the flight log with a pencil. But then he lost consciousness. Partly his wounds, partly the altitude, I think. This is what he left us.'

Jack produced a sheet of rough brownish paper. On one side was a timetable that divided the days into hours and minutes. On the other was a series of words scrawled in a hand that Jill could barely recognize as her brother's.

'He was trying to explain,' said Jack. 'But I just couldn't hear him. I know he mentioned the village, and he mentioned you.'

Jill examined the paper – 'Whitechapel inscription May.' She understood their conversation in the churchyard.

'Does it mean anything to you?' asked Jack.

'Nothing, I'm afraid. Whitechapel's in East London, you know.'

'Jack the Ripper territory.'

'I'm not sure Henry ever went there.' She put down the paper. 'I suppose you can't tell me what these documents were? The ones that got him killed?'

'That works on a need-to-know basis.'

'And do I need to know?'

'You do.'

Jill had expected to be thrown a bone. She seemed to be about to receive the entire carcass. She allowed herself a look at the map on the wall. It depicted Western Europe from Danzig to Dublin. Various points of the map were connected by great lengths of coloured string. The direction of travel was clearly westerly, so they did not describe troop movements – the Allied advance was surging in the opposite direction.

Nor did they seem to be the flight paths of German bombers – they were too straight and uncomplicated. Several sites in the Netherlands were marked. Puzzlingly, so were some deep in Germany and Polish territory, in towns far too distant to send a Doodlebug to London.

Jack looked her straight in the eye. 'You asked me why I'm so interested in your little village. Since late 1940, someone in the New Forest area has been broadcasting encrypted messages over shortwave radio. Long strings of numbers, tapped out in Morse. Very nice and regular, too. He's an eleven o'clock news kind of guy. Transcripts of those messages have now been found in enemy hands. They made it all the way from here to Berlin. We don't have the key, so we have no idea what they mean. They use a system that's very different from the codes we've recovered from the U-boats. But we do know the codename of the operative.'

'The operative? The spy, you mean?'

'Yes. He's Commoner. Or she is.'

'I thought the codenames of spies weren't supposed to give anything away.'

'They're not.'

'Well, this one does. Commoner. Marks him out as a local. There are a lot of Commoners in the New Forest.'

Jack frowned. 'Is this class again? Like U and non-U and which way to pass the port?'

'Much older than that, Captain Strafford. It's positively medieval. Take me and my father, for instance. We have the Right of Common of Mast.'

'You do?'

'When pannage season comes, we can turn out all our pigs for sixty days, and they can eat all the acorns they want. Acorns are poisonous to ponies, as I'm sure you know. And we can do that because the right comes with the cottage. All there in the deeds. Commoners of the New Forest, that's us.'

'How many pigs do you have?' asked Jack.

'None,' replied Jill. 'But maybe our spy does.'

Jack caught himself smiling. He corrected it before she noticed.

'The messages keep coming,' he continued. 'Commoner

has been sending out his screeds of dots and dashes to Berlin since Christmas 1940. But the boffins are getting better and better at this stuff all the time, particularly round here. Two weeks ago, a new and more accurate triangulation was made. So, we've narrowed it down.'

'To Larkwhistle,' said Jill.

'To Larkwhistle,' said Jack.

Jill soaked up this intelligence. 'So, did Henry discover who he was? This Commoner?'

'I doubt it, otherwise he'd have just told me. Or put the name straight down. But I'm assuming that what he did manage to scrawl on that piece of paper are instructions for how to crack the cipher. Well, the start of them.'

Jill looked at the paper again. 'Whitechapel'. 'Inscription'. 'May'.

'We've tried using all these as alphabet substitution codes. You take the numbers from the messages and then use the words as alphabetic keys. So, 1, 2, 3, 4 is A, B, C, D, but you take Whitechapel, let's say, to turn W into A and H into B and I into C, and so on. However, it just comes out as gibberish.'

'It sounds like a piece of advice,' said Jill.

'Advising what, though?' asked Jack. 'And it's rather casual phraseology for a man who knew he was in a life-or-death situation.'

'Somebody in the village must know. And have the

equipment to transmit the messages in the first place.'
Jill turned over the implications of her own words.
'Captain Strafford, are you telling me that one of my
neighbours is a secret Nazi with a radio transmitter
hidden in the attic?'

'I suppose I am.'

'Broadcasting what, though? The Germans are on
the run – what is there for Commoner to do? Tap
out messages saying there's nobody left, they've all
gone off to liberate Paris? Any self-respecting fifth
columnist would already have burned his code books
and thrown his radio into the sea, wouldn't he? What's
the point?'

'Because this might be the most dangerous phase
of the war. Okay, so the Germans never came to
Larkwhistle. You didn't have to fight them on the
beaches. The Home Guard never had to be the
Partisans. But Hitler's getting increasingly desperate,
and the further he pulls back, the more desperate
he'll become. He sent the V1s over. Something worse
is coming.'

'What sort of something? More bombs, you mean?
Rocket bombs?'

Jack nodded. His voice was grave. 'We've seen them
in the aerial photographs. Bigger than the V1s. More
powerful. But they'll still need numbers to find their
targets for tonight. And they can't get that right
without help from agents on the ground. Commoner

and his friends, making their little broadcasts and sending the enemy what he needs to know.'

'But what help do they need? Co-ordinates on a map aren't secret.'

'No,' said Jack. 'But Berlin needs to know where these things are actually landing. That's where Commoner comes in. He'll read about the attacks in the papers like the rest of us, then feed the co-ordinates of the impact sites back to his masters – who will adjust their sights accordingly.'

'How do you know he's involved?' asked Jill.

'Thanks to your brother,' said Jack. 'Henry was on his case. He found references to Commoner in documents stolen from a missile test site. He's one of their most important informers. And he's a neighbour of yours.'

Jill's gaze moved back to the map. Dread coiled in her stomach. She now understood its meaning. Fire in the sky, from one end of Europe to the other.

Chapter 10

Symes and Co. had brought their hearse from Southampton. The men who came with it were kind and softly spoken. It was their job. Their recommendations were informed by decades of experience. Jill, however, was not inclined to listen. She let old Mr Symes speak out of politeness, then demurred. She did not want Henry's body taken to the chapel of rest and thence to Larkwhistle on the morning of the funeral. She had promised her father she would bring him home.

Mr Symes swallowed his disapproval and nodded, then issued instructions to his men. The coffin was loaded into the hearse and pointed in the direction of Larkwhistle; Jack and Jill followed behind in the jeep. It was not a slow, ceremonial drive. Jill wondered if Mr Symes was driving too quickly to spite her. Other motorists, of which there were very few, gave way to the cortège. The New Forest ponies did not. Jack and Jill were obliged to step out and encourage the animals back under the trees. Here was one advantage to bringing Henry straight back to the village: he would not be late for his own funeral.

'There'll be a lot happening in the next few days,' said Jill. 'The inquest, the funeral. But I don't want you to think you can't ask anything of me right now. Because this could start any moment, couldn't it?'

'Yes,' said Jack. 'The first one will be a bolt from the blue. They're supersonic, so there'll be no engine cut-out, no ominous silence. And after it hits, Commoner will be tapping the news back to Berlin.'

'And what do we do when we find him?'

'Treason is treason.'

'He'll hang?'

'That kind of justice is kind of luxurious right now. We need to persuade whoever it is to turn double agent. We'll get him to transmit the wrong numbers so the rockets fall short of the cities. It's worked with the V1s. It's why so many came down in south London and not in the middle of town.'

'And if he can't be persuaded?'

'We'll persuade him. These rockets are ready. We don't know about capacity because they're making them somewhere in the east. Underground, it seems, like something out of H. G. Wells. We can't risk that lot raining down on us.'

'I suppose you can't simply arrest everyone in the village?' said Jill.

'They'd know about it in Berlin as soon as it happened. We need to do this subtly. Gently. We need to find Commoner and turn him without even his neighbours knowing. Then use him to confound the bombers. It's delicate and it requires local knowledge. Henry had that knowledge. You have it too.'

They were approaching the cottage. The hearse was already parked outside. 'What do I call you now I'm working with you?' asked Jill. 'Do I use your rank?'

Jack brought the jeep to a halt. 'No, I think we're on first name terms, don't you? Seems more natural.'

She was surprised by how much the notion pleased her.

Harold appeared on the doorstep. He was ushering Guy Brock through the front door. The two men had clearly been in conference together. They moved to one side as the undertakers carried the coffin into the cottage. It was not the easiest of tasks, but Mr Symes and his men were experts. Harold felt strangely re-assured by the sight. Like Jill, he was comparing the fate of Henry to the fate of Peter Brock and thinking himself fortunate. They discussed the order of service. Guy had proposed nothing experimental. 'All Things Bright and Beautiful', Psalm 23 and 'Jerusalem'. Jill dismissed a faint worry that she might not hit the high note in the second verse – 'Bring me my spear! O clouds, unfold!'

The living then rearranged themselves to accommodate the dead. Guy Brock pocketed his notes and returned to the vicarage to await the return of his own son. Jack informed Harold that he intended to book into a room at the Fleur-de-Lys. The old man accepted the idea without protest and pottered back into the kitchen. Wimsey needed water in his bowl.

At the threshold, Jill put a hand on Jack's arm. 'I'd like you to be one of the bearers. For Henry.'

Jack laid his hand upon hers. 'Thank you, Jill.'

It was the first time he had said her name. He was looking directly into her eyes. Something more than grief now united them; something more than duty.

When Jack walked into the saloon of the Fleur-de-Lys, he thought Wally Speed might refuse his custom. He saw the landlord's eyes move coldly from his kit bag to the sign in the window advertising vacant rooms.

'Well,' Wally said, wiping the bar, which was perfectly clean. 'It's a bit inconvenient. We must be up early to move the furniture, you see. To get the place ready.'

Jack frowned. 'For what?'

'The police called through half an hour ago, sir. The coroner's coming from Southampton in the morning.'

'They're having the inquest here?'

'Always seems to fall to us, sir. When Meg Brent drowned by the bridle path, they had it all out in the public bar. Can't say I liked it very much. All that mortuary talk. Sours the place, you might say.'

'You might.'

Wally cleaned a drip tray as if he was finishing the *Times* crossword. 'Anyway, ain't you got a Nissen hut to go to?'

'I have,' said Jack, putting on his most charming smile. 'It's infested with earwigs. Do you know what some of the men do? They sleep with elastic bands on the cuffs of their pyjamas.'

Effie Speed came in from the kitchen. She had clearly been listening to their conversation.

'The inquest won't be happening up in the bedrooms, Wal,' she said.

'No. But we'll all be witnesses, won't we? Him. Me. You. Maggie. Wouldn't be proper, would it?'

'I don't think the coroner will mind that I'm staying under your roof, Mr Speed,' said Jack.

Wally's forehead creased. 'But we're not supposed to talk beforehand, are we?'

'That's jurors, Wal, you great fool,' Effie said, sighing.

Jack pulled out his wallet. 'Here. Let me pay in advance. I'd be very happy to stay all week, if that's convenient.'

Wally Speed found himself convinced. He put down

his cloth, extracted a key from a hidden place some-where beneath the bar and handed it to his wife.

'Ain't you got any luggage?' she asked.

'It's at the Metcalfes' place. I'll bring it over later. I stayed there last night but I didn't want to get in their way.'

On the landing they passed Maggie, pale and unhappy.

'Miss Speed,' Jack said, smiling. 'I hope you're feeling better.' For a moment she looked at him as if he were a figure from a nightmare who had shown the bad taste to materialize on the stairs in broad daylight.

'They gave me the rest of the week off,' said Maggie.

'Who's that?' asked Jack.

'Mr and Mrs Deever. They said they'd still pay me.'

'Ah. That's very decent of them.'

Maggie shrugged and continued down the stairs.

Effie apologized for her daughter.

'No,' said Jack. 'She was a friend of the boy, wasn't she? Of Peter Brock.'

'She was sick with him, poor girl. It was cruel that she saw him like that. Cruel. She took it bad enough when he told her he didn't want to step out with her no more.' She sighed: this was an old and tender subject.

'Perhaps your husband was right,' said Jack. 'Perhaps I shouldn't really be here.'

'It's not your fault, is it? You didn't know it was going to happen.' The money was in the till: it was staying there. Jack felt secure enough to push further.

'So, Maggie works for the Deevers, does she?'

'Just four days a week,' said Effie. 'Split shifts. She takes Patrick his copy of the *The Times*. Always *The Times*, mind. She took the *Express* once and there was an incident. Then she dusts a bit in the morning. Does errands for them. Goes back later at suppertime. It keeps her out of mischief. Gets her out of the pub for a bit, too. She's a quiet girl. But there's a lot going on up there.'

'Must be interesting, working for someone who writes books.'

'I'm not much of a reader.'

'Tomorrow's going to be tough for her,' said Jack. 'For all of you. I hope the coroner is the tactful type.'

Jack's was a pretty room in the eaves. He nodded his satisfaction and made a mental note not to leap out of bed in the morning and bang his head on the sloping ceiling.

'What would you like for breakfast?' asked Effie.

'What is there?'

'There's porridge.'

'Then I'll have porridge.'

'I can put some jam in it. Make it less boring.'

'That would be amazing,' said Jack. He immediately

regretted this burst of American enthusiasm, which, under the roof of a mediocre country pub, sounded sarcastic even to him.

'Well, I'd best be getting on,' said Effie, gathering her apron.

'Oh, just one thing, Mrs Speed. I'm a bit of a late-night wireless man. If I wanted to listen after closing time, how might I do that?'

'*Forces Favourites* is it? The set's in the parlour. But you best ask Wal. He's the only one up past eleven and he can't abide Vera Lynn.'

Jack listened to Effie disappearing downstairs. Evening opening was two hours away. When it started, and the Speeds were busy, he would search the top floor of the house. In the meantime, he surveyed the reassuring dullness of his own accommodation. A fairly stable Victorian bed, an armchair draped with an ancient antimacassar, a cheap print of a hunting scene, a window – leaded like those in the jigsaws of English country cottages that his mother liked to do when she was ill. The air in the room was hot and heavy. As he moved to open the window, Jack saw he had a perfect view of the vicarage garden.

To his surprise, there was something to see. At the end of the garden, not far from a modest glasshouse, sat a small incinerator for the disposal of waste. From it, a plume of grey smoke was curling up into the clear air. Guy emerged from the back door with a small black object in his hands. A novel? A cash book? He was pulling pages from it and placing them on the smouldering pile of twigs and dry grass cuttings. The paper attracted a lick of fire and was consumed by it. Guy repeated this process several times, watching each page burn to oblivion. Then he looked back to the house. Helena was calling him. Guy scanned the garden as though he suspected that someone might be watching him from a bed of hydrangeas. Helena called again. He buried the little book in the heap of grass cuttings, dusted his hands on his trousers. For a short moment he stopped and looked up. It seemed to Jack that Guy was peering straight at him.

Chapter 11

With death came the small administrative tasks of death. Jill drafted a funeral announcement and phoned it in to the classified departments of *The Times* and the *Echo*. The women on the line were sympathetic. She rang her aunt in Brighton to give her the bad news and half listened to a long explanation about why she couldn't come that seemed to involve a bad leg and a broken tooth, or vice versa. Then there were telegrams to be sent to Harold's Peterborough cousins and the two schoolfriends with whom Henry had kept in touch. This required a visit to the Post Office, which, Jill reflected, would make an excellent base for a spy.

Many Sub-Post Offices have an air of inertia that makes buying a postal order or sending a parcel feel like petitioning a government department. However, the Hills ran a more chaotic establishment. They also sold bootlaces and candles, and liquorice sticks and sherbet lemons by the ounce. The door was half open. Jill could see Ivy Hill at the counter and Pam Sharp from the Copper Kettle leaning against it.

Some felt a little uneasy that Ivy, of all the people in Larkwhistle, was the one who put through calls and received sacks of private letters. Some villagers listened for the sound of breathing on the line. Others manufactured eye-watering gossip in the hope of catching her out. The trick had never been known to work, though Helena Brock, when posting a letter, often wondered if Ivy genuinely believed that the vicar's wife had been present with Leon Trotsky at the Kronstadt rebellion.

Today, however, Pam Sharp was leading the conversation, and Ivy looked thoroughly sick of it. The Bakelite microphone that left her hands free to operate the telephone switchboard curved upwards from her chest. Perhaps, Jill thought, she could use it like a rhino horn to propel Pam from the premises.

'Well,' said Pam, 'I wouldn't kick him out of bed. I'd consider it my patriotic duty. I've always loved America. Everything's bigger and better there.'

Pam fell silent as Jill pushed at the door, making the bell clatter. Ivy looked relieved to see her. Pam offered her condolences for Henry's death. She did it so formally that Jill thought she might curtsey. Pam picked up her tin of Melton shoe cream from the counter and shuffled out.

'How's your dad taking it?' asked Ivy.

'You know him,' said Jill. 'Policemen have a manner when it comes to these things. They're so used to dealing with other people who've been struck down that they don't know what to do if it happens to them.'

'And what about you, Jill?'

'Pretty blitzed, to be honest. But you have to struggle on, don't you? I've seen it on posters at the bus stop.'

Ivy nodded. Jill passed over a scrap of paper bearing her messages, which Ivy began transcribing onto a telegram slip. She licked her pencil. Halfway through the first address, a familiar sound came roaring from the parlour. It was Martin, the Hills' disconsolate baby.

Ivy began to hum and shush in the direction of the baby. 'All right, Martin,' she cooed. But he wasn't reassured at all. Ivy frowned. 'I've just fed him and put him down,' she said. 'And he's been exhausted all morning. I thought I was good for another half hour.' Her pencil broke. She looked forlorn. 'Damn,' she said. 'Let me start again. I've just told this lady in Brighton the wrong day.'

'Let me see to him,' said Jill. 'You carry on.'

Ivy looked for a moment as if she might protest, but it didn't last long. 'Oh, would you?' she said. Her gratitude suggested to Jill that not all customers were so tolerant. 'He can't be hungry,' she said. 'He probably just wants a cuddle.'

Jill ducked under the counter and headed into the back parlour. Martin was in his basket, little arms flailing. Jill scooped him up. Much to her relief, he was dry. She brought him up to her shoulder and cradled the back of his head. Martin had a foul temper, but he smelled as nice as a sponge cake just out of the oven. She jogged him gently up and down. He continued to cry and grumble until he produced a milky burp that seemed too loud for so small a creature. Jill felt his little body relax with relief. His head nestled contentedly against her shoulder. In moments he was asleep with his little fists curled. The quiet was so deep that Jill could hear the scratch of Ivy Hill's pencil, the thump of her rubber stamp, the rattle of her fingers on the Morse mechanism. She was, thought Jill, fast as lightning with the machine.

Jill sank into the horsehair armchair with Martin draped over her shoulder. The baby's contentment was infectious and she felt her own tensions easing away. Martin, who was so often cross and unhappy, seemed to be pacifying her. Her breathing synchronized with the rhythms of his warm little body.

Ivy looked round the parlour door.

'It's quiet here now,' said Jill.

'I turned the sign,' said Ivy. 'They can wait. I expect you need a bit of peace and quiet. Keeps you busy, doesn't it, when someone dies? I remember when my mum went. All the forms. All the arrangements. The grave matters.'

'Guy and Helena are looking after all that,' said Jill.

'Ah,' said Ivy. 'They'd know what to do.' Her eyes were suddenly full of tears. 'There I go,' she said. 'It's embarrassing really. I haven't lost anybody. And here I am, blubbing away. And you holding my baby.'

Jill thought she had a point but did not say so. 'Really, Ivy,' said Jill. 'Little Martin is doing me the power of good. It must be absolutely exhausting, looking after him all day and running this place at the same time. Getting packets down from the top shelf. Listening to everyone's dull little messages. All those impatient people on the switchboard.'

'Well, Sam helps me,' said Ivy.

'Where is he now?'

'Doing the four o'clock collection.'

'He's a man of habit.'

'He has to be. Up before five o'clock, round over by nine. I do his tea for half past five and then he's off to the Fleur-de-Lys at six thirty, prompt, while I put the little one to bed. Put myself to bed sometimes, too.'

'He's not a night owl, though, is he?'

'Dunno, Jill. I'm usually dead to the world when he gets back. He's got his friends in the pub to entertain him.'

'Drinks with Patrick, doesn't he? Old loyalties die hard.'

'Well,' said Ivy. 'Some old loyalties must be pretty close to death. I don't think my husband has paid for a pint since the evacuation. And that's quite the thing, given how much Wally Speed has put up his prices.' Disapproval crossed her face. She shook it away. 'I better get the pudding on,' she said. 'Steak and kidney. Well, kidney. They'll never put suet on the ration, will they? Thank goodness. Men seem to need all that heavy stuff.'

Ivy looked at Martin, happy on the shoulder of a relative stranger. She was suddenly nostalgic for the time in her life when babies were mere line illustrations in soap adverts and male habits were an exciting, unsolved mystery. She let out a groan of frustration.

'Oh, Ivy,' said Jill. 'What's the matter?'

'I'm so fed up with it, Jill. It's Sam. He's so angry. They all are, aren't they? The ones who came back. They're eaten up with it.'

'With what, do you think?' asked Jill. She kept her voice low, hoping not to break the baby's sleep.

'Envy. That's what I see, anyway. They'd rather be a line on a memorial than another broken soldier back from the war with no idea what to do with himself.'

'We can't know what they went through, I suppose,' said Jill. 'Dunkirk. Imagine it. The waiting. The bullets from the air. Seeing their pals go under.'

'It's the women who have to pick up the pieces, though. Tread on eggshells. Listen to them talking in their sleep. Or tell them it's okay if they flinch when the door bangs. I hope this is all worth it, Jill. I hope victory feels like victory when it comes. Or I don't know what I'll do. Run off, I suppose. Into the trees.'

'You mustn't despair, Ivy. Think of Martin.'

'I am thinking of Martin. I didn't say I would run off on my own, did I?' She gazed down at her son. 'He's my victory,' she said. 'I got him. Nobody else did.'

Ivy gathered herself, crossing to the stove, lighting the gas and putting a pan of water on to boil. 'Let me just do this,' she said, 'and I'll take him.'

Jill nodded her agreement. Why, she wondered, had she stayed so long? The baby's warm weight was comforting. So was the less generous thought that she had calmed him more efficiently than his own mother. An easier labour, perhaps, than being in the cottage with her father, Henry's coffin and grief.

As Jill shimmied upwards, Martin in her arms, a hard object slid from the gap between the cushion and the arm of the chair. It was a children's book. Or, better to say, *the* children's book. *The Boy Among the Trees*. The most ubiquitous book in Larkwhistle. Perhaps Ivy had been reading it as a way of mourning Peter Brock.

The pages were torn. Violently, Jill thought. Many of them had been ripped in half.

Ivy took the baby from Jill's arms and glanced down towards the book.

'The baby did that,' she said. It was clearly a lie. 'He's an absolute terror.'

'They have such strong little hands, don't they?' Jill smiled.

Chapter 12

Sam Hill should have been drinking up and going home. But there was Patrick Deever, his former commanding officer, leaning at the bar of the Fleur-de-Lys, offering, as ever, to stand him a drink. The loss of a hand and an eye, Sam thought, had enhanced Captain Deever's military bearing. Since standing easy was no longer easy, the Captain kept his left arm straight and delegated ordinary physical business to the right side of his body, which, as he fished money from his trouser pocket and snapped it down on the counter, moved with a strength and precision he had not possessed before the war.

'A whisky for Sam before he goes, I think, Wally,' said Patrick, with the cultivated hail-fellow-well-met manner of landless men who fancied themselves the squire. 'And one for me, and one for yourself.' Wally Speed took the bottle down from the shelf, poured three measures by eye. He was used to this routine. He had learned to ignore Sam's brief and unmeant protests long ago.

'To the fallen and the few,' said Patrick, knocking back his whisky, undiluted. Wally Speed followed suit. Sam, who usually added water and took his slowly, did the same.

'You could pour me one, too, if you wouldn't mind.' Jack had descended from his room and was standing at the bottom of the stairs. 'Do put it on the bill, though. I won't presume on the Captain's generosity.'

'God bless the strength of the dollar,' said Patrick, raising his empty glass.

Wally Speed obliged. Jack made a show of asking permission to sit with Sam and Patrick at the bar, though refusal would have been difficult. It was the only sociable space remaining. During the hour that Jack had been lying on his bed, the Speeds had reconfigured the furniture in the public bar. The tables were pushed together at one end and the mismatched chairs and stools had been arranged in rows. Anyone walking in would assume that the pub was to be used for a lecture or a hustings.

'All we need now is the coroner, I guess,' said Jack.

'He's coming early,' said Wally.

'Reassuring to know that someone diligent is on the case,' said Jack.

'I think he just likes pubs,' said Sam. 'The Verderers'

Hall would be more convenient, but it doesn't have beer on tap.'

'Verderers'?' repeated Jack, feeling the distance from Philadelphia to Hampshire, but knowing that it gave him licence to ask any question he liked.

Sam pointed at Patrick. 'He's one of them. They go back to the Normans. Verderers and agisters.'

'And little lambs eat ivy?' said Jack.

'It's our court system, do you see?' explained Patrick. 'Have unrung pigs eaten your lobelias? Bring your case to us. Has the MOD dropped a shell in your orchard? We'll do our best to sort it out. But the present tragic matter, well, that's rather beyond our jurisdiction.' He produced a packet of Capstan Filters from his jacket, extracted one with his lips, returned the cigarettes to their place and took a box of matches from his trouser pocket. Jack watched him curl his fingers around the box to take a match and strike it into life. His prosthetic hand stayed perfectly still. Jack imagined him developing the skill, like an actor preparing for a part.

'So, how do you like Larkwhistle, Captain?' asked Patrick, as if his family had been collecting its tithes since 1066. He blew a line of smoke from the side of his mouth.

'I'd like it with a little less death,' replied Jack. 'Otherwise, it's as perfect as a picture book. Under any other circumstances I'd happily waste a few days here.'

'You'll be off after the inquest, I suppose?' asked Sam. 'Off to France?'

'Well, there's the funeral first . . .' He corrected himself. 'Funerals.'

Patrick Deever ignored his serious tone. 'You must come to dinner before you go, Captain,' he said breezily. 'Meet the good lady wife. Sunday night? Bring Jill.'

Jack found himself accepting the invitation. But he also noticed a hard look in Sam Hill's eye. Patrick also caught it.

'And you and Ivy must come too, of course, Sam,' he added. It was very clear that this had not been part of his original plan. Jack's eyes darted between the men. Did Sam have some power over Patrick Deever?

'Let's drink to the new world,' said Patrick. 'To the end of deference.'

Jack looked hard for a trace of irony. He raised his glass.

'The end of deference,' he repeated.

Sam took his final sip of whisky. He looked ready to leave. But Jack was not done with him. This was a good opportunity for his own inquest. 'Tell me about Peter Brock,' he said. 'Was he a particular friend of yours?'

Sam seemed slightly thrown by the question. 'I've known him all my life.'

'Well enough for him to, say, visit your home and steal your service revolver?'

'My home is the Post Office, Captain Strafford,' said Sam. 'It's like Piccadilly Circus with stamps. People never stop coming and going.'

'Peter, particularly?' asked Sam.

'Yes. He used to deal with the parish mail for his father. And he was a member of clubs and societies. Always wanting postal orders to send off for bits and pieces. Glass microscope slides marked "fragile". He liked nature, you see.'

'When did the gun go missing?' asked Jack.

'Two weeks ago,' said Sam. 'And I reported it straight away. It was in a locked drawer. I've no idea what happened.'

'Where did you keep the key?'

'You sound like the police.'

Jack did not respond.

'In the till,' Sam said.

'I'm sure you followed all the rules, old man,' drawled Patrick. 'Nobody can hold you responsible. I keep my own locked up in the bedside drawer. But there are such things as skeleton keys and hairpins. Every victory roll contains a neat little burglary kit.'

Wally Speed nodded as if this remark contained some deep truth about the nature of women.

'Did Peter have any enemies?' asked Jack.

'He used to sit in here complaining about his dad,' said Wally.

'Because of his politics?' asked Jack. 'I'm told they disagreed about the war.'

'Vicars are supposed to want peace, aren't they?' said Sam. 'But I draw the line at the Duke of Bedford's lot.'

Jack's face showed his ignorance.

'The vicar joined them in thirty-seven,' said Sam. 'The Peace Pledge Union. Appeasers. When Munich was signed, they couldn't have been more pleased. Threw their knickers right over the windmill. Got a bit more difficult when war broke out, though. Like it did for the Communists. Until Russia came in and we all had to cheer for Uncle Joe.'

'Are there many Communists in Larkwhistle?' asked Jack.

'There's always a *Daily Worker* in the newsagent's,' said Wally. 'I reckon they get it in for Helena Brock.'

Jack raised an eyebrow. 'The vicar's wife is a Communist?'

'She's an intellectual,' said Wally. 'And they're worse, in my experience.'

'Did Guy Brock ever preach this stuff from the pulpit?' asked Jack.

'He came pretty close,' said Wally. 'But not in those words. And he changed his tune after he did for that Nazi parachutist. We forgave him then. It was a real act of courage. He's a good man and he was a good father. Peter didn't always appreciate him.'

Jack turned to Patrick, who had remained silent throughout this exchange. 'Did you ever hear him?' he asked. 'Espousing defeatism? That's the phrase, I think.'

'I'm not sure whether Sam and I can really help you much with this, Captain Strafford. We were absent from Larkwhistle at that time. We went on a little tour of France, didn't we? Took us a while to get home.'

Sam concurred. 'Like it's taking me, tonight,' he said. 'So, if you'll excuse me, gentlemen?' Jack tried to persuade him to stay, ordered another round and told Sam he wanted to hear his war stories. 'If you want all that,' said Sam, 'you'll have to speak to someone of your own rank.' He turned to Patrick Deever and saluted. Jack could not say whether this was an expression of loyalty or something more sardonic. Then Sam was gone, the pub door thudding behind him.

Patrick Deever took his glass and raised it. 'Let's drink that toast again!' he declared. Jack's eyes stayed on him.

'Oh,' exclaimed Patrick. 'You're serious. You really want to know.'

'I do,' said Jack, in a tone that was polite but unarguable.

'Well,' said Patrick, 'I'm at a bit of a disadvantage

because Sam was conscious throughout the whole episode . . . and I was not.' He lifted his left arm and tapped his prosthetic hand on the top of the bar. 'Do you talk much about your own war experiences, Captain Strafford?'

'They're not over yet, Captain Deever,' said Jack.

'But you can imagine yourself in the peace, back in civvies, once the service is done with you?'

'I can,' said Jack. 'Happily.'

'And do you think you'll be the sort of soldier who sits in pubs and rakes over his past glories? Because I don't think many of us are like that. In fact, I've never met a single one. And do you know why? It's not, in the main, because we're too modest or because we have been sworn to secrecy, or developed the habit of secrecy. It's because we *did things*. Those things that men do when they go to war. Our fathers did them in the First War and we did them in this one. Those girls in French towns who we lied to. The refugees we tried to help who didn't want our help. The small things we did just before our pal got a bullet in the skull. Miscalculations.'

Jack indicated Patrick's prosthetic hand. 'Was that the result of a miscalculation, sir?'

Patrick flicked his glass with a finger. 'So, I think about this once a day, I'd say. An old girl in the refugee convoy, about the same age as my Aunt Molly. Carrying all her worldly possessions in two bundles slung on a broomstick. Which broke. I saw it happen. She dropped her stuff on the ground and I picked it up for her. And do you know what she did? She slapped me across the face. I suppose in war, a chap's got to take that. You don't know what people have gone through.'

'Where was this?' asked Jack.

'Just north of Bergues. Last day of May. We'd been manning an artillery position on the other side of the town. There were twenty of us still standing. Not bad, really. But this lot, this column of people, were blocking our way. They were slowing us down with their donkey carts and their prams full of blankets and bric-a-brac. And we needed to get to the coast, me and Sam and the men. So, I ordered the boys to cut across the fields. And then he came down. Jerry. In a Stuka. Down over the road. Over the heads of the refugees. But he didn't bomb them, he only strafed them. You could see the bullets dancing on the ground. Chucking up the dust. I saw that old girl go down, kiddies running in the wrong direction, and I thought, *Why are they using bullets? Why aren't they bombing them? Why aren't the bastards dive-bombing them? That's what a Stuka is for.*'

'Because they were keeping the road good for the tanks,' said Jack.

'Exactly,' said Patrick Deever. Was there a tear in his good eye?

'Were you hit?'

'I was. But the Sergeant sorted me out. Patched me up. Took me for a little beach holiday to recuperate. Place called Dunkirk. You might have heard of it.'

'How was the weather?' asked Jack.

'We were very lucky in that respect,' said Patrick. 'But the accommodation wasn't up to much. Lying in the sand and being bombed. Not my idea of a good time. We decided to leave after one night.'

'And he got you out? Sam Hill?'

'Saved my life by not taking me to the field hospital on the beach. The doctors were drawing lots by the end, you know, as the Germans advanced. Telling the chaps there that all would be well. Finishing some of them off, I've heard tell. And I don't blame them. Sometimes it's a chap's duty to put another chap out of his misery. Don't make a disapproving face, Captain Strafford, we both know it.'

'How did you avoid being put out of your misery, Captain Deever?'

'Sam got me on a boat. And even that was a near thing. We were on one of the piers. It was in a terrible state. Missing sections joined by single planks. A bloody death trap. We got to the end eventually, though. But down came Jerry again, spitting mouth-fuls of fire. We both went under, into the briny. But Sam got me out. Dragged me out. At some expense to himself. By the time he got back to Dover he was one lung down on the bargain. So, that's why when Sam Hill is in here, the drinks are on me.'

'You should write all this down,' said Jack, 'for posterity.'

'I tried, actually. But my wife said my prose was rotten. And she'd know. Only room for one writer in a marriage, I suppose.'

The life had ebbed from the conversation. Patrick Deever said his goodnights and began the walk back to his house on the edge of the village. Wally Speed put the bottles away and closed the pub: he would serve no more customers tonight. Effie Speed appeared from the back kitchen with a cold supper for Jack. He ate it alone in the saloon and watched the light withdraw from the village green.

At nine o'clock he went upstairs and sank down on the bed. The room contained a small bookshelf. Guides to the New Forest. The Gideon Bible. A dog-eared Captain Marryat. The inevitable copy of *The Boy Among the Trees*. He picked it up and saw Maggie Speed's name written on the inside cover in childish, spidery letters. He began to read.

Chapter 13

The Boy Among the Trees

There is a village in England that all of us know, even if we have never set foot there. It is the village of our imaginations. The village that comes to our minds when we think of cricket on the green on a Sunday in July; when we see a honeysuckled cottage painted on the lid of a tin of biscuits; when we put our hands together and say, 'Here's the church and here's the steeple'.

It really exists. And I would let you in on the secret and tell you how to get there, were it not for the feelings of its inhabitants. They are a quiet people and have asked me not to draw attention to them. Though they are kind to visitors, they would prefer them not to arrive in charabancs, asking for ices and cream teas.

The village lies on the edge of a wood – a great and ancient wood where kings once hunted the hart and the boar. It has a church – a fine old church with an old and sonorous bell. It has a shop, where they will be pleased to sell you confits and penny candles, though only for ready money. Credit is usually refused. There is a limit to their generosity.

This tale concerns a boy from the village. A sunburned boy with yellow hair. At one time I knew him very well. He was familiar with all the woodland ways and byways and would lead me down them to show me where the badger kept his sett and where the woodpecker made his nest. He was a fine and proper boy. He closed the gates. He addressed the cows as ladies. He could tell a fair mushroom from a foul one. He always looked upwards, listened to the conversation of the birds and whistled back, hopefully. This boy was a true Commoner. Whether he was happy or whether he was sad, he walked in the woods.

One morning the boy woke up very early. While his mother slept, he had rolls and milk and blackberries for breakfast. But he was careless and knocked the milk jug from the table. It shattered on the flagstones of the kitchen floor. The boy mopped up the spilt milk, put the china fragments in the ash dump behind the gooseberry nets and went out into the woods. He did not want to face his mother. He had broken her favourite jug.

The boy climbed over the stile and followed the path into the trees. If you look at the map on the facing page, you will see his journey. The asterisk shows the place where he began his walk. The broken line shows his progress past the great fir tree, the dell and the sand bank where the rabbits have their warren. And at the end of that broken line is where the boy met a monstrous crow, as big as a tar barrel.

The crow was scratching at the ground, hoping to find some ant eggs. He cocked his head when the boy arrived. He was curious.

'Why are you crying?' asked the crow, in his strange, dry voice.

'I broke my mother's favourite jug,' said the boy, weeping, 'and I cannot go home now.'

'No matter,' said the crow. 'All boys leave home, sooner or later. They don't stay boys forever. They leave the village and they leave the woods.'

'And what do they do?' asked the boy.

'Oh,' said the crow, spotting an ant running across the ground. 'Some become clerks, some work on the farm, some go down dark mines, some go to war.'

'Do some stay in the woods?' asked the boy.

'Few,' said the crow. 'Vanishingly few. I can only take one apprentice at a time. But you are fortunate. I have a vacancy at present.' The crow shook an oily wing. 'It is yours if you wish it.'

The boy thought of the broken jug hidden in the ash dump.

'What would be my duties?' he asked.

'To listen,' said the crow. 'To be among the trees. To help those who get lost in the woods. Sometimes I will need you to go south, or to dig in a certain place, or to check my snares and traps. But your predecessors have all reported that it is a good life, with fresh air and freedom and good, simple food. You have a day to consider my offer, and then I must make it to another candidate.'

The boy thanked the crow. 'I will meet you here tomorrow morning and give you my answer.'

The crow concurred. 'And I will wait for it.'

The day passed. As the sun fell and night crept in, the boy went home to face his mother. He could see that she had been weeping. She gave him some biscuits and a glass of milk, poured from her second best jug.

'Mother,' said the boy, 'when I am a man, what shall I do?'

'Cousin Edmund went to the town,' said his mother. 'He works in a great office by the harbour and puts figures in a ledger. Spices and bales of cotton. And Cousin Edgar went to Hannant's farm. There's a machine there that pulls the turnips straight from the ground. And Cousin Edward went to France and was lost.'

The boy ate the last of his biscuits. 'I'm sorry for my clumsiness, Mother,' he said.

'No matter,' said his mother, and threw her arms around him and kissed him.

The next morning the boy rose early. He untucked his bed sheet and made a bundle of his favourite things. He opened the door quietly, so as not to wake his mother. On his way he went to the ash dump behind the gooseberry nets and retrieved a fragment of the broken jug. Then he went to the woods.

He found the crow waiting for him. The bird cast a beady eye over the bundle that was slung over the boy's shoulder. 'I see you have decided to make the woods your home,' he said, in his strange, dry voice.

The boy nodded. 'Mother forgave me for breaking the jug, but I do not care for ledgers, or for the turnip field, or for France.'

'Then come with me,' said the crow, 'and never leave the woods. We can walk its paths forever, a crow and his boy. We can roast rabbit over the fire, and wake early every morning, as the dew forms on the grass.'

They did. The boy had his desire. And the shade and the light of the woods were always upon him.

I do not visit the village as often as before. Other shops have better confits, and to my ear, the bells of the new church at Brockenhurst produce a sweeter sound. But sometimes I walk the woodland paths where that boy showed me where the badger kept his sett and where the woodpecker made his nest. And I whistle to the birds, and hope for a reply.

129

Chapter 14

Jack saw the coroner at breakfast the following morning. He was in the saloon, eating toast and marmalade and making pencil notes on the pathologist's report. To Jack's surprise, he was also drinking a small glass of beer. The surprise showed.

'My seventeenth-century predecessors,' said the coroner, in a reedy, sententious tone, 'rarely drank water.'

Jack decided not to be embarrassed. He was American. It was expected. 'You'll be on the beer all day, then, sir?'

'No,' said the coroner. 'Breakfast time and bedtime. Moderation. Regularity. Best thing for a man in my position. If I make a mistake about a corpse, well, that would be mortifying, wouldn't it, Captain?' The coroner moved his eyes from Jack's stripes to the document on the breakfast table and realized he was talking to one of his witnesses. He too decided not to be embarrassed.

'Your very good health,' he said, raising his glass and downing the rest of the beer. Jack answered him with his cup of tea.

'Mind you,' said the coroner, 'he doesn't mind putting his prices up. I was here in November, and it's gone up thruppence since then.'

Once the proceedings began, the coroner appeared to be the most sober man in the world. He greeted the room and laid out the details with the smooth, unhurried manner of a museum guide. 'As the coroner,' he said, 'it is my duty to establish the circumstances surrounding Mr Brock's death. I will aim to deliver a verdict on the cause of death, but this is not a trial. I am not a judge and there is no jury. Our purpose is solely to establish the facts.'

The pub was not large. This, thought Jack, might be another reason why the coroner disliked the Verderers' Hall – the Fleur-de-Lys was not big enough to accommodate a circus. The witnesses sat in a row – Jill, alert and analytical; Harold Metcalfe, leaning on his walking stick, talking in low tones to Len Creech; the Brocks, side by side, not touching, betraying no obvious tenderness, but visibly in alliance. Pam Sharp arrived early and occupied the seat next to Helena Brock, hoping to inhale some of the drama. Mrs Brunton, frowning as she did when late for Evensong, was an unwitting rescuer. Pam Sharp felt obliged to vacate the seat in her favour and cram herself into a space by the cellar door. Two rows back, Captain Deever and his sergeant sat like mourners at a memorial service who fear seeming to make too strong a claim upon the dead.

Beside Patrick was his wife, Mary Rose Deever. A rare sight under the roof of the Fleur-de-Lys. She wore a black hunting jacket and matching hat, and carried a leather-bound notebook on her lap, the kind that has a loop to carry its own slim pencil. Her lipstick was a shade unknown to other women of the New Forest. Hawaiian Fire had yet to spread beyond Bond Street. Her presence in the room caused a ripple of interest. Despite having his back to her, Jack registered the disturbance.

Maggie Speed was the first to be called. Her smallness and slightness seemed to bring out the coroner's paternal side. He asked her about her movements through the woods as if he were in need of advice for a nature walk. Maggie said she liked to gather heather. She liked the smell of it in her room. So did the coroner. What did she take with her? An apple and a copy of *Wuthering Heights*. The coroner approved these choices, making it easier for Maggie to bear the inescapable questions about broken bodies and blood spots on bracken, and a man in a green jacket taking off his shirt in the woods. Her only serious upset came when the coroner asked about the time. Maggie had no wristwatch and could only say that she had been out for a couple of hours and thought it might have been time for lunch. She looked suddenly very young and lost, but the coroner told her that he also measured his days by mealtimes, and that several important French philosophers did the same.

She was more confident on the detail of her duties in the Deever household – the emptying of the ashes, the ironing, the preparation of meals. She mentioned that Mary Rose had given her advice on how to become a writer. However, once the coroner understood that Maggie's was a part-time position, and that she had been nowhere near Woodlander House on the day of Peter's death, he abandoned this line of inquiry, thanked her and asked her mother to take her from the room.

Now Maggie's elders began to unroll the story. When Patrick Deever came to the stand, Jack realized that the coroner's manner was not adopted specially to spare the feelings of the young. He spoke to the Dunkirk veteran, visibly war-scarred, with just the same tone of gentle generosity.

'What took you on that path on the day in question?' he asked.

'I had a letter to post,' said Patrick Deever. 'I wanted to make the lunchtime collection.'

'Is this the most direct route from your house to the Post Office?'

'No. But it's only a slight diversion. The day was hot. I'd already been to the village and back during the morning, and in the middle of the day the main road is unshaded.'

'May I ask if the letter was urgent?'

'It was a letter to a prospective employer in Southampton,' he said, with evident embarrassment. 'I am seeking a position.'

'I see. And is it now sent?'

'I put it in the box yesterday. I imagine it has reached its destination.'

The coroner consulted his notes. 'Were you alone when you left the house?'

'No, my wife was upstairs in her study. Working.'

'How do you know?'

'The sound of her typewriter, sir.'

'She is a typist?'

'An author.'

'Oh, I do beg your pardon.'

Some in the room – Pam Sharp among them – turned to look at Mary Rose Deever. The Captain's wife did something with the angle of her head that was both minuscule and gracious.

'Could you describe what happened on that walk, Captain Deever?'

'Nothing, sir,' he said, 'until I heard the shot. I was

a hundred yards or so from the fork in the path, so I ran towards it.' Patrick's eyes fell upon the Brocks.

'I thought the lad was asleep at first,' he said, 'under the tree. I saw who it was, of course. Despite the injuries. Peter Brock was a figure in our house, do you see? Pictures of him everywhere. My wife used him as a model in one of her books. She painted him under the very same fir tree, when he was quite small. That made the sight doubly shocking. It seemed like a horrible sort of statement. *The Boy Among the Trees.*'

'What do you mean by that?'

'It's the title of the book, sir.'

'I see. Did you find a weapon?'

'Not until the Reverend Brock moved the body of his son. It was underneath him. Hidden in the roots of the fir tree.'

'Was he dead when you arrived?'

'I thought so. I was convinced of it, really. But I didn't want to be accused of not trying, so I attempted to dress the wound. With my shirt.'

'How long were you doing this before Miss Maggie Speed saw you?'

'That's a very hard question to answer, sir,' said Patrick. 'Ten minutes? But if you told me it was only a few seconds, I would find it hard to contradict you.'

'Could you say what time you left the house?'

'Geraldo was on the wireless.'

'Geraldo?'

'The band leader.'

The coroner wrote down the name.

'Wasn't that impressed with him, to be honest,' continued Patrick, unbidden. 'Seems to have lost a bit of his pep, so I switched him off, which is fortunate, I suppose. I wouldn't have heard the gunshot otherwise.'

The coroner thanked his witness. Sam Hill followed Patrick Deever. He described the pattern of his early-morning delivery round, his progress from the Post Office to the pub, over the ford to the charcoal burners' cottages and the manor house (now requisitioned), then back towards the vicarage and St Cedd's. He was, he said, just about to empty the pillar box when the bad news reached him.

The coroner pressed him on the question of the gun.

'I saw immediately that it was mine,' said Sam.

'Was this a surprise to you?'

'A horrible surprise, sir.'

The coroner looked at his notes. 'I see that you reported it missing two weeks ago. When was the last time you saw it?'

'About a week before, I think. I rarely look at it.'

'Why did you keep it, may I ask?'

'When I came back from France, sir, an invasion was on the cards. We – men like Captain Deever and myself – thought we'd be defending this village from the enemy. Sitting in the trees and waiting for the Jerry parachutists to drop.'

'We give thanks that the moment has passed,' said the coroner. 'May I ask why you were discharged?'

Sam tapped his chest. 'I came back from Dunkirk down a lung, sir. Asked for a recount but nothing doing.' The coroner smiled ruefully.

The procession continued. Wally Speed disappointed the room with his poor command of the details: breathlessness seemed to have robbed him of any useful impressions. Jack was better received, as much for the cut of his uniform as the clarity of his testimony. As he stood before the coroner, he felt like an exhibit – an exotic act imported to liven up the village gang show – but it gave him the chance to take in the sight of Larkwhistle as a body of men and women. He looked from face to face, reading pain and prurience, the lines and scars of war. These were the Commoners of the New Forest. Perhaps Berlin's Commoner was among them, daydreaming of rocket bombs and Allied defeat.

When he returned to his seat he was given another object of contemplation. Jill Metcalfe, giving her account of the day. He knew the facts: he'd been there. He knew her insights: he had heard them already. Perhaps this was the reason he found himself listening not to her words, but the clear music of her voice, and watching the way the light fell on her face and hair.

When the Brocks gave their testimony after lunch, the room was quiet enough for a séance. Helena spoke first, pale and unemotional, as if she were reserving her grief and anger for another day. She related the details of an unexceptional morning in the vicarage – some wrangle over the flower rota, a mild dispute about the storage of donations for the summer bazaar, a visit from a farming parishioner who wanted help to fill out a form from the Ministry of Supply. The coroner then encouraged her into more painful territory. She spoke of her son's nature and character, the depth of his feelings about the world and the war, his frustration with the doctor who told him that his heart was too weak for service. She described his relationship with the woods; how they were a sanctuary for him; how he would disappear into them, particularly during the warm months, sometimes declaring his intentions, sometimes slipping out secretly at strange hours. Perhaps, she suggested, Peter told the trees what he could not bring himself to say to people. Perhaps one of those things, she suggested, was a desire to take his own life.

Her speculation changed the temperature in the room. 'Mrs Brock,' said the coroner, 'what evidence did you have that he ever entertained such a notion?'

'Because he said it,' returned Helena. 'Like a black joke, mostly, if things weren't going his way. And sometimes as if he meant it. He was full of passions, Peter. And the tragedy of the matter is that I don't know what they were. Not the deepest ones.'

Helena was released and returned to her seat. She had created a space of pain and regret into which the coroner now summoned her husband. Guy Brock described the rough terrain of his relationship with Peter; told the story of their political disagreement and how it was resolved by a violent encounter with a German parachutist.

'We saw eye to eye after that,' said Guy. 'The world made sense to us, in the same terms. War couldn't be avoided; it had to be fought to the end.'

There was no element of self-aggrandizement in the telling. Nor of resentment when he gave an account of his son's ambivalence towards the book with which his history was entwined. Peter, he said, disliked the illustrations in *The Boy Among the Trees* because he thought them old-fashioned and effeminate. But he recognized himself in the melancholy tone of the story and, when he felt lost and uncertain, which was often, said that it contained some prophecy about his life. One which now seemed to have been fulfilled. 'He always said he would never leave the forest,' said Guy Brock. 'And he was right.'

'Are you suggesting, Reverend Brock,' ventured the

coroner, 'that this book may have influenced his behaviour on the day of his death?'

Guy Brock looked across the room. His eyes met those of Mary Rose Deever. It was hard to say precisely what was exchanged between them, though half the room craned its neck to read the moment. Those familiar with the experience of the confessional understood it best. Mary Rose was asking for absolution. It seemed possible that Guy Brock was granting it.

'It's not so simple,' he said. 'The book is not to blame. The book is a beautiful thing. I've looked at it a lot in the last two days. For me it's not a source of horror, it's a kind of consolation.'

It was a different story to the one he had told in the Metcalfes' cottage, in which the book had been a dark shadow, an albatross around the neck of his son. Perhaps loss had given Guy Brock time to change his mind. Or perhaps he had decided that even in these circumstances, the vicar of Larkwhistle should follow the prayer of St Francis, and not so much seek to be consoled as to console.

The final witness was a stranger, and not a welcome one. A thin-faced septuagenarian in a chocolate-coloured jacket who had been sitting silently at the edge of the room, almost hidden by the bar. The police pathologist described, in detail unloved by his audience, the catastrophe that had befallen the body of Peter

Brock. He spoke of the progress and the angle of the bullet, the destruction of tissues, the flow of blood. He gave a list of figures – time of death, liquid volumes – that were customary in the morgue, but an affront to a country pub, whatever business is being conducted under its roof. A sad tale to be told by the fire, about an unhappy boy who went into the woods in despair, had been disrupted by the particularities of human organs inspected with a magnifying glass.

'Was there any evidence of a struggle?' asked the coroner.

'None,' returned the witness.

'What, in your opinion, caused this man's death?'

'A bullet to the head,' said the pathologist, 'penetrated his left frontal lobe just above the eye. It was fired by the gun that was collected in evidence.'

'You're sure of that?' asked the coroner.

'That's what my examination of the bullet concluded,' replied the pathologist. 'Death was instantaneous. This aspect of the case is very uncomplicated.'

'And who, in your judgement, fired this gun?'

'It may have been the deceased. But the fingerprints of at least four people were found on that weapon. There is nothing in the ballistic evidence that can show, conclusively, that the deceased was the author of his own death.'

'Is it possible that the crime of murder may have been committed?' asked the coroner.

'Certainly,' said the pathologist.

There were no howls of protest. Nobody in the room said anything aloud. But the people gathered in the saloon of the Fleur-de-Lys registered the jolt of this pronouncement and objected to its casual tone as much as the sudden shift it brought to the narrative of the day. They thought they had been hearing the story of a melancholy young man who, like the picture-book boy from whom his life could not be disentangled, had come to some bleak and irrevocable choice. Another possibility presented itself, like a fresh wound.

The English liked their etiquette. Jack knew enough about his hosts to understand that. What he saw when the coroner concluded the inquest upon the death of Peter Brock was something like the business following a church service. The men and women who had spent the day in the saloon of the Fleur-de-Lys gathered on the green in knots to judge the coroner's questions as they might have assessed the quality of a Sunday sermon. The effect of the pathologist's remarks was palpable. The butcher expressed disgust at what had been said. Pam Sharp was struck by a giddiness that led her, wisely, to conclude that she was better off at home. Harold and Len Creech paired up and sat in conference at a pub table.

Guy and Helena Brock were treated with nervous

deference. Some offered their condolences. Others nodded or tipped their hats and returned home.

Sam Hill and Patrick Deever did not approach the Brocks. They stayed together in their own little platoon of two. Mary Rose Deever, however, broke from the formation. For the first time, Jack was able to examine her closely. Her nails, he noted – painted but very short – spoke of her devotion to the type-writer. Her hunting jacket was expensively tailored and betrayed no contact with an animal body other than her own. Her expression was tight and concen-trated: Mary Rose was presenting her best face to the world. As she had recently emerged from a room in which a grieving father had defended her from the charge of being an indirect cause of his son's death, there was, thought Jack, plenty that it might be concealing.

Mary Rose was now approaching Guy and Helena Brock and pulling something from her blue leather handbag. A small board-backed envelope. She offered it to Helena, who accepted it, Jack suspected, because refusal would have produced an embar-rassing scene.

'I wasn't sure if I ought to give this to you after what was said in there,' said Mary Rose. Her voice had a smooth depth and resonance that came from elocution lessons, public lecturing and Black Cat cigar-ettes. 'It's so awful to see your greatest friends in pain. I tried to call the day before yesterday. I'm sorry if I intruded.'

'No,' said Helena, 'I'm sorry. I should have let you in.'

'I wanted to give you something. Just something. As a keepsake, if you like it.'

Helena passed the envelope to Guy, who opened it. Inside was a line illustration mounted on stiff yellow card. A drawing of their son, aged about eight. Not one of the idealized images from *The Boy Among the Trees*, but a portrait from life, executed in loose and confident pencil strokes. It was perfect. It captured Peter's expression and manner, the movement of his eyes, the ironic wrinkle of his mouth. The longer Helena looked at it, the more she felt the acid stir of rage and affront. Her son was dead. She would bury him tomorrow. And now this woman, who had stolen his image and become rich from it, was standing before her, in her Mayfair jacket, offering evidence that she too had thought about him, gazed upon him with a parent's concentration. Could she not see the obscene tactlessness of the gesture?

'Thank you, Mary Rose,' said Helena. 'It's very kind of you. Isn't it, Guy?'

'Oh, yes,' said her husband. 'I do hope that we're going to see you tomorrow, and I hope that after the service you'll join us in the vicarage for tea.'

Mary Rose smiled like a saint in an alcove. 'You're both very brave,' she said. 'If there's anything that I can do for you, please let me know.'

As the Brocks retreated, Mary Rose noticed Jack. She flashed her eyes at her husband who, as if on parade, flowed forward to effect an introduction. Sam Hill moved beside him, the loyal lieutenant.

'I'm so sorry that you should be seeing us all like this, Captain,' said Mary Rose. 'We're usually quite a cheerful bunch.' Her fluting voice cracked slightly. Mary Rose's confidence, Jack saw, was effortful. The boy's death had shaken her.

'I think Captain Strafford might have seen us at our best today,' said Patrick. 'Poor Maggie did very well, I thought. She's a good girl. For an odd girl. She was hopelessly in love with Peter Brock. Did you know that, Jill?'

'Oh, I don't know whether we should drag all that out, dear,' said Mary Rose, closing the subject. 'Ancient history.'

'Thank you for your card,' said Jill. 'It was terribly sweet of you.'

'I hope you didn't think the invitation in poor taste,' said Mary Rose. 'One scarcely knows what to do. As if the war wasn't enough of a test for us.'

'No,' said Jill. 'I should be very glad to come.' Mary Rose and her husband made a gracious acknowledgement.

'About seven?' said Mary Rose. She seemed about to depart, but then, as a visiting dignitary might notice she had forgotten to shake hands with someone in the line, she turned to Sam.

'Sam,' she said. 'I picked out a few things that I thought Ivy might like. Patrick can bring them over. Just some old skirts and blouses. If there's anything that takes her eye, I'd be delighted to pass them on.'

'I'll tell her,' said Sam. Patrick and Mary Rose moved off. Sam departed with a grunt. Jack and Jill retreated to a bench on the green.

'Must we?' muttered Jill, once the couple were out of earshot.

'I can say you're ill,' said Jack.

'I never get ill,' said Jill.

'It's a good opportunity. I'm not like poor Len Creech, you see. I don't need a warrant. But I would hate to upset you or embarrass you.'

'Why would it embarrass me?'

'Because I'm going to need to keep those two talking while I look around the house for evidence of espionage.'

Jill tried to imitate his professional coolness. 'What form will it take, do you think?' she asked.

'The household copy of *The Boy Among the Trees*, for instance,' said Jack. 'It might be marked up in some way.'

'Are you looking for my approval?'

'I suppose I am.'

'You have it,' said Jill. 'And you have my promise of help, too.'

Something, she felt, had shifted. She had done more than enter his confidence: she had become his co-conspirator. She and Jack now occupied a space of secret knowledge. It had a high wall, and on the other side of it was everyone she knew.

'Won't we have to do this everywhere in the village?' she asked. 'Look inside every garden shed and inside every wardrobe? Every fireplace? It's usually the fire-place, isn't it? I saw it in a play. Chap in a boarding house on the Isle of Wight had a wireless hidden there. And there's a Sherlock Holmes. They let off a smoke bomb and Irene Adler leaps for the piano where she's hidden all the letters from the King of Bohemia.'

'I don't think we're going to do this with a grand gesture, Jill,' said Jack. 'It'll be more modest and mundane. I'll be scanning the shelves for references to Whitechapel and May. I'll be looking in the lava-tory cistern. Checking the wardrobe to see if there's anything hidden behind the winter coats. It's quite vulgar, when you think about it.'

'Not as vulgar as treachery,' said Jill. 'Not as vulgar as selling out your country.'

Chapter 15

It was hard to know how to behave with a coffin in the house. Harold Metcalfe, however, had chosen to dispense with the help of the undertaker and did not have the brisk timetable of Catholicism to speed the process or fill the house with sympathetic guests. Both he and Jill were relieved that there was only one more night to be endured before they could give Henry to the Anglican earth. Wimsey seemed restless, too, wandering between his bowl of water on the kitchen floor and his favoured spot beside the bay window in the parlour.

'Why don't you take him for a walk?' said Harold.

Jill concurred. His usual route was through the woods, passing the fir tree where Peter's body had been discovered, but perhaps Wimsey could be persuaded to forgo the pleasures of squirrel territory for a circuit of the village.

As she walked over the green, she saw Jack sitting alone at a table outside the Fleur-de-Lys. The business of the inquest concluded, the Speeds had rearranged the furniture and were attempting an evening of normal service. Jack was their only visible customer. Beside his glass of bitter was a plate of sandwiches, his military-issue satchel and a copy of *The Boy Among the Trees*. Jill had the strong impression he was waiting for her.

'Commoner,' said Jack, as though they were already in the middle of a long conversation. 'Commoner.' He tapped the cover of Mary Rose Deever's magnum opus.

'Where did you get that?' asked Jill.

'I borrowed it from the pub. It was there in the guest room. Next to the guidebooks. Local colour, I guess.' He indicated the cover illustration. Little Peter Brock beneath the great fir. 'The boy,' said Jack. 'The boy among the trees – he's described as a Commoner.' He flipped to the relevant page. 'This boy was a true Commoner,' he read. 'Whether he was happy or whether he was sad, he walked in the woods.'

'As I told you, Captain, we're everywhere in these parts,' said Jill. 'But I don't think the Brocks had any of those rights. They're ancestral. Conferred by family and property. Vicars don't own their own vicarages, and the family only arrived here a couple of decades ago.'

Jack raised an eyebrow.

'I know,' said Jill. 'Madly feudal, isn't it?'

Jack invited her to sit down. 'I need your help with something,' he said. He put the book down and spread it open at its middle pages. Jill saw that there was now a number written beside each word of the text. The sequence was consecutive, assigning each word of the story a value between 1 and 1,171.

'I had to vandalize Maggie's book,' he said. 'It's autographed, too.'

'In Larkwhistle,' said Jill, 'it's unsigned copies that are rare.'

Jack pulled a notebook from his jacket pocket and opened it at a place marked with a ribbon. He showed it to Jill. Each page contained a neat column of numbers written in Jack's hand. Each set of numbers was headed by a date.

'Why don't you make a start while I go to the bar?' he said, pressing the notebook into her hand.

Jill understood instantly. These numbers were the messages transmitted by Commoner. If they were a book code, perhaps *The Boy Among the Trees* was the key.

'I'll have what you're having,' she said. 'And a bag of crisps. The ones with the little blue bag of salt, please.'

Jack disappeared inside the pub. Jill put the story book and the code book side by side. Wimsey had stopped to investigate the potted geraniums that lined the whitewashed wall of the pub. Jill would normally have pulled him away, but it was not a day for discipline. She allowed him to nuzzle among the plants, and soon forgot him altogether as she paired numbers with words and saw sentences emerging like the coloured ink from the pages of a magic painting book.

Arms dump in field south of church.
Visitors arrive second night. Will wait.
Harbour line broken answer tomorrow.

Coded messages transmitted from Larkwhistle to the enemy, all of a portentous and military character.

Jack was back. He put a glass of beer and a bag of crisps down on the table.

'Interesting, isn't it?' he breezed. 'How many have you done?'

'Three,' said Jill. She was excited. 'All sounds very ominous. Who are the visitors? Parachutists, I suppose? And the harbour. Which one does he mean? Lymington? Southampton? Portsmouth?'

'Do another.'

Jill got to work, flipping through the pages to find the words she needed. The fourth sequence was less satisfactory.

'Badger conversation asterisk biscuits.'

'That's nonsense.'

'Complete nonsense.'

She tried another. And frowned again.

'Shattered eggs facing progress. Perhaps we need to count from the other direction.'

Jack shook his head. 'I've tried that, but it's no better. It works for the first few in each sequence, and then stops. And once you start trying to test whether there's an extra key that shifts the correlation between the number and the word, you're into something with millions of possibilities. You might as well do a jigsaw puzzle in the pitch dark.'

Jill put the pencil down and took a sip of beer.

'Did Peter Brock know Morse code?' asked Jack.

'I've absolutely no idea, but I know Henry learned it in the Scouts. They used to practise with torches across the village green at night. Peter never wore the uniform, though. I think he was a bit mistrustful of things like that. Not a joiner.'

'He tried to join the Army, though.'

'That's different. You can't go and fight the Nazis in a freelance capacity. But if they had come to us – as we thought they would before you lot came riding in – well, Peter would have made an excellent Partisan. He'd have been setting traps in the woods, I suspect. Catching the bastards like snipe.'

Jill noticed Jack trying to disguise his reaction to her use of the word. Perhaps there were no bastards in Philadelphia. She opened the crisps and fished out the blue sachet of salt. 'Are you suggesting that Peter Brock was sending those messages to the Germans?' she asked, tipping the salt into the bag. 'That he killed himself out of remorse? Or fear of the hangman?'

'I'm prepared to add him to the list. If there's no broadcast tonight. Our friend Commoner always puts something out on a Friday evening.'

Jill put two crisps in her mouth at once. 'That's a bit dog-that-didn't-bark, isn't it? I agree that if something does go out on air tonight you can strike Peter off the list, but nothing is evidence of nothing.'

Wimsey had grown bored of the flower bed. He ran to the stile that led to the woods, wagging his tail. Then he jumped clean over it. He had decided to stick to his usual route. If Jill followed him, there would be no avoiding the scene of the crime.

'That dog has no sense of decorum,' she said, getting to her feet.

'Is he a good detective, though?' asked Jack.

'Hopeless.'

'But he's named after a detective.'

'We had high hopes of him as a puppy,' said Jill. 'But he's not like one of those dogs in the films who digs up important evidence and growls at the killer. He only really growls at squirrels.' She gave Jack a conspiratorial look. 'You must never tell him this, but between you and me, I suspect he's quite stupid. But he's so jolly that I forgive him with pleasure. He's

154

kept me in good spirits for years. Even this week.'

She drained her drink and passed Jack the packet of crisps. 'Here,' she said. 'Put those in your satchel. There's no use arguing with him.'

They followed the dog. Jack offered Jill his hand as she went over the stile. She smiled at him, but ignored it.

'Are there more?' she asked. 'Messages from Commoner? Or did you chaps get them all down?'

'From the point we detected him. After that we never missed a show. Transmissions like this aren't subtle. If you're tuned into the right wavelength, he's as loud and clear as the Home Service.'

'Badger conversation asterisk biscuits,' said Jill. 'Perhaps there's a secondary code. Maybe you have to do something else to those words to get them to make sense.'

'Bit fussy, isn't it?' said Jack, with a sceptical sniff. 'The nonsense is probably a decoy. They often use trash to hide the gold.'

'Unless,' Jill said, 'the sensible ones are the trash. I mean, what's a harbour line when it's at home?'

'A boom, maybe?' suggested Jack. 'Something to stop U-Boats getting too close to the coast?'

Jill was pulling at a thread. 'Has it been broken? And is there an arms dump south of the church? What church?'

Jack could not muster an answer.

'Would Mrs Brunton's shopping lists make a good code book?' she asked.

'Not unless the Abwehr was keen to receive information about sultanas and Bovril.'

'And Mary Rose's book isn't much more useful,' said Jill. 'A children's story about a talking crow? Why not choose a book with some good war vocabulary? *Biggles Flies West*? *The Thirty-Nine Steps*? I think the most you can say about these messages is that they're just about plausible.'

'So why choose it?' asked Jack.

Jill's eyes glittered. 'We know that the spy is in Larkwhistle. Well, the population is five hundred or so – and almost everyone in the village owns a copy of this book. If the key to Commoner's code is *The Boy Among the Trees*, that's five hundred suspects to rule out. So, I think it's a distraction. The real messages are the ones that don't translate, so they must have some other key.'

Jack's eyes were wide. 'You're wonderful,' he said.

'I suppose I must be,' said Jill. 'I never really thought about it before.'

They had reached the big fir tree. To Jill's relief, Wimsey did not pay it special attention but went off into the bracken to pursue some obscure animal trail.

'It's a great survivor, this one,' Jill said. 'They took most of the firs for timber. For pit props, I think. Taken underground to meet the ancestors.' She gazed up into the canopy. 'I wish you'd seen the Forest before the war. Before they flooded the fields and cut down so many of the trees. It's hard to imagine it ever going back to how it was.'

'Well at least all those troops are out of your hair.'

'I thought I would feel glad to see them go. But I'm not. Before D-Day you had the sense of something important happening here. Something you could feel part of. The evacuees bussed in from the towns on the coast. All the tents under the trees. Even the whizzbangs going off on the artillery ranges. Now we're just left looking at the scars. Those lumps of concrete on the village green. The dragon's teeth on the roads. It's going to take a long time to heal.'

She moved closer to the tree, examining its cracked and mossy trunk. She was, Jack noticed, avoiding the ground where the corpse had lain. He moved closer. He wanted to comfort her, but the words forming in his mind sounded like platitudes even before they were spoken. Jill turned away from him. She did not want him to see her fighting the tears.

'Yesterday I had such a jolly conversation with my dad. He was reading all the good news from Normandy and thinking about the return of those civilized little treats that make life seem so much more bearable. And now Henry's dead and Peter Brock is dead and when I think of peace, I don't think of Hitler defeated, I think of him safe in Germany with all his rockets, and England on fire.'

Jill turned to face Jack and he tried to read her expression. He thought, for one wild moment, that she was going to kiss him.

'I think Peter was here to meet a lover,' she said.

She was pointing at the tree. About four feet above the tangle of roots, someone had carved a tiny heart shape into its bark.

Beside it were two pairs of initials. The first was 'PB'. The second had been chiselled from the bark and was illegible.

Jack came closer. 'Why didn't we see it before?'

'Because it's the scratched-out part that draws the eye,' said Jill. 'It's white and fresh. Whoever removed these letters did it after Peter's death.'

Propriety, like the East End of London, had recently been shaken by the Luftwaffe. War relaxed the regulations of courtship. As soon as the Blitz began, the kissing started – and the prospect of victory had yet to make it stop. Perhaps, in peacetime, there would be some kind of retrenchment. But the discussion had been postponed, at least until VE Day, or perhaps the day after, once the bunting had come down and the empties had been returned to the beer-off shop. Or perhaps it would never happen.

For Jill, the timing of the crisis had been poor. She

had danced her way from the Anschluss to the Munich Crisis to the declaration. She knew her way around the Monseigneur club and the Grosvenor House Hotel. She knew the acronyms that declared a man safe or unsafe in taxis. She could foxtrot without losing her step. Just at the point at which she was ready to be serious, war broke out. Her engaged friends married in haste or broke off their arrangements. Her single friends kept dancing. She tried to do the same, but teacher-training college was a poor source of partners.

Under different circumstances, Jill might have gone to the Fleur-de-Lys to hear a late-night radio broadcast in the company of a good-looking American captain. She might even have enjoyed being the subject of gossip. Henry's death, however, had altered the rules, as it had altered everything.

The clock ticked towards eleven. Harold Metcalfe had already twice fallen asleep on the sofa.

'You get off,' said Jill. 'I'm going to stay up for a bit. Might listen to the wireless.'

Harold nodded through a yawn. It felt unchivalrous, somehow, to go to bed before his daughter, but this reluctance bore little examination. The shock of loss robbed some people of their sleep; others it inundated, and Harold now found himself in the latter category. Sometimes the body knew best: sleep was a space grief found hard to penetrate.

Jill listened to the rattle of his toothbrush in the mug on the bathroom sink, the click of his bedroom door. She opened the writing desk drawer and pulled out a pencil, a piece of scrap paper and Henry's Morse code guide from the Scouts. On the Home Service, Billy Ternent and his orchestra were taking the 'A Train', though it seemed to Jill highly unlikely that they would know what to do with themselves if they got to Harlem. She lowered the volume and pushed the dial beyond the familiar frequencies of the British Broadcasting Corporation. Enemy territory. Waves of static yielded to a fruity, traitorous voice. 'The United States is completely under the Hebrew thumb,' it said, with undisguised disgust. 'The so-called "Wise Men of Washington", or "Brains Trust of the President", are all Jews . . . the financial conference at Bretton Woods, the food conference at Hot Springs and the reconstruction conference in London were all over-poweringly represented by Jews.'

The mantelpiece clock chimed eleven. Jill shifted the dial to the frequency favoured by Commoner. The ghosts of the ether shrieked and warbled. Then she heard it. A stream of dots and dashes, tapped out with cool regularity. The numerical code was not so hard to render as alphabetical Morse. If a dot began the sequence, it was below five; if a dash, then higher. She took her hand from the dial and began to transcribe, struck by the strangeness of the enterprise; the idea that Jack was doing the same in the parlour of the Fleur-de-Lys, and somewhere in Larkwhistle, Commoner, whoever they were, was responsible for these pulses, and confident they would be relayed to Berlin.

After a few minutes, the dits and dahs fell silent. Surging shoals of static took their place. Jill's paper was now filled with a column of numbers. She pulled her copy of *The Boy Among the Trees* from the shelf and considered attempting a translation. No. Better to wait until morning and use the copy marked up by Jack. She re-tuned the radio to the Home Service and pushed the volume a little higher to allow the sound of Robin Richmond and his Swinging Sextet to spill into the parlour.

The night was warm and moonless. Jill opened the front door and stood on the threshold, looking out across the gloom of the village green. Was Commoner at work behind one of these windows, concealed by blackout curtains?

She breathed in the night air. Somewhere in the woods, an owl screeched.

A man was walking towards her across the green.

For a second Jill panicked, imagining that this was Commoner, come to take revenge upon an eavesdropper.

It was a friend.

'Did you hear?' asked Jack.

'I did,' said Jill. 'I wrote down the numbers, but I haven't tried to decipher them. Have you?'

'Yes,' said Jack. 'Same form as before. A preamble from *The Boy Among the Trees*, followed by something not yet crackable. The Whitechapel May part.'

'Anything interesting?'

'Not good news, I'm afraid,' he said. 'He's lost his taste for plausible junk about arms dumps.'

Jack produced the paper upon which he had made his own transcription.

Beady Eye On You. Go Home Now.

Chapter 16

'I think it's perfect,' said Mrs Brunton. She was sitting on the edge of Jill's bed, examining the text of her eulogy for Henry. 'It's the sort of thing I imagine saying about Michael.' She checked herself. 'I'm so sorry, Jill. It's the not knowing. It's been so long now.'

'You mustn't apologize,' said Jill. 'I know where Henry died and something of how he died. And for you – for Michael – well, the answers are all blank. Except for one, I think. Whether Michael is lost or whether he comes back, he'll be one of those boys who gave us victory. All that darkness that fell on us – well, it's lifting at last. Thanks to Michael and Henry and millions like them.'

'You always know how to put these things,' said Mrs Brunton.

'No I don't. It's the way we all talk and think these days.' She gave Mrs Brunton's hand a squeeze. 'Won't that be one of the most liberating things about peace when it comes? That we can just be ourselves with each other? When we're talking about our fears and hopes and what we love and want, we'll sound like ourselves and not like Winston bloody Churchill.'

Mrs Brunton gave a snotty and involuntary laugh. 'You're so brave, Jill. You always have been. Always had to be, I suppose.' She drew away from Jill to blow her nose.

Jill got to her feet, smoothed her dress, checked her hair. 'Well, I had you to look after me, didn't I?'

'You look beautiful,' said Mrs Brunton. 'Just like your mum. We should be going to a wedding, not a funeral.'

Male voices rose from the parlour below. The pallbearers had arrived. Jill and Mrs Brunton went down to greet them. Ben Twist, septuagenarian chief bell-ringer of St Cedd's, was in the middle of telling Jack how he taught Henry to master the front crawl and backstroke, and how glad he was to have let him call the changes on the last Sunday before the war. The bells had since been silent, their voices reserved for warning of invasion. Jill had the feeling that Jack had stopped asking Ben to explain the technicalities early in the conversation. Beside them, Henry's Lancing schoolfriend G.G. Johnston, whose given names were a mystery, was kneeling on the floor and petting Wimsey. 'He's a capital chap,' said G.G., whose expressions of enthusiasm were always followed by the worry that he'd done or said the wrong thing. 'Just like his master.'

Harold Metcalfe was straightening his tie. 'Is this all right, Jill?' It was.

Jill looked at the men gathered in the parlour. They were good and kind. She felt a pang of sadness. Commoner had turned Larkwhistle into a field of judgement. Every neighbour, every friend and acquaintance was now a locus of mistrust. Last night's message had added new anxiety. Commoner seemed to know his enemy: she and Jack did not.

It was hard to find an opportunity to speak to Jack. While the bellringers went outside for a smoke, Jill found it quiet enough in the kitchen.

'Perhaps it's a bluff,' she said. 'Perhaps he sends this message out regularly, just to see if it gets a response.'

'It's new. I think we can assume he's watching us.'

'Why tell us, though? He knows he can't scare us away. We're not kids stealing apples.'

'To flush us out. He has suspicions he wants to confirm. Perhaps he's hoping that we'll call in reinforcements. Maybe he's planning to cut and run as soon as he knows for sure. So we must try to give him nothing. Make him think he's safe.'

'That sounds a bit optimistic to me,' said Jill. 'What if a threat is a threat? He knows we're on to him and he's going to do something about it.'

Jack nodded. 'It might be worth watching what you eat and drink over the next few days. And avoid being alone. This doesn't seem the right moment to be saying this, but perhaps we should . . .'

He trailed off. He was not looking her in the eye.

'Perhaps we should what?'

'Go about together, as if we were . . .' The words eluded him.

'Courting?' said Jill. 'Stepping out?'

'I'm sorry. It's a poor idea and it was crass of me to say it while—'

G.G. Johnston was in the kitchen doorway. 'Sorry to disturb you chaps,' he breezed, Wimsey at his heels. 'It's almost time to go. Should we put this good boy in the kitchen?'

'Yes,' said Jill. 'I think it's a good idea. You're quite right.' She was not looking at G.G.. She was looking at Jack.

The church bell struck ten. The day was hot and cloudless. The sun would make back-breaking work for the sexton and hurt the eyes of the mourners. Jack had a pair of aviator sunglasses in his pocket, but he did not put them on.

As the strikes ended, Henry's coffin began its final journey. Harold and Jack led the bearers; G.G. and Ben Twist followed, two of Ben's bellringers keeping the balance. At the same time, Peter Brock was borne from the vicarage. Beneath his coffin walked two senior men from Symes and Co.; Guy Brock's brother, on leave from the Fleet Air Arm; Derek Wray, Peter's second-best village friend, stationed at RAF Sopley, his best friend being out on the Atlantic convoys. There was also Helena's cousin Robin, who worked in the Recorded Talks department at Broadcasting House and had once met Eleanor Roosevelt, and Simon Pinn, the curate of St Cedd's, emergency substitute chaplain at RAF Beaulieu and Stoney Cross, Peter's favourite fishing companion and the shortest of the six.

The two parties converged on the church and the two sons of the village were laid side by side in the chancel. St Cedd's was not a large church. Its awkward shape spoke of a millennium of adaptation and conflict. Jack noted the roll of the dead from the Great War, the black woodwork salvaged from the carcass of a Spanish galleon. It seemed that the entire population of Larkwhistle – bar those not dispersed around the world in khaki – were crammed into the box pews and choir stalls. So many beady eyes.

Much to Jill's surprise, Uncle Vincent, her late mother's younger brother, made an appearance just before the service started. Harold attempted to look grateful, but really, he would rather he had stayed away. Vincent was an awkward presence in the family. He regarded the law as a series of guidelines and suggestions, and a string of court appearances were evidence for his sincerity.

Larkwhistle tried to forget its animosities that morning, though some undercurrents always flowed. Martin Hill cried, of course, and had to be carried from the church by Ivy. Jill watched Helena's impatience with the baby, even in the depths of her grief.

Jack turned his eye to the Speeds. When they arrived, Maggie walked down to the front as if she meant to find a place among the chief mourners. Her mother placed an arm on her shoulder to guide her gently back to some more obscure position in the church. Maggie, he saw, took her place on the aisle nearest to Peter's coffin, ensuring that no human obstruction came between her and the object of her feelings. She was three rows back from Jack, but with a quick turn of his head he read her face easily: despair and longing.

The bulk of the praise that day was for the Reverend Guy Brock, who had come to bury his own son and to perform the same office for his neighbour. From the pulpit, his hands pressed hard against the eagle lectern, he described Peter's love of fishing, his eye for nature, his mastery of the common and Latin names for the life that thrived in the forest. Jill knew some of his stories, but not all. She remembered the fire at the magnesium factory at Marchwood; how it had burned for three nights with a pale white blaze, making a beacon for the Luftwaffe. She did not know that during those nights Peter had wandered through the woods, calming the horses worried by the strange, milky light in the sky. She knew that the boy had been deeply upset when he received the letter confirming him medically unfit for service. She remembered Peter outside the pub, sloshing his cider and shouting at the air. But she did not know that he had spent the following month camped in a haystack, waiting for invasion from sea and air, his rifle ready.

'We should not think of him sad,' pronounced the Reverend Brock. 'We should think of him in the woods. He knew the code of nature. He knew how to read the forest. He knew the pattern of the year.' At no point in the service did he mention *The Boy Among the Trees*. There was a moment, however, when he seemed to stare straight at Mary Rose Deever. She was sitting with her husband at the edge of the north aisle, and might have remained inconspicuous had she not chosen to wear a jacket trimmed with black fur.

When it was Jill's turn to take the pulpit, she found her eye drawn in the same direction. Mary Rose's combination of discretion and extravagance was compelling, and perhaps she was an easier sight than the bereft, ghostlike face of her father. Jill began by talking about the day during the Battle of Britain when a Messerschmitt with a mortal wound came careering out of the sky above Larkwhistle, machine guns blazing, just as the congregation were leaving St Cedd's. Henry, heedless of his own safety, had pushed people out of range of the gun. But the story Jill really wanted to tell was not about heroism. It related to Henry's last period of leave, six months ago. Larkwhistle at that time was crowded with GIs from the air bases, training for the rigours of D-Day. They drank the Fleur-de-Lys dry and offered compensation in the form of flirtatious remarks for the women and Mars bars for the kids. Not all the soldiers present, however, were preparing for Normandy. Some were burned airmen and tank crew who had been patched back together at the hospital in Marchwood. They were sent out into the villages as part of their treatment in the hope that they would gain some confidence and, perhaps, learn how to endure tactless local stares. Henry, forewarned of the visit, gathered the Larkwhistle children after church and explained that some men were coming to the village whose faces might, at first, shock them. He told them to try to look through the wound and see the man beneath.

'That afternoon,' said Jill, 'the children were playing football on the village green and they came over to the soldiers outside the pub. The GIs from the bases, fit and ready for war, and the men from the hospital, whom war had scarred so profoundly. And they played together for the rest of the afternoon, with Henry running about as referee, blowing his whistle.'

170

There were solemnities and hymns before the two coffins entered the bone-riddled earth of the church-yard, where Peter and Henry joined the ranks of soldiers, labourers and Commoners, and introduced two new names to the ancestral population of Larkwhistle. Ashes were added to ashes, and dust to dust. Of all the mourners, Mrs Brunton found it hardest to leave the graveside. She stood and gripped the handle of her handbag, and imagined the day her son would join them.

Once she had gone, however, a final mourner came forward. The sexton had done his work. The soil was piled upon the coffins. Most of the congregation were taking tea in the vicarage garden. Maggie Speed waited for her moment. She moved to the plot where Peter Brock lay. She knelt. She pushed her face to the turned earth. She breathed in deeply. She sank her hands into the soil. Let the dirt slide under her fingernails.

Maggie thought she was unobserved. Maggie thought wrong.

Patrick Deever stubbed out his cigarette on an illegible tombstone and returned to the vicarage garden.

Chapter 17

Under ordinary circumstances, the women of the parish of St Cedd's could be relied upon to do their duty – a well-established set of tasks that included cutting sandwiches, heating urns, counting knives and forks out and back from canteens of cutlery. The deaths of Peter Brock and Henry Metcalfe triggered action on a scale not seen since the 1936 coronation. Ladies in floral prints shifted the big trestle table from the Verderers' Hall to the vicarage lawn and covered its scratched surface with the combined resources of their linen cupboards. So many salad bowls and plates of scones arrived that Guy Brock, walking out into his own garden, wondered if he would be obliged to hand out prizes. Obligations, however, turned out to be sparse. To their relief, the Brocks discovered that they had been cast as participants rather than overseers.

Harold Metcalfe felt equally unburdened. Thanks to the preferences of the Brocks, funeral tea at the vicarage was a teetotal affair, but it spared Mrs Brunton and Jill the trouble of catering for the mourners. It also spared Harold the discomfort of a parlour crowded with acquaintances. Here, in the faintly municipal space of the vicarage garden, he could even manage a friendly conversation with his brother-in-law. Under the low roof of his own home, that would have been much more difficult.

'So, there was an inquest on the other bloke?' asked Vincent, biting into a sausageless sausage roll.

'Yes,' said Harold. 'Yesterday.'

'And what was the verdict, Harry boy?' Harold winced. Vincent was a dog track man. Harold thought it showed in his manner as much as in the wide cut of his suit.

'Not handed down yet, Vince.'

'Too many guns around these days, aren't there?' muttered Vincent. 'All these soldiers running back from France. Service revolvers falling into the wrong hands. They're a temptation to the criminal element.'

'I'm glad you're concerned,' said Harold, wondering how many of these revolvers were now in the pockets of Vincent's business associates.

'So, what are you thinking, Harry boy?' asked Vincent, as if he were pursuing a racing tip. 'Come on, it's your trade.'

'Suicide,' hissed Harold. 'So, let's be subtle, eh?'

'Not murder then? Have they ruled that out?'

'No convincing case was made.'

Vincent cast a leering eye over the guests. 'There's a few possible suspects here, I reckon,' he said. 'What about the vicar's wife? She's an enigma, ain't she? An enigma in a neat little frock.'

'Put a sock in it, Vince,' said Harold. He looked around the garden, but nobody appeared to have overheard. Mary Rose Deever was pressing her condolences upon Helena, whose smile, Harold thought, was a thin cover for a desire to jump onto a chair and scream. The book club ladies, Helena's principal allies in the village, read the same story in her face and made an intervention with a plate of egg-and-cress sandwiches. Helena broke away from their orbit and disappeared through the back door of the vicarage.

Sam Hill and Patrick Deever were under the apple tree, stationed together, as ever. They were talking to Helena's cousin from the BBC Recorded Talks department. 'It's much less formal than it once was,' Robin was saying. 'Dinner jackets no longer required for drama. No more Shakespeare in dickie bows. But Alvar always reads the news in one.'

'I suppose it's proper,' said Patrick. 'You'd want to dress up for the fall of Berlin, wouldn't you, Sam?' Sam Hill said nothing. He seemed not to be listening.

Beyond them, Simon Pinn, the curate, was regaling

Jack and G.G. Johnston with stories of his hours at the riverbank with Peter Brock. Pike, perch, golden afternoons, the scriptural references in *The Compleat Angler*. 'You haven't told us anything about the fish you actually caught,' said Jack.

'Well,' said the curate. 'Perhaps that's not so important.'

'I think you've discovered the main difference between us, Mr Pinn. An American angler would only describe his victories. And show you all the marlin heads on the trophy room wall. An English angler tells you about his heroic failures. What do you think, Jill?'

Jill had appeared with a plate bearing the last of the jam tarts. 'I'm sick of heroic failures,' she said. 'Finish these off, would you?' The men obliged. 'Anyway, you always threw them back, didn't you, Simon?'

'Always,' said the curate, holding his jam tart without eating it. 'It was enough to look at them. Watch them quicksilvering away through the stream. You don't have to kill everything and bring it home for dinner, do you?' His voice cracked with emotion. 'Sometimes,' he said, 'you just have to see a fish move in the water to know that you're looking at the work of God.' He nibbled the pastry, which collapsed in his hand, then moved towards the trestle table in search of a napkin, grateful for a reason to excuse himself.

'He was talking about Peter,' Jack said. 'Not a pike.'

'Hopelessly in love, I'd say,' breezed G.G. Johnston, licking strawberry jam off his fingers.

'Simon Pinn's a harmless chap.' Jill shrugged. 'Some men choose the church for that reason.'

'And what did Peter make of it?' asked Jack, surprised to find himself discussing a subject unbroachable at a comparable Episcopalian gathering in Philadelphia.

'I don't think it gave him any cause for worry,' said Jill. 'Peter was used to attention. Thanks to that book. I think it amused him, to be honest.' She smiled at Jack. 'You Americans are such prudes, aren't you?'

The plate was now empty. 'I'd better take this back to the kitchen,' she said.

On her way she passed the trestle table, where the book club ladies were standing hugger-mugger. 'No more fruit plates,' said Mrs Alder, as though announcing the collapse of the Eastern Front.

'I'll get some,' said Jill, happy to complete the task. She went into the vicarage kitchen and deposited the jam tart plate beside the sink. She was alone. She took a deep breath and exhaled. 'Onward,' she muttered. The vicarage had a large pantry where the Brocks kept a store of crockery, donated over many years. As she stepped inside, Jill heard the voices of Helena and Guy from the hallway.

'Why is he here?' asked Helena, testily.

'Because Patrick is here,' her husband replied. 'They come as a pair, those two.'

'War does strange things to men,' said Helena. 'Look at him. He follows Patrick around like the shadow of death.'

'That's what he is.'

'He's a bloody parasite. Still, his wife's not here. We should be grateful for that.'

'She's with the baby,' said Guy.

'She can't keep that brat quiet. Perhaps Patrick disapproves of her, knows her sort.'

'Really, Helena.' Guy sounded annoyed. And Jill realized that the moment to emerge from the pantry and announce her presence had passed several seconds ago. The couple were now in the kitchen. Jill could hear one of them – Helena, she assumed – opening and closing drawers, clearly looking for something.

'She's less interested in you than she used to be,' said Helena. A drawer slammed shut.

'I never encouraged her,' snapped Guy. 'I'm old enough to be her father.'

An undiplomatic answer.

'Your other one is here, though. Come here in an expensive frock to talk down to us.'

'Rosie, you mean?'

'She'll get rich from this. Richer. Maybe she'll give some of it to you.'

'I hope she does. I've been trying to get her to

donate something to the church for years. I do have to be nice to my parishioners, Helena. These accusations are not kind. But I think you're in shock. You don't know what you're saying.'

'I do. I'm saying I don't trust you with them. These women. All the women. I don't think Peter did either. Perhaps that's why he did what he did. He could forgive you for your being an Appeaser. But the other things—'

'There are no other things,' Guy interrupted.

Helena could see Mary Rose through the kitchen window. 'Look at her,' she said, 'buttering up Robin. Trying to get herself on the BBC. She's so ghastly.'

'You invited her.'

'What else could I do?'

'You could have said that you didn't want her to be there,' said Guy. 'You never say what you think. Rosie considers you her closest friend, you know. You should set her right about that. Tell her what you really think.'

'Guy, most of my life in this parish is spent saying exactly the opposite of what I think. In fact, take it as read. Whatever I say to these people, I'm thinking the reverse.'

Jill heard Helena's heels clatter on the flagstone floor. In the silence that remained, her own breathing sounded inordinately loud. This, however, was not what brought Guy Brock to the pantry door and the sight of Jill standing there, tight with shame, clutching an armful of crockery. Mrs Alder from the book club had entered the kitchen. 'I'm sorry, Guy,' she said. 'Bit of an emergency in the fruit plate department. Where might I find them?'

'In here,' Jill said, emerging from the pantry into Mrs Alder's view. She smiled briefly at the Reverend, walked back into the garden and put the stack of plates down on the tablecloth. She looked around the garden for Jack and failed to locate him, instead finding herself next to Simon Pinn.

'You were very good to him,' she said. Simon Pinn blushed. 'And when he went on about Izaak Walton,' Jill continued, 'you were the only person who knew what he was talking about. I tried to read it myself once. People say it's a classic.'

'It is. It's a religious book, really. It's all there. Psalm 137 – "By the rivers of Babylon, there we sat down, yea, we wept, when we remembered Zion." How many times have you heard that in church? Only Walton thought about the fish in the river. They swam in those tears, I suppose.' He came to a halt. 'He's over there.'

'Sorry?' said Jill.

'He's over there,' said Simon Pinn. 'Captain Strafford. I can see you looking for him. There's really no need to apologize, Jill. There's much to envy in the life of a GI bride.'

Jack was walking towards the house on the path

that ran beside the lawn. He looked as if he had returned from a trip to inspect the compost heap. 'There's a wasp nest under the pear tree at the end of the garden,' he said. 'Someone should remove it.' He was rubbing the back of his neck.

'You need something acidic on that,' said Jill. The condiments on the table provided. She snapped open her handbag, pulled out a handkerchief, soaked its corner in vinegar and pressed it to the back of Jack's neck.

'You know what you're doing,' said Jack.

'Just simple chemistry,' said Jill.

Simon Pinn watched, impressed, as Jill applied the remedy. Nobody else present, however, paid the slightest attention, because Helena Brock was now standing in the middle of the lawn, tapping a knife on the side of her glass.

'I don't often make public speeches,' she said. 'My husband is rather better at it than I.' The mourners, particularly those who knew Helena's predecessor, looked to Guy and were satisfied to find him standing beside his wife, wearing a tender smile.

'But these,' she said, 'are exceptional times. The war. The coming end of the war. And now this great blow – the loss of Peter and Henry. I hope you'll forgive me for not speaking about them. I shouldn't keep my composure if I did. And some thoughts, I think, are for one's secret heart.'

There was a mumble of approval. Mrs Alder wiped away a tear.

'So, what I shall say is this,' continued Helena. 'When I look around the garden here, what do I see? I see a gathering of family and friends. But mostly I see this place – Larkwhistle. A community of men and women joined in a mutual web of responsibility. I know that if one of us – any one of us – suffers a reverse, then the others will come to their aid. We are all of one body. And that is such comfort to me.'

She could say no more. Guy Brock moved towards his wife and folded her up in his arms. It was the first time he had held her in five years.

Helena's speech brought the funeral tea to an end. The mourners began to speak of bus times and family responsibilities and in half an hour most of them had peeled away. Simon Pinn helped the bellringers carry the trestle table back to the Verderers' Hall. Patrick Deever gave Robin a lift to catch the London train. The green light, said Robin, waited for nobody, and Patrick laughed despite having no idea what he meant.

'No rest for the wicked,' said Vincent. Harold walked him back to his car, which was parked outside the Fleur-de-Lys. If Vincent had not been Vincent, but a representative of some much more common species of brother-in-law, this would have been the moment when the two men exchanged fond words about the woman, long lost, who bound them together. But

Vincent was Vincent. He took a handkerchief from his pocket and rubbed at a white mark on the chassis. 'Bloody birds,' he said. 'I thought I'd left them behind in Southampton.'

Harold watched him drive away, then returned to the vicarage garden, where Helena Brock was sitting on a wicker settee. He settled beside her. They held hands and spoke of lost sons in low voices. It was the kind of delicate moment that compelled strangers to withdraw.

The book club ladies volunteered to do the washing up.

'I'll help you,' said Jack.

The book club ladies were thrilled by this idea – and more thrilled when he took off his jacket and rolled up his sleeves before sinking his hands into the washing-up water. Mrs Alder, caught by a feeling she had not experienced since watching Atlanta burn halfway through *Gone with the Wind*, took a wet plate from his hands and immediately dropped it on the floor.

Jill felt the desire to stay and help with the clearing up, but not out of obligation to the Brocks. Jack was at the centre of things. She wanted to be with him. Moving out of his presence felt like leaving a theatre before the fall of the curtain.

'Why don't you go?' Jack said. 'I'll see to this.' He was oddly insistent. 'Your dad will be exhausted.'

'Yes, you're right,' said Jill.

When Jill emerged into the garden, Harold looked up and let go of Helena's hands. They began a small ceremony of condolence and departure. Guy Brock arrived to play his part, smiling and shaking hands, but Jill saw that he annoyed his wife by slipping into the cadence of his pulpit voice.

'I suppose you'll let Simon take the service tomorrow?' said Harold.

'No, I'd rather do it myself. Seems necessary, somehow.'

Jill was frowning. 'Oh dear,' she said. 'I seem to have mislaid my handbag. I could have sworn I left it here.' A brief search of the garden yielded nothing. Everyone agreed it would turn up. And everyone was right: as Guy walked Jill and her father back through the house, Jack appeared in the kitchen doorway.

'You forgot this, Jill,' he said, offering the missing bag.

'That's strange,' said Jill. 'I'm sure I never brought it in here.' She took the bag from his hands. There was something odd about it. She was about to open it up when she noticed Jack looking at her with a peculiar intensity.

'Please come and see us before you go, Captain,' said Harold. 'I'd like to give you a keepsake of Henry. You might pick something out.'

'Actually, sir,' said Jack, 'I'm going to stay on at

the Fleur-de-Lys for a few more days. I'm due some leave, so I thought I would take it here.'

'Then come over for dinner tomorrow,' said Harold, pleasantly surprised. 'Or lunch if you prefer. After church. Not that I'm assuming you'll be there.'

'Ah, well,' said Jack, 'the thing is, Mr Metcalfe—'

Jill cut him off. 'The Deevers have invited Jack and I to dinner tomorrow night, Dad,' she said, sharply aware that she was saying this to her father in front of Guy Brock and an audience of parish ladies, and wishing herself teleported to a remote island.

'Oh, that's nice,' said Harold, trying not to sound wrongfooted. 'Well, you know you're very welcome to call on us, whenever it suits.'

They shook hands. Harold turned to Guy. 'Thank you for everything that you did today,' he said. 'I think we're lucky to have you. Not every village is so fortunate.'

Guy took his hand. 'It's a sad brotherhood we've joined, Harold. We're in it for the rest of our days. You, me, plenty of our neighbours, too.'

Jill opened the front door. As she passed through with her father she heard an indulgent murmur from the kitchen. The performance was going on without her.

Harold offered her his arm as they crossed the green. 'Dinner at the Deevers, eh?' he said. 'I don't mind, you know.'

Jill had been meaning to tell him about the invitation, but the habit of secrecy was already upon her. The same impulse that kept her silent about her new clandestine work had led her to hold her tongue about the dinner. All matters regarding Jack, she realized, were now filed in the part of her mind she did not share.

'You knew he was staying on for the week, didn't you?'

'Yes,' said Jill.

'Seems a decent sort, doesn't he?'

'He does, Dad.'

Harold took a breath.

'Are you and he . . . ?'

Jill nodded before the word could surface, saving her father from embarrassment and herself from an explicit explanation. She was happy to occupy the space of that unspoken word.

Wimsey was scratching at the kitchen door when they returned. Jill offered him profuse apologies and a biscuit, which he found perfectly acceptable. When Harold settled into his armchair, the dog interpreted this as an invitation to join him. Wimsey had a habit of disrupting the careful business of filling a pipe. Ordinarily, Harold would have shooed him away. Today he seemed grateful for the dog's warm and fuzzy presence. Wimsey burrowed against him, quite content.

Jill went straight up to her bedroom and opened

her handbag. Her first reaction was dismay. Her compact was smeared with soot. Something dark and grimy had been stuffed inside the bag and besmirched its contents. When she pulled out the offending material, she saw that it was a wedge of paper fragments that appeared to have been pulled from a fire. One piece had a date printed in the corner. This was the charred remains of someone's diary.

She turned the pages over in her hand. The surviving words, executed in a plain, masculine hand, were mostly banalities. The times of church services and meals; small calculations of pounds, shillings and pence. The margins, however, carried something delicate and beautiful. Illustrations of leaves and flowers, placed in an irregular pattern down the right-hand side.

The final page of the sequence was entirely different. It came from the endpapers. Two words in block capitals, underlined, stood at the top: 'RADIO TIMES.' Below it was a series of dates and numbers. They looked very like sequences from Jack's code book. Whoever kept this diary had also been keeping an ear on Commoner.

'Can I get you anything, Jill?'

Harold was calling from downstairs. Jill gathered up the charred pieces of paper – they were evidence, ready for police examination. There was a former policeman in the room below. There was, however, also the Official Secrets Act.

'I'd love a cup of tea,' she called, feeling sad and bad for accepting her father's offer simply to keep him in the kitchen long enough for her to run downstairs, extract an envelope from the writing desk in the parlour, take it back to her room and stow the burnt papers inside.

Five minutes later, as she held the hot cup, pleasureless, and listened to Bartok on the radio, she began auditioning excuses to see Jack again before the day's end; plausible reasons for leaving the house to ask him why he'd slipped these fragments into her bag and what they meant. The music rose through the cottage. Wimsey slept on the rug. Jill imagined a moment in the future when she might walk through the front door and see all this again, as a visitor. A married visitor.

'He's back,' said Harold.

Jill was barely in the room. 'Sorry, Dad?'

'He's back already. Keen, isn't he?'

Harold was already moving to the door. It seemed to Jill that she barely had time to put down her cup before Jack was in the room, asking if she wanted to come out for a drive. Jill asked her father's permission.

Harold smiled. 'What possible objection could I have? Lots to see round here, isn't there, Jill? The tree walk at Rhinefield is looking rather fine. Might remind the Captain of home.'

'It's a good idea, Dad,' said Jill.

'Off you go, then,' said Harold. 'What has war taught us? We may not have time to waste.'

On the doorstep they spoke of Rhinefield and its redwoods, but once they were in the jeep, Jack drove north, motoring over the ford near the Fleur-de-Lys. Water broke around them.

'Does he mind?' asked Jack.

'No,' said Jill. 'I don't think so.'

'Does he suspect?'

'That we're not out on a romantic drive? I think he believed it.' Jill regretted her words immediately. The evening was beautiful. So was the driver.

'I thought it might make him sad, you see,' said Jack, turning a corner. 'Taking you out today. Does it make you sad?'

'Not in the least,' said Jill. The moment settled between them. 'Thanks so much for finding my handbag. There was something in it I don't remember putting there. Something rather sooty and dirty.'

'I saw Guy Brock burning a book on the day of Peter's death. I think those fragments come from it. I found them this afternoon on the bonfire at the end of the vicarage garden and I needed somewhere to hide them. And there was your bag. I'm sorry, I hope I didn't ruin the lining.'

His contrition appeared genuine. Touchingly so, she

thought, given that he was an intelligence officer who had, she assumed, spent a lot of his time cutting wires and blowing things up.

'It'll recover,' she said. 'Like your wasp sting. How is it, by the way?'

'Fine,' he said, a little sheepishly.

'Never there, was it?' said Jill. 'I thought I couldn't see much. That was a distraction, I suppose.'

'Afraid so. Did you bring the burnt pages with you?'

'This is completely the wrong way for Rhinefield,' said Jill. 'We're going to Stoney Cross, aren't we?'

Jack nodded. 'We are. Hut 22, where we can listen to the radio undisturbed.'

'Well,' said Jill, 'then we can open *this* when we get there.' She waved a manila envelope under his nose.

Jill looked for changes to the map in Hut 22. Had the lines of string multiplied? Or did they just seem thicker and more numerous now she had a better understanding of what they meant?

The room was not empty. A uniformed signalman was setting up equipment on a desk. An ordinary domestic wireless set, illuminated and working, relayed dance band music from the BBC Forces Service. Beside this was a blue box transmitter with a row of sturdy black switches and two sockets, connected to a pair of Bakelite headphones and a Morse tapper. The signalman saluted as Jack and Jill entered, then turned to retune the wireless.

'Just keep it there, Henslow,' said Jack. 'Don't mind a bit of . . . who is this?'

'Louis Levy and his Gaumont British Studio Orchestra, sir.'

'Don't mind if I do.'

Henslow turned it up. 'Ready for you now, sir,' he said. Jack thanked him and waved him away. Once the door was shut, he opened the envelope and laid out the blackened fragments of paper.

'Hmm,' he muttered. 'We need our cryptogam guy.'

'That's ferns and the like,' said Jill. 'Do you mean "cryptogram"?'

'No. He was recruited from the Natural History Museum by mistake but turned out to be great at salvaging U-Boat code books pulled from the sea. If you can believe it.'

'Oh.' Jill stared at the fragments, hoping that some aspect of the case would resolve itself, as the eye can turn a drawing of a vase into the faces of a pair of lovers.

'That's not a woman's handwriting,' she said. 'And the nature drawings seem more Peter than Guy, don't you think?'

'What about *Radio Times*?'

'Well, that's just the magazine you buy if you want to know when to listen to *Monday Night at Eight*.'

'Monday night at eight?'

'*Music While You Work*, then. Or the nine o'clock news.'

'Nine o'clock?'

'If you want to know the details, Jack, the details. Which bit of Verdi will you hear massacred by the Band of the Coldstream Guards? Which ventriloquist will be top of the bill tonight?'

'They put ventriloquists on the radio?'

'Only the good ones. But this isn't a list of his favourite wireless programmes and you know it. I've seen numbers like this before. In your code book. They're from Commoner's broadcasts. I saw it straight away.'

'Absolutely right,' said Jack. He produced *The Boy Among the Trees* from his satchel. 'Let's mark their homework.'

Jack read out the numbers while Jill looked them up in the book and recorded the results. It yielded the customary mixture of the intriguing and the nonsensical.

Traps set for Sunday in France.
Arms ash in field south of church.
Fair hope of freedom in July.
All the way in a dark wood.
Into the village jug jug jug jug jug jug.

'Do you know all these?' asked Jill.

'Like old friends, some of them.'

'So, they're definitely transcriptions. If they were his own messages, there wouldn't be any mistakes. Commoner said "arms dump". That makes sense. He's written "arms ash". He miscounted by one word.' Jill read the last of the sequence aloud. 'That repeat is unusual – "jug jug jug jug jug jug."'

'I guess he gets lazy sometimes.'

'Seems familiar, somehow,' said Jill. 'So, is it father or son?'

'Definitely son,' said Jack. He separated the fragment that preserved a column of calculations in shillings and pence. 'Guy doesn't drink, does he?'

'Only at Communion. Other than that, he's a ginger pop man.'

'I think I know what this is. The cost of a beer in the Fleur-de-Lys. One shilling last November. Up another threepence since then.'

'Pretty steep, isn't it? Considering how much Wally Speed waters it down.'

'I thought all English beer tasted like that.'

Jill ignored the tease. She sifted through the papers. 'So, this is what Peter Brock thought worth recording. What he had for dinner, the church services he attended, the creeping inflation of the price of a pint. It's pretty dull stuff. But's it's all wrapped up in leaves and flowers like an illuminated manuscript. What a queer mixture of the utilitarian and the fanciful. And then he's listening to the radio, just like us, trying to crack the same code that we're trying to crack.'

Jill looked at the blue box transmitter.

'Are we going to reply to Commoner? Is that your plan?'

'Yes,' said Jack, with a grin. 'What shall we say?'

Louis Levy put his baton down. The programme changed. The newsreader delivered sweeter music – the German Seventh Army was in a state of disintegration. US troops had reached the River Orne. British forces were six miles from Lisieux.

'I'd be toasting this if it weren't for that map on the wall,' said Jill.

Jack disappeared to the NAAFI and returned with two bottles of stout pushed into his pockets and two baked potatoes, butterless but comforting. They consumed them with *The Boy Among the Trees* open on the desk, considering how to build a suitable message from the text.

'What do we want him to do?' asked Jill.

'Or her,' said Jack.

'I suppose so,' said Jill. 'I'd imagined a man, somehow. They're always men in the films. Sneaky sorts.'

'Persuade them to meet us. Failing that, panic them into breaking for cover. Either would work, but I'd prefer the former.'

When eleven o'clock came, Jack retuned the dial.

For a moment they thought that Commoner had decided to cancel his broadcast, but then came the familiar jitter of dits and dahs. Jack did not note them down. 'Let's just give him an earful, shall we?' He put on the headphones. His finger shivered on the key.

1055, 11, 683, 84, 106.
We know who you are.
1055, 1056, 681, 84.
We can help you.
1055, 755, 756, 84.
We will meet you.
44, 327, 5, 167.
Sunday morning in church.

They listened for a reply. At first, none came. Jack's hand was moving for the dial when the frequency came alive with numbers. He grabbed a pencil and began to jot them down.

1029, 1030, 1031, 1032.
81, 184, 98, 185, 403.
572, 84, 49.

Jill turned the numbers back into words and read them out.

'I do not care. I will not be broken. Do you see.'

She put down the pencil with a shudder. 'I really don't like his tone. He sounds defiant and more than a little mad. Like someone with nothing to lose.'

She imagined St Cedd's toppled; a great burning crater where the village green had been. The images stayed in her mind as Jack drove her home through the dark. As the jeep rattled over the empty roads, she found herself drawing close to him. The warmth of his body and the clean smell of his skin was consoling.

'Thank you for coming to us,' she said.

Chapter 18

Guy Brock always put up the hymn numbers himself – it was part of the ritual of Sunday. Likewise the choosing of the hymns. However, several longstanding members of the congregation were irked by his indifference to their suggestions. Vera Lynn played requests for the Forces – did Guy Brock not have a similar duty to Christian soldiers on the Home Front? Mrs Parsons, owner and manager of the Copper Kettle, suspected some sectarian loyalty. Why else would he have declined to let the choir loose on 'Love Divine, All Loves Excelling' unless he nursed some quiet prejudice against the Wesleyans? Reverend Brock had been difficult on these matters in peacetime, and war had made him even more intransigent, as if he were acting on some secret directive from the Ministry of Information.

His depth of commitment, somewhere between devotion and bloody-mindedness, explained Guy Brock's presence in the pulpit on the day after the funeral of his only son. Surely, maintained a body of opinion strong among less frequent attendees at St Cedd's, the curate might have taken the service? Simon Pinn would have been happy to do so, if only to silence the muttering about his supposed lack of tact. But those more diligent worshippers, particularly the wafer-taking kind, knew that Guy Brock was unpersuadable. He was like a pilot resolved to fly every mission assigned to him. Indeed, when Guy took the lectern, Simon Pinn could see the vicar's knuckles whiten, as if he was gripping the joystick over occupied territory.

The church was three quarters full that morning. The Deevers sat in their customary place; Patrick opened the door of the box pew for his wife with the silent deference of the doorman at Claridge's. Neither said anything. Helena Brock was nowhere to be seen. Mrs Alder and the book club ladies sat together, which gave the only husband among them the appearance of a minor English painter who had founded a polygamous cult. Wally and Effie Speed, who usually came unaccompanied, arrived with Maggie. Wally was hot and pink, and already smelled of beer. Sam Hill was absent, but his wife and child were punctual arrivals. Martin's tolerance for religious observance was usually low, but today he slept quietly in his mother's arms, and seemed undisturbed by lurching organ notes or the shuffling bodies of the congregation.

When Jill and Harold arrived, they received smiles of understanding that made them both feel they were attending a second funeral for Henry. Jack appeared and sat with them, like a member of the family. As a visitor, he had more licence to scan the church: his desire to check for absences or nervous eyes was easy to hide under a pretence of interest in Gothic spandrels. Did Patrick Deever's face betray a buzz of anxiety? Where was Sam Hill? Why was Maggie Speed staring with such concentration, as though she were preparing for an exam? Could an eighteen-year-old girl be a German spy?

The service began with a hymn. Jack's voice, Jill discovered, was a baritone so sweet and clear that she found herself quite unable to produce a note. Instead, she gazed up at the east window and mouthed like a boy who fears his voice will crack during the low parts of 'O God, Our Help in Ages Past'.

The lesson was from the first Book of Kings. Jill could not recall the last time Guy Brock had taken his text from the Old Testament. The imagery was unfamiliar, the moral more obscure. He asked them to picture the Prophet Elijah, veteran of a bloody battle, fleeing from Queen Jezebel. He asked them to imagine him stumbling through the wilderness and collapsing on the ground in the shade of a juniper tree. There was something unusual, Jill thought, in the timbre and speed of Guy's voice. The smug and bell-like element of his delivery had vanished. It was as if he had something very urgent to communicate and was worried that it might not be properly understood. Usually Jill thought of something sandy when she envisaged the Biblical wilderness. Today her thoughts were closer to home. They were at the fork of the path to Brockenhurst, where the fir tree cast its shadow.

Guy read aloud from the Bible on the lectern. 'And he requested for himself, that he might die; and said, "It is enough; now, O Lord, take away my life; for I am not better than my fathers."'

He looked up from the text. 'Elijah was overcome with fear and exhaustion,' he said. 'And we, who have faced the enemy for so long, can surely understand that feeling. War has taken much from us. It has worn us down. And there have been times, in the watches of the night, when we have all felt despair. Perhaps during an air raid. Or perhaps after one. Perhaps while waiting for news of loved ones lost in action. Those who have given so much for us. Those who have made the greatest sacrifice. We must remember, though, that through all our agonies, through those moments at which we find the plea of Elijah forming on our lips, that God will never abandon us, just as he did not abandon Elijah. God sent an angel to that man in despair beneath that juniper tree. And the angel touched him, and provided him with water, with bread and with meat.'

A smile twitched at his mouth. 'Meat,' he said.

'Some of us might wish for such a visitation today. It gave Elijah the strength to get to his feet and move on through the wilderness for another forty days and forty nights. It brought him closer to God. We know that effort, too, and what it must bring us. Our freedom. New generosities and plenitudes. For who in their heart believes that we can simply return to the lives and the thoughts we had before the war? None of us, I think. We must think better thoughts. And I am convinced that we shall.'

Maggie Speed gave a great, cavernous sob.

Jill wanted to look at Jack. She could feel him wanting to do the same, to confirm that they were hearing the same words. Guy Brock was giving a sermon about the war, but he was also making a statement about his son; about personal despair, and where that leads. What was he saying? What was he giving away?

Jill was still turning these questions over in her mind as the congregation filed from the church. Ivy Hill was before them in the line. Little Martin, now awake, seemed perfectly happy.

'No Sam this morning, Ivy?' asked Jill.

'I thought I'd let him have a lie in,' said Ivy. 'He needs it.'

Jill gave her a sympathetic smile; one informed by her knowledge of Ivy's feelings about the distribution of labour in the Hill household. She gave a different look to Jack.

Ahead of them, Mrs Alder finished giving the vicar the benefit of her views on the Old Testament. It was now Ivy's turn to thank Guy Brock for his sermon. The vicar beamed at the baby and chucked the little roll of fat beneath his chin. Martin seemed pleased with the attention, but not as pleased as Ivy, who gazed at Guy with an expression of warmth and gratitude for so long that she held up the queue.

Once they had walked through the lych-gate, Harold frowned back in the direction of the cottage. Wimsey was sitting in the bay window. 'I'd better take him for his walk,' he said. It was not Wimsey's customary hour for exercise. This was, Jill saw, a ploy to leave her with Jack, unchaperoned. The dog made no such deduction, but as Harold neared the cottage, Wimsey understood the meaning of his owner's expression and leapt up at the bay window, celebrating the unearned win.

'What did you make of that?' asked Jack, once they were alone.

'I thought it was odd that Sam was absent,' said Jill. 'I thought Maggie Speed was beside herself. Wally Speed was drunk. Mary Rose and Patrick didn't say a word to each other. I thought Guy was rather sad. A father giving a sermon about the war and finding his own son in an old bit of the Bible. His wife not even there to hear it. Strange, isn't it, how unconscious people can be of their own motives and desires.'

'I dare say you're right,' agreed Jack. 'But I was talking about Ivy Hill's baby.'

'Oh. It's nice to see him happy for a change. He's usually as miserable as sin.'

'And it brings out his resemblance, doesn't it?' said Jack, as though commenting on the most obvious thing in the world.

Jill frowned. 'His resemblance to whom?'

'To Guy,' he said. 'He's the baby's father, isn't he?'

A snorting laugh escaped Jill. Was this some strange joke? And then she saw it, as clear as day. It had taken an outsider to notice something that, once pointed out, seemed obvious. 'The smile,' she exclaimed, her eyes wide. 'It's exactly the same. We all knew Ivy had her eye on him. And Guy is very susceptible to flattery. But I always thought him rather transparent. Embarrassingly so, sometimes.'

'Good adulterers like to give that impression,' said Jack. 'It inspires confidence.'

'But fathering a child?' hissed Jill, feeling the heat of the gossip on her tongue. 'Do you think Sam suspects he's been – what's the polite word – cuckolded?'

'Well, if he doesn't, it would explain why he hasn't challenged the vicar to a duel.'

Jill shook her head. 'You're underestimating the power of the village. Benign most of the time. Wonderful, actually, if you're in trouble. But it imposes something on us. There are rules. There's the weight of history. So you don't make a scene. You don't cut people if they offend you. There aren't enough of us to keep our distance from each other.'

'He wouldn't feel humiliated?'

'He would. But I can imagine Sam thinking that it would be much better just to tolerate the situation, if nobody mentioned it in his presence, because think what would happen if he did say something. Guy defrocked. Helena getting a divorce. Ivy talked about as a tart. The *vicar's* tart. It'd be three columns and an illustration on the back page of the *News of the World*. Then the Post Office would be closed. The kiddie sent off to an institution. And I dare say Sam would be stuck in a rented room in Southampton, drinking himself to death, like someone in a Victorian engraving. Catastrophe. The status quo is worth a lot round here. It's more powerful than any ideas of personal happiness. We've never been too crazy about those in Larkwhistle.'

Jack inhaled. 'I'm not in America anymore, am I?'

'Jack and Jill!' exclaimed a low, fluting voice, interrupting them. 'It's such a charming coincidence. Take it from a children's author. It has a music.'

It was not the moment Jill would have wished for Patrick and Mary Rose Deever to appear, clearly determined to exchange pleasantries. They had been stony-faced through the sermon, but here they were, out in the light, looking as if they expected a round of applause. Jill arranged her face into something sociable.

'Jack and Jill went up the hill to fetch a pail of water,' said Patrick Deever, helpfully. 'Jack fell down and broke his crown . . . what's the next bit, dear?'

'I'm not for tumbling after him,' said Jill. 'I'm intending to stay on my feet.' It was only when she was halfway through the joke that she realized it sounded like a romantic denial.

'Shall we expect you at seven?' said Patrick. He was lighting his cigarette with a technique that would have impressed an Italian acrobat. 'I hope you like a game bird, old man.'

'Love one,' said Jack.

'Splendid,' boomed Mary Rose. 'I used to get them in from Fortnum's, but we're so blessed around here with grouse and pheasant. Pat just goes out for a walk in the fields with his gun—'

'And dinner has flown up from the grass soon enough,' concluded the Captain. 'Though you need to keep your wits about you these days. Poachers, do you see? They come up from Southampton and they're bloody amateurs.' He tapped a finger against his nose. 'Town people,' he added.

Mary Rose Deever exhaled. 'So looking forward,' she said. The pair moved off. So much of village life, thought Jack, was constituted by these tiny locutions of class and territory. The words didn't matter much.

Mary Rose and Patrick might as well have been robins, trilling their claim to a particular patch of land.

'Tonight,' asked Jack, 'will it be dressy?'

'They're not the Astors,' said Jill.

'So, what are they?'

'Provincial snobs. They subscribe to *Horse and Hound*. But only to keep an eye on the divorces.'

'Patrick's clever with that hand, isn't he?'

'He has the time to practise. Really, what does the man do all day? Apart from keep the pub in business. And post letters for his wife.'

'You only need one hand to operate a Morse key, *do you see*?'

'Do I see?' repeated Jill.

'He says it all the time, Patrick. Like a catchphrase.'

Jill watched Mary Rose and Patrick disappearing down the lane. 'Oh heavens. Could it be him?'

'Why not?' said Jack. 'Perhaps we didn't need to send out that message to Commoner. Maybe his wife already invited us for dinner.'

'Our problem,' Jill said, 'is that we can't see the wood for the trees. There's more than one mystery to be solved in Larkwhistle, and they're tangled up like roots. It's hard for us to work out where one ends and another begins.'

'They meet in Peter Brock, don't they?' said Jack. 'In his body, as it were. And Patrick found that body.'

Chapter 19

Something was wrong in the saloon bar of the Fleur-de-Lys. It was Sunday lunchtime and the natural order of things had been usurped. The drinkers looked at each other as they might if the village clock chimed thirteen. Even a newcomer like Jack, sitting at the bar with a glass of lemonade and a cheese sandwich that looked very like an American cheese sandwich viewed from a considerable distance, registered its strangeness.

Sam Hill walked into the pub on his own. Usually he waited until he knew Patrick was at the bar, ready to perform the ritual of generosity and for Sam to say he didn't mind if he did.

Wally Speed drew him a pint. Through sheer force of habit, he started to draw another.

'Just the one, Wal,' said Sam.

'Oh,' said Wally Speed. 'I thought he might be at one of the outside tables.'

'No,' said Sam drily. 'One and three, is it?' He reached inside his jacket and snapped the money down on the counter.

'Steady on,' said Wally. 'You know I'm on pills for my ticker.'

The butcher was sitting nearby. 'Blimey,' he said. 'Is it VE Day? Funny they never mentioned it on the wireless.' He gave a great belch of laughter and thumped the bar.

Sam ignored them. His face was as still as a photograph. 'I think I might sit outside,' he said. 'It's a nice, sunny day.'

'And we'll miss them in the winter,' said the butcher.

Sam carried his pint of bitter out of the saloon to a table in the garden. The back of his head was visible through the window.

'That was unusual, yeah?' said Jack.

'Round here,' said the butcher under his breath, 'that's like getting an invitation to the Pope's wedding.'

'What do you think happened?'

The butcher felt for his moustache, as if concerned that someone might have stolen it. 'I suppose Captain Deever finally came to his senses and saw Sam Hill for what he is.'

'Which is what?' asked Jack.

The butcher cast an eye around the bar.

'What are you looking for?' asked Jack.

'Just checking if there are any ladies present,' said the butcher.

'There's Effie,' said Wally Speed.

'Takes a lot to disgust me, Reg,' said Effie. 'That's why I'm always in your shop.'

The butcher raised his glass to her and turned back to Jack.

'He's a sponger, sir,' he said. 'A dirty little sponger.'

Wally made his sour lemon face. Not the way for a villager to talk in front of a visitor. 'Come on, be fair. Sam saved the Captain's life at Dunkirk.'

'Really?' said the butcher. 'I don't believe I've ever heard the story.'

Even Effie Speed laughed at that.

'The Lord Jesus Christ saved us all,' said the butcher. 'But He always got His round in, didn't He?'

'Is that blasphemy, Reg?' asked Effie.

'That's John, Chapter Two,' said the butcher. 'Verses one to twelve.' He was warming to his theme. 'What I'm saying is, Sam may have dragged his Captain from the waves or saved him from a Nazi bullet with his name on, but he's presumed too much on it. There's only so grateful a man should be.' He sipped his beer meaningfully. 'And besides, men should take their wives out for a drink.'

This, thought Jack, seemed to be an accusation of impropriety.

'Who'd look after the little one, Reg?' asked Wally. 'Can't bring a baby to a pub. Not that one, anyway. Not my pub. He goes off like an air-raid siren, young Martin.'

'He's quiet sometimes,' said Effie.

'So's a V1,' said her husband. 'Just before it hits you.'

'The Deevers don't have any kiddies,' said the butcher. 'The Captain could bring his missus here, couldn't he?'

Effie rolled her eyes. 'Her ladyship? Slum it here? With people like you sitting at the bar, Reg? Not likely.'

'The Queen went to the East End,' said the butcher, with a low chuckle. 'To wave at all those bombed-out Cockneys. Risking her heels. So I'm sure our Mary Rose could stand an evening under your roof.'

'She was here yesterday,' said Effie. 'To hear about Peter Brock.' The landlady had brought a ghost into the bar and disturbed the butcher's flow of sarcasm. It would have stopped anyway: the door rattled and there was Sam Hill with an empty beer glass in his hand.

The butcher turned quickly to Jack. 'What did you think of *ITMA*, then?' he asked, with enough jollity to draw Sam's suspicious eye. 'I think it's gone off a bit, don't you? Not as funny as it used to be.'

'He won't know about that, you great fool,' said Sam, putting his glass down on the bar. 'He's a Yank.'

'You're probably right, Mr Hill,' said Jack. 'English humour is so . . . English. You know where you are with Bob Hope.'

'Bob Hope's from London,' said the butcher.

Effie began drawing another pint of bitter.

'It's all filth anyway,' huffed Sam. 'They put it in code.'

'Well,' said Jack. 'You can take me through it all over dinner. I like a code.'

'Oh,' said Sam. 'I'm afraid you won't see us there. There's really far too much to do in the Post Office. And the baby's coming down with something. I can't leave Ivy on her own with him for too long.'

'Ah, that's a great shame,' said Jack.

Sam made a noncommittal sound and reached into his pocket. Jack held up a hand like a traffic warden. 'Put it on my bill, Mrs Speed,' he said. 'And perhaps you'd be so kind as to pour me one, too.'

Sam considered refusing, but this muscle was weak in him. And now it was clear that Jack proposed to join him in the beer garden, he became visibly discombobulated, fumbling the latch of the pub's front door. With infuriating ease, Jack reached in and flipped it into the correct position. 'There's really no need, Captain,' Sam said. 'I've been carrying glasses in and out of this pub since I was in short trousers.'

Jack smiled. 'Let's sit here, Mr Hill,' he said. 'We'll keep out of the sun.' Unable to think of a polite reason to do otherwise, Sam settled at Jack's chosen table.

'It's a great shame,' Jack continued. 'You're going to be missed at the party. What's Patrick going to do without his old pal?'

Sam took a gulp of beer. 'He'll be fine.'

'I suppose you're round at his place quite a lot?'

Sam shrugged. Where was this leading? 'From time to time,' he said.

'Nice, is it?' pressed Jack.

'It's all right,' said Sam, in a tone that suggested he had never stepped over the threshold.

'He told me about you,' said Jack. 'Told me the whole story.'

Sam looked nervous. 'Told you what?'

'You getting him onto that boat. The Stukas coming down. You both going under. And then you saving him again. Dragging him out of the waves. Did you climb back on the same boat?'

'No fear,' said Sam. 'That one was burning. It was a steamer out of Margate. The deck was on fire and blokes were jumping off it to save themselves. Even the wounded ones. I saw one chap with bandaged eyes throw himself in, just hoping someone would help. And they didn't. We were all filthy from the oil. I can still taste it. The beer helps.'

He took a long drink. A little line of foam was left on his top lip.

'And you had to keep him afloat, I guess?' asked Jack. 'He was out cold?'

'It weren't no picnic,' said Sam. 'A small boat picked us up. A herring lugger all the way from Polperro. I don't know how long we stayed in the water, me and the Captain. You can't keep track of time when you're in a fix like that.' Something flickered in his eyes. For a moment, he was back there.

'No wonder he looks up to you,' said Jack. 'Admires you.'

His words broke the spell completely. A twitch of animal anger creased Sam's features. Jack had found a soft spot. He pushed. 'It creates a special kind of bond, an act of courage like that. He'll be in your debt forever. He said it to me himself. When we were in the Fleur-de-Lys the other night, toasting you. Toasting the end of deference.' Jack took a sip of beer. 'And now he's uninvited you from his dinner party. What did you do? What happened?'

'Nothing happened,' spat Sam. 'I didn't want to go to his damned party.'

'It was wives, wasn't it?' said Jack, with a conspiratorial grin. 'I bet they don't get on. I heard her. Dispensing her second-hand clothes like blessings. Come on. You can tell me. I was born in a republic. We don't tug our forelocks to anyone. Certainly not to people like Patrick. I mean, he's a Non-Commissioned Officer, right?'

'Yes,' said Sam.

'He's not the King of England, is he?' asked Jack.

'No,' agreed Sam.

'Doesn't even earn his own money, does he? It's all from his wife.'

'Exactly,' said Sam. 'He's bloody bone idle. That cinema will never have him.'

'Cinema?' said Jack. 'What cinema? Is that what the job in Southampton was?'

'Commissionaire,' said Sam. 'Can you imagine?'

'So why put up with it?' pushed Jack. 'Why tolerate it? What's he got over you? Why do you let him talk down to you? Why do you let Mary Rose talk down to Ivy?'

Sam opened his mouth to answer. And stopped. He blinked at Jack. He had been led into something and knew it. 'I need to be with Ivy, tonight,' he said. 'The kiddie's not well. Like I told you.' He drained his glass and got to his feet.

Jack watched Sam follow the road back to the Post Office. Something had happened to alter the balance of power between Captain Deever and his sergeant. It was like talking to a blackmailer who had just discovered that his cache of compromising letters had gone up in smoke.

Chapter 20

Unlike some of her contemporaries, Jill had lost a lot of pleasure to the war. Since Hitler crossed the Polish border, there had been little romantic glory to report. A good-looking pilot had asked her to a dance at the Memorial Hall in Brockenhurst, but his two left feet had left her worrying about the outcome of the Battle of Britain. She had been disappointed by her encounters with the Hampshire men considered her social equals – or who were at least sufficiently middle class to save her from jokes about gamekeepers in D. H. Lawrence novels only available from certain Parisian bookshops – and even more so by the men at the teacher-training college, who were very few and wore corduroy jackets and a faint sense of disgrace. One from her chemistry class had tried to kiss her during a blackout, too soon after his tea of tinned sardines. Another had turned pale at a restaurant menu and asked her to only order the cheapest items. Yet another had taken her to see a comic at the Empire, whose barrack-room jokes embarrassed them both. She knew that a punchline about 'the last turkey in the shop' was obscene, but had no wish to understand precisely why.

Tonight she was making an effort for a provincial dinner party at the home of a woman for whom she did not particularly care, on a mission that made her hot with uneasy excitement. What did one wear, exactly, if the object of the evening was to prove that the host was a German spy plotting to set Southern England ablaze? Particularly if his wife had money, confidence and a wardrobe full of disconcertingly expensive clothes? As Jill brushed out her hair, however, she knew she was not primping herself to keep up with Mary Rose Deever. She looked in the mirror. Applied some lipstick. Not bad.

Jack called for her at six thirty. Far earlier than necessary, but it gave them time to strategize. Had he also made an effort? Men did these things far more mysteriously. Jill would have found it hard to say exactly how he had adjusted his appearance, but his tie was straight, his hair pleasingly sharp, and he seemed to have a glow about him, as if he were projected on a screen. She wondered what it would be like to kiss him.

Perhaps he was having similar thoughts about her. 'You look wonderful,' he said. He was beaming.

'Really? I bought this dress before the Anschluss, and I've repaired it three times.'

'Let me make you a promise, Jill. Any compliment you give me, I'll just take.'

She thought for a moment. 'Your Morse skills are dazzling.'

As they passed through the cottage gate, Jack took Jill's hand. It was a quiet, casual gesture, or would have looked so to anyone passing them on the road. It was rather more to Jill.

'Is this part of our cover?' she asked.

'I would say not,' he replied. 'I like holding your hand, Jill. But what do *you* think?'

'I think,' said Jill, enjoying their closeness, the synchronicity of their steps, 'that I'd prefer the significant events of life to be placed further apart. Just to get a breather. The horrible shocks. The state secrets. The lovely things. You with me, here, on this path, on this evening. Peace won't be like this, will it? Like being on the edge of a whirlpool. We won't have to contemplate love and death every day, will we? It would make me giddy.'

'I think we'll be allowed to do exactly as we please,' said Jack.

They crossed the ford by the Fleur-de-Lys and followed the stream that ran parallel with the road to Woodlander House. There was a fallen tree by the bank; a great deciduous wreck colonized by ferns.

Jill would have perched on it had she not feared for her good dress. Instead, they moved behind it, putting its bulk between them and the road.

'Here's a good place to make a plan of action,' said Jill. 'Also good for sticklebacks.'

Jack broke into a smile that showed the whiteness and regularity of his teeth. Why, thought Jill, did British men, even the handsome and expensive ones, all have teeth like Neolithic stone circles? She was standing close enough to see the pores in Jack's skin and the dark blue shade of his eyes. The stream beside them rushed and gurgled. Nature, thought Jill, was urging her to do something, and probably, she calculated, that something was pushing Jack against the mossy bark of the tree and ruining his uniform.

Jack solved her dilemma: he brushed his hand against her cheek and kissed her.

'Oh,' said Jill. 'Oh, I see. We're in deep cover now, are we?'

'Looks like it,' said Jack. He kissed her again.

Jill rested her head against his warm, clean neck. She inhaled deeply. His arms had found their way around her. Her thoughts would have lit a VE night bonfire.

'Let this be real,' she said.

'It is real,' said Jack.

'We'd better win this war, you know,' she said. 'Or I may never know for sure.' She pressed herself against him. 'Just tell me what to do tonight. Give me some orders, Captain.'

Jack spoke softly. 'We'll need to create as many opportunities as we can. Let me take the lead on that. I'll break something. Spill something. Disrupt the business of the house long enough for me to case the joint. Open a few drawers.'

'Find a transmitter?'

He kissed her again. 'If we get lucky.'

'I feel quite lucky,' she said.

Jill had not visited the Deevers' home since December 1939, when Patrick and Mary Rose had thrown the first Christmas party of the war. Behind the blackout blinds, it had been a muted affair, where guests talked about fifth columnists and Tobruk, and a man from Portsmouth, a writer of cowboy stories who had never been further west than Minehead, swore that he had seen a nun signalling to an enemy plane with a battery torch.

The door was opened by Maggie Speed. Jill could not suppress her surprise.

'It's all right,' Maggie said. 'I don't mind. I'm fed up with sitting in the pub all day. It's mainly peeling carrots.'

Patrick bustled into the hallway. He was ebullient. He was clubbable. He waved Maggie back into the kitchen. 'My lady wife is teaching her how to write, apparently,' he said, in a theatrical whisper.

219

'Yes,' said Jack. 'Effie was telling me. I'm sure there's room in the village for more than one author.'

Patrick had a gin fizz in his hand and was offering his guests the same. How *nice* it was, he said, how *nice* to have some smart and charming company, and not to be spending another evening supping bitter under the horse brasses. 'Don't think me a snob,' he said, snobbishly, 'but I have had enough of the English village pub to last me until the next world war.'

As his wife emerged, smiling, from the kitchen, he called to her extravagantly. 'When this is all over, my darling, let's move to town.' There was, Jill noted, a hint of threat in his voice: they had been arguing and were now putting on friendly faces for their guests. Was this Patrick's second gin fizz or his third?

Most people's homes had become shabbier during the war. Fences went unrepaired, paint was left to peel. The Deever household had moved in the opposite direction. The couple had a new piano – the varnish on it shone – and the drawing room had clearly just been redecorated. Mary Rose saw Jill admiring the wallpaper, which had a pinkish pattern that seemed to reflect her name.

'A reader sent it to me,' said Mary Rose. 'She bought too many rolls in 1939, so she put the rest my way. Charming pattern, isn't it?' Well-to-do people, thought Jill, had found so many subtle ways of maintaining the privileges of the peace. Coincidences involving pheasants and salmon and lightbulbs and soap afflicted them like coughs and sneezes.

'It's a very charming pattern,' she said.

They had drinks in the main living space of the house, which served as both drawing room and dining room. *The Boy Among the Trees* had a legible presence. The original watercolour for the frontispiece was framed on the wall. A row of foreign-language editions filled an entire bookshelf. One publisher, Jill saw, had even translated the book into Latin. 'For schools,' explained Mary Rose Deever, and Jill felt sure she understood why: it was a story about lost boys. She imagined sons and younger brothers stumbling through the text in a stuffy classroom, and feeling the air disturbed by ghosts.

'Never made it into German, though,' Mary Rose said. 'That always disappointed me. But I'm rather glad of it now.'

Patrick sniffed. 'Ironic, really. The Germans are awfully sentimental about forests. They love a bit of the dark sublime. Something of old Europe. And considering the source is German—'

'Not the source,' snapped Mary Rose. 'The inspiration, perhaps?'

Patrick pulled a face.

'What was it that inspired you, Mrs Deever?' asked Jack. 'A folk tale of some sort?'

'Oh, please call me Rosie,' said Mary Rose. 'Like the Riveter.'

Jill almost spat out her drink – she could think of few people less likely to roll up their sleeves and do something vigorous with tempered steel.

Mary Rose seemed about to begin the story, but her husband cut in with a tone that suggested he was exposing an infelicity, not celebrating the achievements of his wife.

'We went on a driving holiday. Baden-Baden through the Black Forest to the Swiss border.'

'My husband is a very keen driver, Captain Strafford,' said Mary Rose, as if asking him to feel her pain.

'Nothing like it,' continued Patrick. 'Anyway, we stopped at the Schloss – try saying that after a pint of something foamy – and went off for a bit of a trek. We had a guide, so as not to get lost. What were we going to pick, dear?'

'Mushrooms, dear.'

'Of course. Hans was his name, wasn't it? He was very honest with us, that chap. Told us about his dad. Foreman on an Autobahn project and very happy in his job. And this is the point – his old *Vater* had left the trenches without a scratch, but after the Armistice he tried to get a job, and no dice. Not *eine kleine* dickybird. Didn't work again until '33. Well, you know what happened then. That's why they all voted for him. They wanted work. They wanted *things* to work.'

'My story,' said Mary Rose, with razor-like coolness, 'hasn't anything to do with Hitler.'

'Well, I'm not saying it has, am I?' said Patrick, with an unexpectedly sulphurous tone. It would not be the evening's last show of hostility. 'When we were in the middle of the forest, do you see,' he said, stirring his drink, 'Hans told us this story. It was something about the last war. Something about his older brother, who never came back. Lost in that last big offensive in the spring of '18. Sent with all his pals into the mud by Ludendorff. Never found his body, he said. Anyway, they'd played in the forest as children, under the trees. Being Buffalo Bill and Tarzan and William Tell. And sometimes, he said, he thought he could hear him. Not his voice. Just the sound of him running over the ground, as if he were about to come dashing in with a pair of six-shooters.'

'Did you pick any mushrooms?' asked Jill.

'I don't believe we did,' said Patrick.

'We did, dear,' said Mary Rose. 'They made you sick.'

'Oh,' said Patrick. 'I thought that was the beer.'

He laughed heartily.

'Where do you do your writing, Rosie?' asked Jack.

She looked pleased to be asked. 'I have a study upstairs. Shall I give you the tour?'

'What a splendid idea,' said Jack. 'What do you say, Jill?'

If this was a ploy by Mary Rose to get Jack to herself, she did not betray any disappointment at its failure. Patrick made a great show of taking on the burden of the final preparations for dinner. He disappeared into the kitchen and began quizzing Maggie about cooking times for vegetables. Her answers were inaudible: if Jack had not seen her with his own eyes, he would have suspected that Patrick was talking to himself, and the servant was a fiction to give an impression of affluence.

Mary Rose led the way upstairs, and for fifteen minutes Jill felt she was being given a masterclass in how to search a property under the nose of its owner. Jack barraged Mary Rose with flattering questions. He took great interest in a coral paperweight and lifted it up to the light as if to examine it. Jill, however, could see that his eyes were darting down to her desk, and that as Mary Rose turned away, he gave its drawer handles an exploratory pull. He was marking up the whole room in his mind. When a floorboard creaked as they crossed the hallway, Jack stepped on the same place again, testing the bones of the building. If he was to sneak back up here later in the evening, he would need to know how to do it silently.

When dinner was served by Mary Rose and Maggie – the maid playing humble assistant to the stage magician of her hostess – Jill watched Jack go to work again. He commended a sour bottle of French wine that Patrick had extracted from the cellar. He picked the pheasant carcass clean, praising it all the way.

'Such a pity Sam and Ivy couldn't join us,' he said.

Patrick cleared his throat. 'I believe the baby is under the weather. Though it rather seems to make its own weather, that child. Most of it like a squall over the Solent.'

'He's not a particularly content little chap, is he?' said Jill.

'He only does it to annoy,' said Mary Rose, 'because he knows it teases.'

'But to be honest,' added Patrick, 'one can spend enough time fraternizing with the lower ranks. I didn't want him getting in the way of our conversation here. He's not much of a reader, you know. Apart from the fronts of envelopes, of course.'

'I thought we drank to the end of deference the other night,' said Jack.

'So we did,' said Patrick. 'Personally, I like the traditions. You won't catch me voting for the socialists, once this war is over. And it will be over quite soon, thanks to you chaps. Though I would have quite understood if you had wanted to sit this one out.'

'Didn't we owe it to the world?' asked Jack. 'To come in and do our bit?'

'Absolutely not. Plenty of Germans in America. It's why you drink cold beer.'

Patrick tapped his glass with his celluloid hand. This, Jack realized, was a habit he used to draw subtle attention to his prosthesis. 'We wouldn't be fighting this one, would we, if we hadn't put their fingers in a vice at Versailles. And then I'd still have mine, do you see?' He chuckled to himself.

Dessert was served. The first of that season's pears. Stewed and cold. Maggie brought them to the table. Jack made further silent contemplation of the mysteries of the British class system. All of them had been witnesses at an inquest into a sudden and violent death. Maggie had seen Peter Brock's blood spilled on the ground. The image of the dead boy, idealized by Mary Rose, gazed down at them from the wall. And here they all were, four with napkins, and one – the youngest, the poorest, the most affected by the tragedy – moving quietly around the table with a dish of fruit.

'You get off now, Maggie,' said Mary Rose. Maggie Speed gave a curtsey as vestigial as the human coccyx.

'I've done the copper and the baking sheets and the dinner things,' she said, 'so it's just what you're using now.'

Mary Rose did not appear grateful for the information. Maggie withdrew from the room. A few moments later they heard the bang of the back door.

'She wants to be a writer, I'm told,' said Jack.

'Maggie?' said Mary Rose. 'Yes, I've been trying to encourage her to write about nature. She loves fungi and bugs.'

'You can tell by the way she scuttles about the place,' snorted Patrick.

'Does she have talent?' asked Jill.

'Not really,' said Mary Rose. 'She never saw an infinitive she couldn't split. I can't abide that kind of solecism. But she has a real feeling for her subject. Knows all the Latin names too. She's a proper idiot savant.'

'Idiot savant?' exclaimed Jack.

'Yes, Captain,' said Mary Rose. 'Like that German boy who was raised in a shed and lived on bin scrapings and did all those marvellous drawings.'

'I know what it means, Rosie,' said Jack. 'I'm just not quite sure how it applies to Maggie Speed.'

'Because Maggie's a fool,' said Patrick. 'She was certainly a fool for that boy, wasn't she, dear?'

'Peter, you mean?' asked Jill.

'It was pure pity,' said Patrick, chasing the last morsel of pear around his plate. Jill winced at the cruelty of the remark and put down her spoon.

'Oh, come on, Jill,' said Patrick. 'He barely came to the pub these last few months because she was always there staring at him with those dreadful cow eyes, like he was something in a cake shop window. She was totally infatuated. Wasn't she, dear?'

'I don't really go to pubs, dear,' said Mary Rose. Patrick snorted.

'But I pity her too,' she continued. 'Stuck in that place all day with the stink of brewer's yeast and those awful old men from the village. Wandering through the trees. Talking to them, probably. It's why I gave her the job. Why I encouraged her to write.'

'She's Rosie's philanthropic project, do you see?' said Patrick, tapping at the tablecloth with his spoon. 'What else would the girl be doing? Getting herself into trouble and producing some idiot child, I dare say.'

He was silenced by a knock at the dining room door.

Maggie Speed was standing there, her face like an Easter Island statue. She was in her outdoor clothes.

'Sorry to interrupt,' she said. 'But I thought I'd better check when you wanted me tomorrow.'

Naturally, silence followed. Mary Rose broke it.

'Nine, dear. If you're feeling up to it.'

Maggie thanked her employer. She did not, however, leave immediately. Instead, she walked across the room and placed her apron on the low divan that occupied the space in front of the bay window. Then she turned on her heel and left through the front door. It was a peculiar act, but clearly one of defiance.

Mary Rose gathered her strength. 'I want to hear a story from you, Captain Strafford. Tell us how you got your wings. That's the expression, I believe?'

Jack tackled the request with an enthusiasm that surprised Jill. Perhaps it was the alcohol that made him garrulous. His first pilot's lesson, he said, had taken place at a Philadelphia aerodrome under an instructor who had learned his craft in the Marie Meyer Flying Circus. Jack illustrated the progress of a nosedive executed more to scare than educate the pupil. As he did so, his hand upset the bottle of wine on the table. To Jill it seemed, and seemed correctly, that Patrick had the best chance of preventing its fall – but Jack made contact first, and with such apparent clumsiness that he succeeded in propelling the bottle harder towards himself. The contents hit his shirt and the tablecloth. Jack now had a burst of red across his belly, as if he had been gored by a bull.

A flurry of shame and apology followed. With no maid to assist, Patrick and Mary Rose were obliged to deal with this small domestic catastrophe. 'I don't suppose you could lend me a shirt, could you, Patrick?' said Jack. It was, Jill later reflected, a virtuoso move. Most Englishmen would have been too embarrassed to ask such a question. Jack, however, knew that there were few things more alien to a middle-class British household than a display of American directness. He stood up, slipped out of his jacket and hung it over the back of the dining chair. For a moment it seemed as if he might take off his shirt in the living room. He had a strong sense of himself as a distraction; a bomb thrown into a room. The effect compelled the Deevers to usher him upstairs. Moments later Patrick was looking through his wardrobe and Mary Rose was in the kitchen, looking for some caustic soda to soak the wine-stained shirt.

Jill, alone in the sitting room, felt like an unrehearsed actor left on the stage to deliver an important soliloquy. She opened the drinks cabinet, hoping to discover a secret wireless radio set. She felt over the chimney breast for evidence of a secret compartment, then felt ridiculous: it had seemed an unlikely hiding place even in that hoary old play about the spy on the Isle of Wight. She scanned the shelves. She noticed several German books and tried to commit the names of the authors to memory. A run of volumes with swastikas on the spine turned out to be the collected works of Rudyard Kipling, printed when Hitler was in short trousers and the symbol, to British eyes that knew it, was synonymous with Indian religion. A peculiar English-language title caught her eye: *Weeds in the Garden of Marriage*. It appeared to be an advice book with a eugenic angle, and was inscribed by the author, Archibald Ramsay Pitt-Rivers. She knew the name. They were Dorset landowners and connected with the Museum in Oxford where you could see dinosaur bones and shrunken human heads. There was some scandal, too, the details of which Jill could not quite recall.

Jill slipped the book back into its place and moved over to the shelf that recorded the international progress of *The Boy Among the Trees*. She opened each copy, hoping to find something inside. A note of thanks from a Spanish publisher. A congratulatory postcard from Enid Blyton, from which Jill detected the tang of sour grapes. Nothing with any bearing on the death of Peter Brock or the identity of Commoner.

However, when Jill ran her hand behind the row of books she found a concealed object: a cardboard sleeve that had once contained a presentation copy of the French edition of *The Boy Among the Trees*. The book had been removed and replaced with a sheaf of letters.

Most were single sheets bearing a few lines about meetings urged, arranged or postponed. They were not obviously amorous, but clearly intimate. One bore an urgent-sounding message: 'George Vatine arrested – did he keep your name?' None were signed. Several longer examples remained in their envelopes, which were brown, typewritten and dull. On the basis of these wrappers, a person would think that they contained business letters or bills. She peered inside one and found a notification from the National Westminster Bank about the withdrawal of £50 in cash. A second envelope revealed something that made her catch her breath: a delicate pencil illustration that turned the cracked bark of a fir tree into a new margin for the page. These were not letters from the bank. They were expressions of powerful feeling.

Jill had the letters in her hand when she heard the door click behind her.

'I'm afraid all my shirts need cufflinks,' said Patrick. He had returned to the room alone. 'They won't survive the war, will they? Cufflinks. Not very suited to the utilitarian age. I wonder if Churchill will keep his siren suit. Looks a damn fool in it I've always thought. Like a mechanic who'd be too fat to get under the car.'

Jill pushed the letters back into the case, hoping her body would block Patrick's view.

'Borrow it if you like,' said Patrick. 'She won't mind. Rosie loves to discuss her work with readers.'

'It's so interesting to see all the different editions,' said Jill. She could not return the cardboard sleeve to its hiding place. If Patrick saw her fumbling behind the row of books, it would be as good as telling him that she had been searching the room. She put it on the shelf with the other translations, the spine facing outwards.

'I'd offer you some more wine,' breezed Patrick, 'but I think we'd have to suck it out of the Captain's shirt.' He reclaimed his place at the dinner table. Jill followed, trying to tear her eyes from the bookshelf, on which the cardboard case now seemed to broadcast evidence of her tampering as obviously as the bleeps of the RKO transmitter.

'All gone now,' said Mary Rose, returning from the kitchen. 'Bit of salt works wonders. I'll get my husband to bring it to the Fleur-de-Lys in the morning. I'm sure it'll be as good as new.' Jill kept her eyes on Mary Rose. Would she notice the change on the bookshelf? She gave no sign that she had registered it.

Once Jack had returned to the room, Jill felt less anxious: his confident manner and the faint comic value of his borrowed shirt changed the atmosphere of the room. But the good humour did not last. The final half hour of the Deevers' dinner party would become distinct in Jill's memory, brightly lit as a department store window before the war. Mary Rose was the principal illuminated object. It was as if something within her, a fragile spot subject to attack over a long period of time, had been left suddenly undefended, and become overwhelmed.

'Is it a parable, Rosie?' asked Jack. 'Your book. Is it about the war? The last war?'

'You've read it?' Mary Rose sounded surprised.

'Of course.'

'I suppose it is. But I didn't set out to do it. Not like Beatrix Potter, who made her hero a piglet and had its mother and father wave it off to market. You read that and you see the pictures and you know it's the trenches.'

'I know it,' said Jill. 'The pigs are at the garden gate. And the piglets have bundles on sticks with peppermints wrapped up in them.'

'Brave of her, I think,' said Mary Rose, 'to keep the idea of slaughter. But she was a proper country-woman. Not like me. I was born in the Victorian suburbs. Ever been to Birmingham? I miss it rather. And that's why I write children's books about chil-dren, not frog fishermen and puddle ducks. Couldn't draw one of those to save my life.'

'So you drew a boy instead?'

'Yes,' she said, quietly. 'Peter Brock is everywhere in this house. That little apple-cheeked lad I remember when we first moved here a decade ago.'

She was right. Peter Brock was on the wall and on the shelves. On the sideboard, Jill noticed a china figurine in his likeness, mounted on a little wooden stand.

'He wasn't bloody Peter Pan, though, was he?' said Patrick. 'He grew up. Into a moody young man who gave his father hell.'

'He was sad,' said Mary Rose, her voice cracking. 'And he was young.'

'When you're that age,' said Jill, attempting to pour some oil on the conversation's troubled waters, 'I suppose you don't know that sadness passes. If you have time to wait it out.'

Mary Rose gazed up at a watercolour on the wall. 'This boy will reproach me from every page, forever. And not just the page. He's out there, among the trees.' She turned to Patrick. 'The story we were told in Germany – well it's come true, hasn't it? I've hardly dared to be in the trees these past few days. I've walked the tarmac way on the main road, not the dirt path through the trees. I'm afraid of seeing him, I think. Or hearing him, like Hans could hear his brother.'

It was then that Jill saw the thing that she had been dreading. Mary Rose was staring at the bookshelf. It was as if she had seen a ghost. Jill could not help herself following her gaze, to check her suspicions – which had the effect of making Patrick and Jack do the same. For a moment, an expression of hopeless defeat fell over Mary Rose's face, as if she had lost some invisible battle. It passed so quickly, however, that Jill wondered if she had seen it at all.

'We've been thoroughly mangled by this war, haven't we?' said Mary Rose. 'It's marked our minds and our bodies. I'll be glad to be rid of it. In some new world.'

'Your lot will be paying for that, I suspect,' said Patrick, looking at Jack. 'We won't have anything left in the bank.'

'Patrick, you will bring that shirt in the morning,' said Mary Rose, 'won't you, dear?'

Jack and Jill went out into the night, arm in arm. It was hot and close, ready to be threshed by rain and thunder. Something had bitten Jill before they had even left the Deevers' garden. Her discovery of the letters was also biting her.

'I hope you didn't mind the amateur dramatics?' asked Jack. 'Subtlety isn't always the best policy.'

'They were very professional,' said Jill. She had yet to decide what to make of his conduct. It was daring. It was exciting. It had a cold streak. It left her wondering about the extent of Jack's talent for deception. 'Did you find anything?' she asked.

'Patrick keeps his service revolver in his bedside drawer,' Jack reported. 'Same make and model as the one that killed Peter Brock.'

'There aren't that many kinds, are there?' said Jill. 'Standard issue, surely?'

'Unlike his cufflinks,' said Jack.

'He was talking about cufflinks when he came back downstairs,' said Jill.

Jack bit his lip. 'I wondered if he'd noticed me noticing.'

'And what did you notice?' asked Jill.

'He had a pair with the lightning flash,' said Jack. 'You know, the sign for the British Union of Fascists.'

'Do you think he was a member?' asked Jill.

'You don't know?'

'Well,' replied Jill. 'He likes correcting people. Shooting things in fields.'

'But you don't seem that surprised by the idea.'

Jill shrugged. 'We had a few Mosley men around here. I remember when they had a bring-and-buy sale in Brockenhurst, and nobody batted an eyelid. The butcher was in on it. He used to wear the pin on his tie. It was unnerving when he was holding a knife. I think he recanted. But it was the ones who passed through who worried me. Fascists do love their hiking, don't they? I suppose they pretend they're annexing places. Or that they might come back one day and give a hard time to people who looked at them in a funny way.'

236

'Did you ever see anything to suggest that Patrick was one?' asked Jack.

'A hiker?'

'A Fascist.'

'Well,' said Jill. 'I saw his bookshelves tonight. Does the name Archibald Pitt-Rivers mean anything to you?'

'It does,' said Jack. 'He was a guest of His Majesty, under the powers granted by Regulation 18B. Spent a long vacation behind barbed wire. Suspected Nazi agent.'

'Patrick owns a signed copy of the magnum opus. Jolly sort of work about racial degeneration in Europe and what to do about it.'

She was affecting jolliness herself. Jack detected it. 'What happened at the end there, do you think? To Mary Rose?'

'She seemed broken. I think we saw her break.'

'What was she looking at, though? Something on the wall? It wasn't the watercolour of the boy.'

'Jack,' said Jill, 'I'm afraid I did something very amateurish.'

She told him about the cache of letters inside the cardboard sleeve. The news produced a barrage of questions. What kind of sleeve? What was on the spine? How was it concealed? Did she steal any of the contents? What kind of paper were they printed on? Were there dates, names?

Jill struggled to answer. They were notes arranging

meetings. One was a business letter from the bank about a fifty-pound payment. But the personal letters – love letters possibly – were also sent in plain brown envelopes with typewritten addresses. One was illustrated in a style that resembled the fragments of the diary recovered from the vicarage. She remembered the name of George Vatine.

'I would have looked longer. I might even have taken something, but Patrick came back into the room and saw me looking at it, so I had to pretend it was a real book from the shelf and just put it with the others.'

'Oh,' said Jack, darkly. 'So that's what she was looking at.'

'I'm afraid so,' said Jill. She could see lines of frustration on Jack's face. She had disappointed him.

'Well,' she said, 'it was an excruciating evening but at least you got your favourite dinner. I can't bear pheasant.'

'I hate it too,' said Jack. 'It's like someone found a way of making a bird out of all the parts of a turkey that nobody wants.'

Doubt fluttered inside Jill. She pulled her hand away from him. 'I believed it when you said you liked it. I believed it completely.'

Her reaction seemed to shock him. 'It's just strategy, Jill,' he said. 'To put people at ease.'

This answer did not please her. 'Is this part of your strategy, Jack? Doing this? Holding hands? Kissing me?' They were passing the fallen tree. Jill felt wracked with shame at the difference between that hot moment and this cold one.

Jack began to apologize; he asserted his sincerity, but his words sounded stale and flat. They sounded like the things a professional liar would say when protesting his innocence to a dupe. 'Like you say, Jill,' he said, 'we need to win this war.'

Harold was in bed when Jill's key turned in the latch. She went upstairs in the dark. She did not brush her teeth or her hair. She did not hang up her dress but draped it carelessly over the chair. She lay awake, her heart leaden and disconsolate. When the sound of the telephone disturbed the silence, she felt a lurch of dread. It was after midnight. No good news ever arrived so late. As she fumbled with her dressing gown, Harold was already descending the stairs. She heard him pick up; conduct a conversation in low, grave tones. When she heard the receiver rattle in its cradle, she opened the bedroom door and went out onto the landing.

Her father's face was sombre.

'That was Len Creech,' he said. 'The coroner's returned his verdict on Peter Brock. Murder by persons unknown.'

It rained that night in Larkwhistle. The heat broke with the morning, sending a cool fusillade against the windowpanes and thatched roofs of the village. Around St Cedd's, rain brightened the moss on the tombstones of the Mays and the Hills, and blackened the earth above the bodies of Peter Brock and Henry Metcalfe. The great green canopy of the forest welcomed the rain like a lover. It softened dry leaves, disturbed the dust of paths and root-boles, reddened the bark of the fir tree by the fork in the path to Brockenhurst and washed the blood from the corpse of Mary Rose Deever that lay beneath it, gazing sightlessly at the dawn.

Part Two

Chapter 21

The news came to Jack first. It arrived with the muffled sound of someone banging on the front door of the Fleur-de-Lys, and his bleary assumption that this was somebody else's problem. Then came a voice from the landing. Wally Speed, arriving like the Porter in *Macbeth* to tell Jack that Patrick Deever wanted to speak to him on an urgent matter. The clock showed 5.30 am. Jack pulled on his vest and trousers and went downstairs to find Patrick sitting on a chair in the public bar. He was holding Jack's shirt from the night before, now clean and dry. He was pale and strange and breathless.

'She went away in the night,' said Patrick, giving Jack the shirt like a present. 'Walked out on me, do you see? I don't know where. She must have got out of bed while I was asleep. Or perhaps she never came to bed. I'd had a bit to drink, you see, Captain

Strafford. You'll say that, won't you? I couldn't be expected to wake up, could I?'

Wally went behind the bar and drew a measure of brandy from the optic. Patrick seemed to have lost his co-ordination as well as his composure. He accepted the drink but tried to pick it up with his prosthetic hand and almost knocked it to the floor. Rescuing it with his good hand, he drained the glass with a shudder.

'Would Harold Metcalfe have a home number for Len Creech?' he asked. 'I really think it best that he handles this.'

'Handles what, Patrick?' asked Jack, pulling on the shirt – which was, he noticed, freshly pressed and ironed. Had Mary Rose done this as her husband slept?

'We need to find her. We need to find Rosie.'

'So, she's gone off somewhere without telling you?'

'In the small hours.'

'Well,' said Jack, kneeling to lace his shoes, 'the hours aren't so big yet. Tell me what happened. When did you go to bed last night?'

'About half past midnight, I suppose. Quarter to one, possibly. Not more than an hour after you left. The gin knocked me out, you see. I should stick to beer.'

'Did you two have some sort of argument after we left?' asked Jack.

'No. I mean she didn't seem very happy, but she often isn't.'

'I thought she seemed unhappy, too. About the death of Peter Brock. Understandable, don't you think, given his place in her work? The events of this week?'

Patrick did not reply. He flashed a wary eye at Wally. There was something he did not wish to say in front of the landlord of the Fleur-de-Lys.

'What was Mary Rose doing?' asked Jack. 'After we left?'

'She went to her study. I could hear the typewriter. Drives me nuts, that typewriter.'

'Does she often use it so late at night?' asked Jack.

'It's part of her,' said Patrick. 'Never off it. It's like the sound of a deathwatch beetle in our house. Writers, you see. They don't have timetables. Not like us with reveille and drill or the licensing laws. When inspiration strikes, she has to get it down.'

'Doesn't it keep you awake?' asked Jack.

'I use earplugs. Only need the one these days, though.' He tapped the left side of his head. 'This one was lost in action.'

'Did you put one in last night?' asked Jack.

'Yes,' said Patrick. 'I woke up at four with a terrible hangover. The front door was wide open.'

Jack fastened the top button of his clean shirt.

'What makes you think she's not just gone out for a walk?' he asked.

Patrick reached into his jacket and pulled out a crumpled page of typing paper. He pressed it upon Jack like a court summons. 'Because I found this on the dining room table. Next to your ironed shirt.'

Jack unfolded the paper. It was a letter, handwritten and signed by Mary Rose. The ink was faint in places, but the message was clear. It was a final goodbye. It also contained a confession that made Jack catch his breath.

Patrick watched him absorb this information. 'Would you come back to the house?' he asked. He sounded meek. 'Perhaps you'd help me look for clues to her whereabouts? I'm afraid I'm a bit distracted.'

'Of course,' Jack said.

'Or,' continued Patrick, 'just to keep a chap company until she comes back.'

The intimacy of the remark took Jack by surprise. 'Sure,' he said. 'And we'll call in at the Metcalfes' on the way.' He refolded the letter, slipped it into his back pocket and mustered a friendly smile. 'I'll look after this, if you don't mind. We don't want to lose it, do we?'

Patrick Deever shook his head obediently, as if he were glad to be receiving commands rather than giving them. He was lost in some hostile territory, hoping for the instructions that would lead him out to safety. 'I'm sure you're right about Harold having a number for Inspector Creech,' said Jack. 'We can ask him or Jill to ring him. It's a good thought. He knows the family and he knows the village.'

'Should I be doing anything, Captain?' asked Wally Speed.

'I don't think so, Mr Speed,' said Jack. 'Not just yet.'

He turned to Patrick. 'Just give me a moment.' He disappeared upstairs. When he returned, he was wearing his cap, his jacket and his pistol.

Jack ushered Patrick out of the Fleur-de-Lys. 'That note,' said Patrick, as they crossed the rain-washed green. 'I don't want any of that in the papers.'

'I'm sure Len Creech will use his discretion,' said Jack.

'And what about you, Captain?' said Patrick. 'I hope I can trust you, officer to officer. This really is a matter of the utmost delicacy.'

'Of course,' said Jack. He waved the letter. 'Could you tell me what you think this means?'

'I think it's called a "Dear John", isn't it?' said Patrick.

'Has Mary Rose ever walked out on you before?' asked Jack.

'Once. Last year she accused me of having an affair with a girl in Boscombe. But it was a misunderstanding. She read my diary and thought she'd found evidence of an assignation. "Jane at the Hippodrome."'

'Oh,' said Jack, understanding. 'Jane was the name of the show, right?'

'The Forces' Favourite. The one from the *Daily Mirror*. There were nudes in it, but none of them moved.'

'They didn't?' asked Jack.

'No,' said Patrick.

'Does she often read your diary?'

'I've got nothing to hide,' said Patrick. 'Unlike some I could mention.'

As they reached the Metcalfes' cottage, Jack could see there was already someone awake. The parlour curtains and the kitchen window were open to the morning air. He could hear the whimper of a boiling kettle being removed from the gas. His first thought was of Harold, habitually early to bed, but as he opened the gate, he saw Jill standing at the kitchen table. She was wearing a pale green nightshirt. She had been crying. When her eyes met his, she recoiled out of instinct, clearly wishing not to be seen. Then she registered the presence of Patrick, standing at the end of her garden path, blinking like someone who had just emerged from an air raid.

She came to the kitchen window.

'What's happened?' she asked.

Jack moved closer. Patrick remained at the gate,

nervous, agitated, looking mainly at the ground. 'Might you do something for me?' asked Jack. 'I'm sorry to impose on you, but Patrick needs our help. He's in a spot of bother. Mary Rose has gone wandering off.'

'Wandering off where?'

Jack shrugged. Jill looked at him carefully. The casual manner of his voice was not, she saw, reflected in his eyes. He was like someone in a prison yard or at a checkpoint, trying to communicate something in plain sight of the guard.

'I have some news too,' she said.

'It'll keep,' said Jack, breezily. 'Might you do us a great favour? Ring Len Creech and tell him to come over to Patrick and Rosie's place? We're just heading over there now. See if we can find any indication of where she went.'

Jill agreed. Much to her surprise, Jack thanked her by leaning through the window and planting a kiss on her cheek. Patrick, already ill at ease, turned his head away. The small distraction allowed Jack to reach into his back pocket and press something into Jill's hand. Mary Rose's letter.

Jill watched the two men walk towards the main road, following the route she had taken with Jack on the previous evening. Once they had disappeared from view, she unfolded the letter.

Dearest Patrick,

Tonight was really the end, wasn't it? I really can't go on. Since Peter died – and I <u>will</u> mention his name – I have been trying so hard to be brave and strong. And this evening, darling, somewhere towards the end of that dinner, I realized that it was no longer possible.

I have drafted this letter several times, but it does not improve. So, goodbye. Do try to forgive me. None of this was mentioned in our marriage vows, and I am sorry I was compelled to break them. I loved him. That's all there is to it. And once I had seen that, I realized that my love for you had died without my quite noticing. Perhaps I drew his picture once too often. Perhaps it was the war. Perhaps it was the silence in the bedroom. Perhaps it was the crime I committed against him, which is the greatest regret of my life.

But I grow tired of asking these questions and wish to be free of them.

Rosie

Chapter 22

Patrick had stayed silent at the cottage gate, but beyond sight of the village, he began to lose some of his inhibitions. Jack could hear the panic in his voice.

'People will know she was unfaithful to me, that she slept with that boy. And he *was* a boy. We really must do our best to stop them talking. Saying that she was with him. I can't have that.'

'How do you know that she slept with him? Nothing in that letter says so. It might have been entirely unrequited. There's no evidence that they were having an affair, Patrick. Like you and the Forces' Favourite. Don't read too much into it.'

Patrick put a hand on Jack's shoulder and moved closer to him than he would have liked. 'You're going to help me, aren't you?'

'Of course,' said Jack. 'We'll find her and then you can settle all this between yourselves. You've been married a while, Patrick. These things happen in marriages. Rows. Infidelities. Perhaps you can forgive each other. And even if you can't, well, divorce isn't a death sentence.'

'It would be for me,' said Patrick. 'I don't own a thing. Everything belongs to Rosie. I'd only have my Army pension.'

They had arrived at the front door of Woodlander House. There was no need for Patrick to extract his keys: he had left the front door wide open. The walk had soaked their shoes. They slipped out of them and left them on the doormat. Crossing the threshold, it struck Jack that he and Patrick were already treating the house as a crime scene. They spoke in hushed voices. Neither of them was inclined to sit on one of the many inviting chairs or sofas, or handle objects that might bear the mark of the last few hours.

The dining room looked much as it had when Jack and Jill had departed. The red wine stain had darkened on the tablecloth. The ashtray was heaped with Mary Rose's cigarette stubs, bearing traces of her lipstick. Jack made a subtle study of the bookshelf that held the foreign editions of *The Boy Among the Trees*. No presentation copy of the French edition was visible. He moved closer. When he felt that Patrick's attention was elsewhere, he ran a hand behind the row of books and found nothing.

In the kitchen, the ironing board was up and the

iron still hot and connected to the mains electricity. Jack yanked the plug from the socket. The washing up from the previous night was waiting in the sink for Maggie. Pheasant bones had been left on a plate, not scraped into the dustbin. Jack noticed a fly dining on the remains.

'Maggie is due at nine, yes?' asked Jack.

'She makes my breakfast and brings a paper from the village. I'll send her away when she arrives. I'm not in the mood to eat anything.'

'How long has she been with you?' asked Jack.

The answer seemed effortful. 'Oh, since the summer of '40. I didn't engage her. It was when I was in France. The other girl left and joined the WAAF. She's an ack-ack gunner in Plymouth now. Rosie managed for herself, mostly. I mean, she still does. Maggie's not a natural domestic.'

'Oh?'

'She didn't cook that bird last night, you know. That was all Rosie's doing. I think Maggie would prefer to make friends with pheasants rather than stick them in the oven at gas mark four. I've seen the look she gives me when I'm cleaning my rifle.'

'She must like working for you, though?' asked Jack.

'I don't know. I think she just likes to be around this stuff,' he said, waving a hand towards the paraphernalia associated with *The Boy Among the Trees*. 'She adored him, you know. That *boy*.'

They went upstairs. The floorboard creaked as Jack remembered. He moved to open the bedroom door, but Patrick suggested they look first in Mary Rose's office. On her desk they found an address book and an appointments diary. The coming week was blank except for a note of Maggie Speed's working hours and a line about a lunch engagement with the writer of cowboy stories from Portsmouth. They rang him from the office phone. Once he had stopped complaining about the ungodly hour, it became clear that Ray Spain, author of *The Purple Sage Rustlers*, was still expecting to meet Mary Rose in the British Restaurant near the harbour.

'No, Ray, everything's fine,' said Patrick. 'I just didn't want to double-book her.' Jack was struck by the authenticity of his tone: Patrick was a good liar.

'Does she often have lunch with him?' asked Jack, after he had hung up.

'Oh, once a week,' said Patrick. 'In the Portsmouth Grand. Not quite as grand as it used to be. Though they do have oysters sometimes.'

'Once a week?' queried Jack.

'Nothing to worry about there, though. Ray's an unspeakable of the Oscar Wilde sort. You can tell it from those awful Westerns he writes. All those cowboys and their six-shooters.' A thought came to Patrick. 'Could you do something for me?' He indicated a large black portfolio propped against the wardrobe. 'Hard for me to untie the knots with the old false hand. But I think there might be something important in there. It's where she keeps things like her passport and birth certificate. It might indicate whether she's intending to come back any time soon.'

It was a reasonable thought. Jack pulled the portfolio from its place, laid it flat on the floor and undid the string that kept it closed. The space inside was tightly packed with drawings and illustrations. They were the work of Mary Rose Deever, but they were not in the naïve style of *The Boy Among the Trees*. These were life drawings, charcoal lines on paper describing the soft architecture of a human body. There were dozens of them, but only one subject – a young man, quite naked, his hair in his eyes, stretched out on a divan like a sunned cat. The divan belonged to the Deevers. Jack had noticed it in the dining room in front of the bay window. The body belonged to Peter Brock.

Patrick Deever dropped to his knees and slapped the portfolio shut. The muscles in his face contorted as if he had just swallowed a mouthful of bleach.

'Christ,' he spat. 'No wonder she kept them in something I couldn't open.'

'You knew these were here?'

'I thought it was some dirty secret,' Patrick muttered.

'Do you mind if I . . . ?' asked Jack, gesturing to the case.

'Before I burn them, you mean?' asked Patrick.

Jack ignored the remark. He turned the portfolio around so that when he opened it, the cover would shield the contents from Patrick's view. He could understand the man's desire to erase them from the world. They were evidence of a fixation. The folder contained around a hundred sketches and drawings. The complicit expression in the boy's eyes suggested that these were something more than the product of Mary Rose's imagination. She had drawn these from life.

Jack turned over a smallish head-and-shoulders pencil portrait and held it up to Patrick. 'This is like the one she gave Helena Brock.'

'Well, I can see why she chose it,' he said. 'He's in the bloody nude in all the others.'

'How long do you think this was going on for?' The question was a calculated one. As he went through the papers, Jack could see that each one was signed and dated.

'While I was in France?' Patrick suggested. 'And then while I was in the nursing home for months learning how to use the new arm. She had plenty of opportunity. As did he. That lad wanted to fight, you know. But the business with his heart, that put paid to it. Though this stuff suggests that he wasn't entirely unfit for active duty.'

Jack was surprised by the joke. Patrick seemed to

have recovered his equilibrium. 'I suppose the police will have to see all of these,' he went on. 'Do you think there's any way of stopping them going any further? I don't want to look at them in the *News of the World*. That would be more than I could bear.'

'Mary Rose owns the copyright. They'd be foolish to print anything without her permission.' Jack used the present tense. If Patrick thought his wife was dead, he betrayed no sign of it.

'That's good,' Patrick murmured. 'It would kill Rosie's reputation. If there's anything left of it.' He allowed Jack to give him a consoling pat on the shoulder.

'Let's look in the bedroom,' Jack said. 'Something in there may help us.'

He closed the portfolio. Both men got to their feet. For a moment Patrick had to steady himself against a chair, like someone reaching for the guardrail on a listing ship.

'I'm fine,' he breathed. He crossed the landing and pushed open the door to the marital bedroom. The curtains were drawn. The space inside was warm and gloomy. Jack looked at the bed. One half was disturbed; the other did not appear to have been slept in at all.

Patrick seemed compelled to explain his sleeping arrangements to Jack. 'Lot of couples have separate rooms. Never us. Wasn't that kind of marriage. Not at first, anyway. You only realize later, perhaps. When you start to turn your backs on each other before you go to sleep. And when that kiss before lights out becomes the only one of the day.' He had drifted away to the early years of his marriage. He looked as if he wished to stay there.

'You're not married, are you, Captain?'

Jack shook his head. 'Let's cast a little light on the situation, shall we?' he said. He moved to the window and pulled open the curtains. His eye fell upon the table on Patrick's side of the bed. There was a white, bullet-shaped object beside the reading lamp. Some kind of pill or capsule? No. This was Patrick's discarded earplug.

Something more dramatic then caught his attention. The wood around the lock in the bedside drawer was splintered, as if someone had forced it. The previous night, he noted, it had been unlocked.

Jack looked up to press Patrick on the matter and saw that the owner of the house was standing at the bedroom door, wearing a faintly apologetic expression. What was he about to do? For a split second the two men stared at each other. Then Patrick whipped the key from the door, slammed it shut and, without a fumble, turned it in the lock, trapping Jack inside the bedroom.

'What on earth are you doing, Patrick?' Jack spoke through the door, trying not to make things worse by showing his anger. The question, however, was unnecessary. Jack was perfectly capable of identifying the sound of a man running into the next room, grabbing a large portfolio and carrying his burden downstairs. The creak of the floorboard marked his progress.

'It won't do you any good, you know,' Jack yelled, realizing how hard it was to shout and sound reasonable at the same time. 'It might even prejudice your case, if the police decide that there's one to answer.'

He rushed to the window and saw Patrick lugging his burden over the gravel path. Jack looked at the bedroom door. It was thick and heavy. He considered kicking it down or shooting out the lock, but concluded that the room offered a quicker and simpler option. He wrenched open the window and assessed the possibilities of the side of the house. It had a drainpipe. It had ivy. The porch looked capable of supporting his weight.

He hauled himself over the windowsill, tested the strength of the pipe and judged it worth the chance. Gripping the edge of the flat roof of the porch allowed him to find a foothold on the ledge of the stained-glass window below, and, in a couple of seconds, he had crashed down onto the gravel and tackled Patrick to the ground.

Patrick kept such a tight hold of his prize that the folder remained closed, the contents unspilled.

'Come on, Patrick,' said Jack, catching his breath. 'Don't be a fool.'

'Nobody must see this stuff,' Patrick whimpered. 'Nobody.'

'Bad luck, old man. You can't destroy it. Not yet, anyway. I've got a question I need to ask you. If you don't mind?'

Patrick, caught by the ankles, lying flat on his back outside his own home, clutching a portfolio to his chest, was not unaware of the absurdity of his position.

'What?' he spluttered.

'Your bedside drawer,' said Jack. 'What do you keep in it?'

'My service revolver,' said Patrick.

'And you keep it locked?' asked Jack.

'Of course I keep it locked,' said Patrick. 'Them's the rules.'

'It's been forced,' said Jack. 'Someone's taken the gun.'

Patrick sat up. He let the portfolio fall to the gravel. His hand went to his mouth.

'Oh my lord,' he said. 'Oh my lord, she's done it too.'

Jill took the short cut to Woodlander House. The undergrowth and the trees were slick and sodden, but the path, baked hard by weeks of sunshine, was already dry. Jack had not asked her to follow him, but once Jill had delivered her message to Len Creech, the compulsion was unignorable. She woke up her father. Wimsey followed her into his bedroom and jumped up onto the eiderdown, pleased that everyone was up so early.

'The first train is at 6.10 am,' said Harold. 'Perhaps she'll be on that. She's not much of a walker, is she? Does she drive?'

'No,' said Jill. 'Can you imagine Patrick letting her behind the wheel? I'll check the station.'

'Whose help would she seek, if she came to the village?'

'Helena Brock, I think.'

'I'll ask at the vicarage, then,' said Harold. 'And I'll meet you over at the Deevers' place.'

When Jill arrived at the station, there was nobody on the platform but a couple of soldiers, dazed from long hours of duty or pleasure, and a woman who was telling a sullen child that he had no choice but to stay with his aunt for the day, and he was not to comment on the smell of the house. Jill gazed down the track. Perhaps Mary Rose had departed by other means: might someone in the village have driven her into town?

Soon the news would be all around Larkwhistle. Patrick, she thought, would be seen as the wounded party. The women of the village would be at the door of Woodlander House to offer him their home-baked commiserations and long-nursed doubts about his absent wife.

But when Jill tried to imagine Mary Rose's sudden act of leaving, she found it easy. The exhilaration of slamming a door and getting out into the air of the world. Who did not want it?

This was her last thought before she found Mary Rose's body.

It was at the foot of the great fir tree, in the same place where the corpse of Peter Brock been discovered. Mary Rose was wearing an expensive-looking rain-coat, still belted, beneath which was visible the same floral frock she had worn at the dinner table the night before. A small black leather handbag was at her side, its clasp shut. There was a black streak at her temple, where her hair dye had run. She wore no lipstick or face powder: the rain had extinguished her Hawaiian Fire. It struck Jill that she had never seen Mary Rose without her make-up.

Jill sank to her knees in shock, reeling with the churning, seasick feeling of events repeating them-selves. Mary Rose, she saw, had also been killed by a bullet. Her pale fingers were wrapped around a service revolver, exactly like the one that had killed Peter Brock. Her other hand was pressed against her chest. Through a hole in the waterproof fabric of her coat, Jill could see an open wound, cleansed of blood by the rain, as if in preparation for a surgeon – and also, she suspected, cleansed of any evidence that could be taken to a laboratory.

The nearest telephone, she calculated, was at Woodlander House. It was the logical place to go. She gathered her breath and ran on down the track. The noise of her progress disturbed a squirrel, which squealed and skittered through the bushes. When she looked back up the track, she saw two figures up ahead. She knew them immediately. They were also running.

Jill stopped, allowing them to reach her.

Patrick stared at her as if she were a basilisk – some monster that might turn him to stone with a look – then abruptly cast his eyes downwards. 'Have you found her?' he stammered. 'Have you found Rosie?'

Jill nodded. 'Don't look, though, Patrick. Don't look.'

She did not expect him to heed her. She did not even think it right that he should. Jack walked towards her and enclosed her in his arms.

'Are you okay?' he asked.

'Just let me stay here for a moment,' said Jill. She burrowed into him, raising her arms to pull his head down towards her.

'You need to know something,' she said. 'Peter Brock was murdered.'

Jack looked up and watched Patrick belting breathlessly down the path, towards the body of his wife.

Chapter 23

Len Creech had known better mornings, and better nights before. The coroner's judgement had reached his desk just as he was putting on his coat to go home. If the Inspector had been a betting man – which he wasn't – he would have put money on a verdict of suicide whilst of unsound mind. The Larkwhistle people had described a boy who seemed the type. They had produced no evidence of the presence of another party until after the shot had been fired. But the expert witness disagreed, and the coroner sided with expertise.

A verdict of murder made home a distant prospect for Inspector Creech. Another awkward conversation; another spoiled dinner. It also stirred gloomy reflections about his chances of finding men with the skill and experience to conduct the investigation. The late-night conversation with Harold Metcalfe had helped to put his mind at rest. The early morning call from Harold's daughter about the missing Mary Rose Deever, however, had the opposite effect. A long and painful day of interviewing and reinterviewing witnesses in the Peter Brock case awaited him. Now a spanner had been thrown into the works by some domestic bother with consequences no more serious than a *decree nisi*. Perhaps Harold would be able to help him oil the machinery.

On the way to Larkwhistle, Len and his constable stopped to give a presentable young flight mechanic a lift to RAF Beaulieu. When she threw them a cheerful wave from the main gate, they felt they had done their good deed for the day. Had the car been equipped with a radio, they might have put on more speed. But the Hampshire force was not the Met. On his visits to the capital, Len always felt a faint pang of jealousy when he heard a crackling voice calling all cars or saw the insistent flash of a London Metropolitan Police Box. So, it was with a sense of shame and frustration that he registered the ambulance parked on the gravel drive of Woodlander House, and Jill Metcalfe standing at the beginning of the path that led to the woods, urging him to hurry, as if he were late to an appointment.

Jill filled him in on the events of the past few hours. The dinner party and its revelations. The cache of letters hidden on a bookshelf in the dining room of

Woodlander House. The rain-rinsed corpse of its mistress lying beneath the tree, echoing the death of her lover. The arrival of the ambulance and its crew.

Len took in this new information. 'Did your father tell you about the verdict on Peter Brock?'

'He did.'

'And does Captain Deever know?'

'No,' she said. 'But I told Captain Strafford.'

'Do you have Mrs Deever's letter?'

Jill pulled the sheet of typing paper from the pocket of her cardigan.

Len held it up to the light as they walked. His constable walked dutifully behind him.

'What are you looking for?' asked Jill.

'She says she revised it many times,' answered Len. 'I can see the impress of an earlier draft. Reads a bit differently now, doesn't it?' he said. 'This isn't her saying that she's going back to Mother. It's a suicide note.'

'It does look that way,' said Jill. 'What are you thinking?'

'I'm thinking,' he said, stuffing the letter into his waistcoat pocket, 'that she did this in response to Peter Brock's death. She's following him on. You know. To the next life. Like Cleopatra.'

'If you think there's something romantic at the end of this path,' said Jill. 'You'd better prepare yourself.'

'I don't believe in romantic death,' said Len.

'I have to tell you that my father is on his way here.'

'That might not be a terrible thing. I'm a bit short-handed this morning. He's dealt with more murder cases than I have. I'd appreciate his advice.'

'He thinks it's a missing persons case,' said Jill.

'Your dad worked the patch around the docks for thirty years,' said Len. 'I'm sure he'll be able to take it.'

'I think he's bringing the dog.'

Len sighed.

They arrived at the fir tree like a boy and a girl in an uncollected Grimm fairy tale. Patrick Deever was standing with his hands covering his face, shaking his head. Jack had placed a supportive arm around his shoulders and was telling him all would be right in soothing tones that did not match his steely and interrogative expression. Mary Rose's body lay twisted on the same spot occupied by Peter Brock less than a week before. The tree itself had an almost guilty look to it, though the gun clasped in the dead woman's right hand spoke of an obvious culprit. The ambulance crew, two war-toughened women in blue serge uniforms, were hunkered over the body, entirely aware that the scene demanded little of them but porterage duties. Their stretcher was laid flat beside the corpse.

'We closed her eyes,' said the younger of the two. 'But we thought we'd better wait to move her.' Jill felt grateful for the smallness of the scene. The removal of Peter's body had become a horrible village festival. Mary Rose would be permitted to leave Larkwhistle without an audience.

Len removed the revolver from Mary Rose's hand and wrapped the weapon in a clean white handkerchief. Jill wondered if he kept a supply for such purposes and imagined a pile of them on his sideboard at home, ironed by his mother. The ambulance crew loaded the body onto the stretcher.

'One, two, three,' said the older of the two. 'Roll her, Enid.' Len's constable, a taciturn sixty-year-old called back into service from his allotment, was left to guard the scene of the crime.

'You girls can get her off to the morgue,' said Len. The ambulance crew did not seem to mind being spoken to in this way. They said nothing as they raised the stretcher in a notably ungirlish fashion and began to walk down the path to Woodlander House.

'Captain Deever,' said Len, 'I'd very much like to ask you and your friends a few questions.' Patrick narrowed his eyes. He looked like a man who had just heard some alarming news on the wireless and was hoping that he'd misunderstood.

'I'm aware that this will be very distressing for you,' Len continued, 'but if we could go back to your house and work through the events of the last few hours, that would be of great help to us. And a service to your late wife, too. We need to understand what has happened here. Better we pursue that in your own place than at the station, don't you think? I shouldn't like to put you through that. The chairs are very hard.'

Patrick sank beneath the logic of the argument. He nodded dumbly.

'Is there anyone who might come and stay with you?' asked Len. 'You might need some company in the next few days.'

'Very kind of you to think of it, officer,' said Patrick, 'but I'm fine.'

'Perhaps your friend from the Post Office?'

'No,' said Patrick, firmly.

As they followed behind the ambulance crew, Jill attempted to offer Patrick some words of condolence. Something, however, prevented her from doing so wholeheartedly. She might have walked beside him to give comfort – perhaps even a supportive arm – but instead she paired herself with Jack and let Patrick walk with Len Creech, and did not feel guilty.

Chapter 24

The ambulance dragged its wheels over the gravel drive of Woodlander House. Jack, Jill, Patrick and Len watched it go, as if they had gathered to wave off weekend guests.

'Right,' said Patrick. 'Shall we go in?'

'I'll use your telephone, if I may, Captain Deever,' said Len.

As Patrick opened the front door he stumbled over a small obstacle at his feet.

'Sam Hill's been,' frowned Jill. 'While we were down the path. Did he not see the ambulance?' She picked up a sizeable stack of letters and cards, all of which were addressed to Mary Rose. One, with rabbits drawn on the envelope in coloured pencils, had clearly been sent by a child.

'I suppose I'll have to answer these,' sighed Patrick, taking them from Jill. 'A load came yesterday, too.

Full of stuff about Peter Brock. The bloody public. Most of them are lunatics.' He dropped the correspondence on the hall table, and, in doing so, noticed the muddiness of his hands.

'Excuse me,' he muttered, and disappeared inside the cloakroom lavatory.

The taps ran. Len was on the telephone, asking the station to strengthen his arm, warning the pathologist to expect a guest. When he replaced the receiver, Jack came in close and, with a movement of his finger, also brought Jill into a conspiratorial huddle.

'Inspector,' he whispered. 'There's some valuable evidence in this house that Patrick is planning to destroy. I think some if it has already gone. Jill discovered a cache of letters last night. They're now missing. And upstairs there's a folder full of material that Patrick has already expressed a desire to burn. I had to fight him for it.'

'What is it?' asked Len.

'Pictures,' said Jack. 'Evidence that Mary Rose and Peter Brock were more than friends.'

'Oh dear,' said Jill, already imagining an inquest, given the horrible vigour of scandal.

Len Creech chewed his moustache. 'Shocking what goes on in the countryside,' he said. 'Old women and young boys. I'm glad I live in Southampton.' Len was a Primitive Methodist, and was ungenerous towards those who did not possess his talent for continence.

He pulled out his notebook. 'Where are these pictures now?'

'I put them back in Mary Rose's study,' said Jack. 'They're in a portfolio. I tied the ribbon. He says he can't open it.'

'Is he lying, do you think?' asked Jill.

Jack shrugged.

'And what about these letters?' said Len, his eye on the lavatory door. 'Are they significant?'

'They were agreements about meetings,' said Jill. 'Assignations, perhaps. And there was one note from Peter about someone being arrested. Someone called George Vatine.'

Len Creech wrote down the name. 'Sounds like you've already done a number on this house,' he said.

'The place needs tearing apart,' said Jack. 'There might be more letters. Diaries. Secrets under the floorboards. Mary Rose was a writer. She wrote things down. All the more important now. Jill told me about the coroner's verdict on Peter Brock.'

'Well,' said Len, doubtfully, 'I would need Captain Deever's permission.'

'I don't think he'd give it,' said Jill.

'How long would it take to get a warrant?' asked Jack.

'A couple of hours,' said Len.

Jack gave a whistle of frustration.

'Some of us, Captain Strafford, have to operate within the letter of the law.'

The taps stopped running, and after a few seconds of audible fuss, Patrick emerged, checking his finger-nails. Jill saw that he had been trying to tidy his hair, but without much success. His face was frosted with white stubble. She had, she realized, never seen him anything less than neatly shaven.

'I'll try not to trouble for you for long, Captain Deever,' said Len, throwing open the dining room door. Patrick, however, was already troubled. He rubbed nervously at his chin. He moved as if the carpet carried an electric current. When Len directed him to sit on the divan in the bay window, he winced. Only Jack could read this moment and understand why. When Len allocated Patrick a dining chair and settled on the divan himself, his interviewee seemed even more agitated. The ghost of Peter Brock was here, bloodied and naked, for his lover's husband and for Jack.

'Is this a formal interview?' asked Patrick. The possibility did not delight him.

'No, Captain Deever,' said Len. 'It's just a simple chat. I've a couple of men on their way so we can take a statement later.' He cast an eye over Jack and Jill. 'Shut the door, would you? I'll talk to you two separately, if you don't mind. Please don't leave the house.'

Jill led Jack out into the hallway, where they perched on the stairs. There was a moment of silence, then the sound of muffled voices.

'Patrick's going through hell,' said Jill. 'Ninth circle stuff. His wife is dead. Funny thing is, I used to like him a little, but right now I've never liked him less.'

'Is that because you think he killed her?' The bluntness of Jack's question shocked her. She summoned the idea in her head, imagining a furious argument in the middle of a storm.

'I think he hated her. That he was hurt by her. But Mary Rose left a note. And if you're asking brutal questions, I think it more likely that Patrick killed Peter.'

'Since last night,' said Jack. 'Maggie Speed has been on my mind. If she discovered that Peter and Mary Rose were having an affair, that gives her motive in both cases. What did you do with Mary Rose's note?'

'Gave it to Inspector Creech. But I took a copy first.'

'Excellent,' said Jack. He was visibly pleased. Jill felt that her homework had been marked with a big tick and was surprised by how much pleasure it gave her. She would not, she vowed, take Jack's approval as some women took packets of American tan tights.

The test was not over. 'Those letters,' said Jack. 'They were definitely on the same shelf as Mary Rose's foreign editions?'

'Yes, in their own cardboard case. Which was taller than anything else on the shelf. Stuck out like a sore thumb.'

'It was gone when I checked. Perhaps it's already been consigned to the flames.'

'Mary Rose saw it, I'm sure,' said Jill. 'It was right in her eyeline. She looked mortified. I'm sure it was because she was afraid that Patrick would see them. They were a secret hidden from him.'

'In their own dining room? Behind copies of her most successful book?'

'The perfect place,' said Jill. 'Patrick had absolutely no interest in his wife's literary work. He knew nothing about it. Resented it, I think. If she were trying to hide something she wouldn't keep it in her desk drawer or put it in her handbag. She'd put it next to the fruits of her success.'

The sound of Patrick's raised voice – an insistent but controlled protest – bubbled through the dining room door.

'Clever chap, your Len Creech,' muttered Jack. 'He's absolutely within his rights to interview Patrick alone, and to do it in the house. And asking us back here, there's also nothing wrong with that. Nor would we be breaking any law but the law of good manners if we had a look for those letters.'

'Shall we?' asked Jill.

'Let's,' said Jack.

As they went upstairs, Jill felt that a boundary was being crossed. She was invading the private space of a married couple, in the company of a man she had kissed. There he was, one index finger on his lip and the other pointing to the place on the landing where the floorboard creaked, warning her not to make a sound; leading her into Mary Rose's office and opening the portfolio that lay on the floor; showing her the evidence that the boy among the trees was also a boy on the divan.

'It must have been an obsession,' Jill said, the contents of the portfolio spread before her. 'The sort that Doctor Freud might have to talk you down from.'

'Evidence of an affair, do you think?'

'These are done from life,' said Jill. 'She wasn't getting it out of her head. You were with Patrick when you found these?'

'Yes.'

'And how did he react?'

'Like he'd looked into his own grave,' said Jack. 'I know some husbands don't mind this kind of thing. But Patrick isn't one of them. There's no way this happened with his knowledge.'

Jack stopped rummaging through the papers.

'Are you all right?' asked Jill.

'Something just caught my eye,' he said.

'I bet it did,' said Jill.

Jack lifted a pencil sketch of Peter Brock lying on

his belly on what appeared to be a tartan picnic rug. Beneath the drawing was a document. Three pages of typescript, with a handful of pencil annotations.

'What is it?' asked Jill.

'A story,' said Jack. 'I think it's the sequel to *The Boy Among the Trees*.'

'Give me your notebook,' said Jill. 'Read it aloud.'

Chapter 25

The Pact Beneath the Trees

I thought I did not know the language of crows. When I hear them arguing in the treetops, I never feel able to take a side. When they make an insolent remark on the village green, I never know how insulted I should be. They regard us, I believe, with an amused sort of tolerance. Do they really fear a rotten turnip with coals for eyes, wearing a dead man's hat? I doubt it. Such objects scare us more than they scare them.

I think the birds know this and humour us. They fly away. They come back. They laugh at us.

So, naturally it came as a great surprise to find myself, one restless night in summer, deep in conversation with one of these creatures. I knew him by sight. He was an oily-feathered gentleman who thought it no affront to his dignity to wait upon a telegraph wire at the crossroads, hoping that the thunderous progress of a tank might provide him with a meal of carrion. I do not judge such conduct. When the children of the village shriek for chocolate bars tossed from the backs of Army trucks, I never click my tongue at them. We have adjusted our standards to the time. The war is not yet over. Perhaps when peace comes, our self-respect will be restored.

The crow came to bring bad news. So he came at night.

My husband was asleep beside me, and did not wake, because he rarely does.

The crow rapped on the window with his shiny beak and spoke a few dry words through the glass. There is, I am aware, a poetic precedent for this. But when these events occur in real life, they cannot be resisted simply because some dead poet imagined them first.

The crow came to tell me of my poor conduct. I listened because I like to give a fair hearing to any parties thoughtful enough to speak to me. Moreover, I suspected he was right. His critical remarks regarded my behaviour towards a boy with whom we had enjoyed a mutual acquaintance. We did not name him, for that would have made our discussion too painful to pursue.

The case against me seemed strong. It was alleged

I had taken something from this boy. I called it his likeness, but the crow said it was his youth and his hope. Displaying a rigour that could not but impress me, he proposed that many other of my errors should be taken into consideration. The crow averred that I had allowed this boy into my house. That I had loved him, which I admitted. That – worst of all, in the judgement of my prosecutor – I had allowed him to love me back, and all that this entails.

Coyness on this matter, I think, marred the crow's argument. He should have been blunter. He should have upbraided me for the pain caused to those who loved the boy more hopelessly than I. He should have mentioned the advantage I took of the absence of my husband, who was at that time abroad, fighting the enemy on the other side of what the French call 'La Manche'. He should have mentioned my holiday in London, during which I dealt with the consequences of our love. I had the help of a distinguished gentleman in Chelsea, who had, he said, my best interests at heart, and an account at Bell and Croyden.

The crow put his argument so forcefully that his talons rattled the glass in the bedroom window. My husband began to stir. I had to slip out and meet the bird on the front doorstep to hear his concluding remarks.

'The boy we mourn is one with the woods now,' he said, his head turned to one side. 'He is in the

rustling leaves, the crawling insects and the very breath of the forest. Although you must take your share of the blame for his death, there is no need to say goodbye to him. You may detect him in the revolutions of the earth, in the sound of the wind and in the voice of the forest.'

I am sceptical about ideas like this – partly because I have in the past pressed them upon others. At this stage of my life, I am no longer persuaded. Railway bookstand pantheism is, I believe, bafflegab of the first water, and I would not insult the intelligence of any reader – human or animal – by asking them to waste their time on it.

'Stuff and nonsense,' I told the crow. 'There is nothing in the forest. And it is to nothing I must go.'

The crow said nothing. I took this to be an expression of amazement, but it is hard to really tell with crows. A hard beak and beady eye are not efficient carriers of feeling.

'Do not try to follow me,' I warned the crow. 'I will walk alone to the tree. I was invited there days ago, and I should have kept the appointment.' The crow let loose a long and arid caw of disbelief. He had yet to formally pronounce his verdict. His thunder had been stolen. The accused had made her own judgement, boldly issued and quickly enacted.

'The punishment will fit the crime,' I informed him. 'Not the same gun, but borrowed from the same

regiment, and a veteran of the same conflict. Never fired a fatal shot until this morning.'

'Tsk, tsk,' the crow complained, scratching at the flagstones on the doorstep. I left him there, fiercely clawing and cawing his disapproval, as I followed the path to the trees.

'The court has not risen,' he protested. 'You do not have permission to just depart. I shall remain until judgement has been passed.'

I suspect he does so still. My husband may throw him bacon scraps, thinking he is begging when, in truth, he is making a point of order. I have some sympathy with his position. But as the woman in the dock, I can say that I have judged my own case deaf to any special pleas. And if I am also the executioner, none can complain that I showed undue mercy to myself. Quite the opposite, I think.

Chapter 26

'It won't be for long,' said Harold Metcalfe. 'I promise.'

Wimsey had heard these words before and had grown sceptical, but he also had the good taste not to bark. The doorstep of Woodlander House gave shade, and his lead was not too short to prevent him investigating the sensory possibilities of the boot scraper.

Harold had seen Len Creech and Patrick Deever through the bay window; Len with his back to the world, Patrick doing the talking. Harold gave a businesslike nod in their direction and, assuming himself welcome, bustled into the dining room without knocking. The expression on Patrick Deever's face told him that the case had entered a more serious phase. Len Creech supplied the details.

Harold shook his head in disbelief. 'Jill found her?' He put a hand on Patrick's shoulder and offered his condolences with an unforced sincerity that made Len think of the words his own father used when comforting the bereaved. Men of the Somme generation, he reflected, knew what to say in these circumstances.

Patrick had not been an easy interviewee. Len was torn between postponing their conversation and taking him to Southampton to conduct it more formally. Harold's presence, however, seemed to calm Patrick's nerves. Perhaps it was the tone of his voice.

'When we had the inquest on Peter Brock,' said Harold, 'there was no bother with the press. Nobody made the connection between him and Mary Rose's book. We won't be so fortunate this time. It'll be a big deal for the papers, even with all the news from France. So, if you want me to look after that aspect of it, then I'd be very happy to do so.'

'That aspect?' said Patrick, blankly.

'People will be ringing the house,' said Harold. 'You're in the phone book, aren't you?'

'Yes. Rosie liked it that way. She thought only snobs went ex-directory.'

'Then you might want somebody just to answer the phone and tell them where to stuff it. There'll be another inquest in a couple of days, and I dare say that the gentlemen of the press will not have the patience to wait that long. You could do with a bit of help, I think.'

Patrick groaned with dread: public exposure was his greatest fear.

'Be thankful there's a war on, Captain Deever,' said Len. 'In peacetime the papers were twice as long and there were no checkpoints in the New Forest.'

Patrick's eyes moved in the direction of the hall. Jack and Jill had appeared in the doorway. Jill rushed into the room and threw her arms around her father.

'I'm sorry, Dad,' she said. 'I didn't know it was so bad. Poor Mary Rose.'

Harold waved away her apologies. 'I'm an old hand at this,' he said. 'You've seen such things in the past few days. I wish I could undo them.'

Jack had Mary Rose's typescript in his hand. 'What's the procedure here?' he asked. 'May we all speak freely, as it were?'

Len motioned for him to sit down. 'I've got two constables on their way to take statements,' he said. 'So right now we're just talking. Nobody's taking notes.'

Jack chose the chair directly opposite Patrick. 'Do you mind if I ask you a few questions?' he said. 'I'm not the police, so you mustn't feel under any obligation to answer, but I'd be very grateful. It may have some bearing on a military matter that I'm investigating.'

'No,' said Patrick, a little dazed. 'It's fine.' Len and Harold looked equally bemused. Jack laid the typescript on the table in front of Patrick. Only the first page, blank apart from the title of the story, was visible – *The Pact Beneath the Trees.*

'Who would you say typed this?' asked Jack.

Patrick's eyes fell upon the paper. 'Where did you find this?' he asked.

'In that portfolio upstairs,' said Jack. 'Whose work is this, do you think?'

'Rosie's, of course,' said Patrick. 'This is the typing paper she always uses. Comes from a stationer in Southampton. She won't use the stuff Ivy Hill keeps in the Post Office. Too thin, she says.'

'Is she profligate with paper?' asked Jack.

'Absolutely not,' said Patrick. 'She uses it very carefully. Don't you know there's a war on?'

Jack accepted his answer. 'Might I see that note again, Inspector?' he asked. 'Mary Rose's note?' Len extracted the paper from his jacket pocket. Jack placed it beside the typescript. 'The same paper, would you say?'

Patrick nodded. Jack pulled the paperclip that fastened the pages of the story together and spread the document out like a fan.

'Every typewriter is subtly different,' he explained. 'They all have their idiosyncrasies. Particularly if they get used every day. What do you think? Is it definitely hers?'

'Really,' said Patrick, looking blankly at the paper.

'I couldn't say. I just go to the shops for her. I'm not an expert.'

'Does the name Whitechapel mean anything to you, Patrick?'

'The first square on the Monopoly board,' he said. 'One of those brown ones nobody wants to buy.'

'One more thing, Patrick – how many wireless sets do you have in the house?'

Patrick was growing testy. 'How can this be a military matter?'

Len Creech had also lost his patience. 'What's all this about, Captain Strafford?'

'I'm afraid I'm not at liberty to say anything more,' said Jack. He got to his feet and put the typescript into Len's hands. 'This document is probably more part of your investigation than mine.' The Inspector began to read.

'It's very sad,' said Jill. 'And I think it's of a piece with the note that Mary Rose wrote to you, Patrick. It's told like one of her stories for children, but really it's an explanation of her state of mind. And perhaps an explanation of what happened last night. What happened last night, Patrick?'

'I heard her typing,' said Patrick, quietly. 'But I always hear her typing. She hits the keys so damn hard.'

As he spoke, they heard the crunch of gravel from outside. Two constables, called in from neighbouring villages, arriving by bicycle. They looked older than Harold. One was having trouble getting down from a saddle that seemed to require some downward adjustment. Len shared a private word with them on the doorstep, then brought them into the house to do their work.

'Strike me pink,' said one, as he entered the dining room. 'It's Harry Metcalfe.'

'All right, Alan,' said Harold. 'How's the knee?'

'Rotten,' said the constable.

The business of taking statements proceeded with tiresome slowness. Len Creech dealt with Jack, but Jill was not so lucky. As she sat at the kitchen table watching her allocated officer lick his pencil, she could not help thinking of the men who turned up in *Much Ado About Nothing* to investigate a conspiracy at the big house. Perhaps, when the war was over, Len Creech would face the sadness and cruelty of the world with the support of younger, brighter, taller men.

It was midday when Jack and Jill left Woodlander House. Len made a careful examination of Mary Rose's study, then locked the door and took away the key, which Patrick surrendered without comment. A constable collected the black portfolio and put it in the back of the Wolseley. Len and Harold conducted a conversation in the hallway in low tones. The small constable with the tall bicycle sat on a chair, tidying his notes.

Harold returned to the dining room. 'I'm going to stay here with you for a bit while Inspector Creech goes back to Southampton,' he said.

'Why?' asked Patrick.

'So it's not just you and some old coppers.'

'You are an old copper, Harold.'

'It's true,' he conceded. 'Hungry?'

Patrick nodded. His prosthetic hand, it seemed, was far less useful with a wooden spoon than it was with a cigarette and box of matches. Harold led his host into the kitchen and began scrambling eggs. It was the limit of his culinary competence, but the result was received with gratitude. The telephone, as predicted, had already begun to ring. Harold suspected careless talk at the morgue.

'To whom am I speaking?' said the voice on the line.

'Betty Grable,' said Harold, and slammed down the receiver.

Jill had assumed that they would take the main road back through the village, but Jack strode off towards the woodland path. Wimsey, who had views on the relative abundance of squirrels on the two routes home, did not question his decision.

'Why did you do that?' Jill asked, as they walked

beneath the trees. 'Swish your cloak and show your dagger?'

'Show my what?' said Jack.

'Tell Patrick that you were working on a military investigation. If he is Commoner, he'll know you're on to him, won't he?'

'Absolutely he will,' said Jack. 'He might even try to use tonight's broadcast to tell Berlin that he's hit a reef. We've also got your dad on the scene. If Patrick does anything suspicious today, then he'll be sure to spot it.'

'Is Patrick telling the truth, do you think?'

'About what happened last night? He told me they didn't have a row. That Mary Rose was upset about the death of Peter Brock, and that she stayed up writing while he put in his earplugs and went to bed. An average night in the Deever household, I should say. And it's consistent with what we saw that evening.'

'So, he's saying that he slept through the noise of her typewriting and also through the noise of her breaking into the bedside drawer and taking his gun?'

'He did have earplugs in,' said Jack. 'Well, *an* earplug.'

'What about the portfolio in the study? Was he lying about that? Did he really need your help to open it?'

'That's begging for your *A Scandal in Bohemia*

test,' said Jack. 'The knot was tight. He might have undone it with one hand, but it would be a hard job to tie it up again.'

'He could have cut it with a pair of scissors.'

'He could,' said Jack. 'If he didn't mind anyone seeing the damage.'

'Patrick's very clever with his injury,' said Jill. 'You see him in the pub and around town and you forget how badly wounded he was. It's miraculous, really. But the other day, Wimsey nearly sent him tumbling in the street. Just a little dog running near his feet. He dropped his shopping, and I had to pick it up for him.'

Jack grunted. 'I fought him for that portfolio. Physically. He locked me in the bedroom and made a run for it. I had to tackle him to the ground like we were in college football. It was farcical, really. But he didn't go down without a struggle.'

Jill was astonished. 'Did you put that in your statement?'

'Not in so many words,' said Jack. 'I said that he was upset when we discovered the contents and intended to destroy them. The constable didn't ask me for more detail.'

'I'm surprised they remembered to take our names,' said Jill. She might have said more, but they had reached the sight of the fir tree and could see Len Creech's constable standing guard over the crime scene.

'Patrick didn't have much to say when Len took all

that stuff away,' said Jill. 'Mary Rose's drawings. He didn't even seem to care when you put that story in front of him. It was there on the dining table. He'd been told it was a companion piece to his wife's suicide note. But he didn't even turn over the first page.'

'We know he's not interested in his wife's work.'

'Well,' said Jill, 'if they ever make spousal indifference an Olympic sport, that's one gold medal in the bag.'

They had reached the tree. The constable gave them a half-hearted salute.

'What's he doing, the guv 'nor?' asked the constable.

'Having a chat with Captain Deever. No drama yet, but that may change.' Jack tapped the pistol holstered at his belt. 'In fact, it may change very soon. Jill, I assume Wimsey is not a fan of loud and sudden bangs?'

'He hates them,' she confirmed.

'Then perhaps you could take him back and I'll join you in five minutes.'

'Ah,' said Jill. 'Is this an experiment?'

'It is.'

'I hate to miss out on one of those,' she said, 'but owning a dog has its responsibilities.'

Wimsey was already racing ahead.

Jack made small talk until Jill had disappeared from view, during which time he heard that the constable had a great admiration for American people, particularly Carole Landis and Veronica Lake. This established,

Jack took the safety catch off his revolver and fired it into the air.

He listened to the boom fade, nodded with satisfaction and walked back towards the village.

As Jill emerged from the woods, she saw Simon Pinn cycling across the green, his face creased in a frown.

'Nothing to worry about,' said Jill. 'Ballistics.'

'Oh, yes?' Simon said, entirely baffled. He had not even registered the faint sound of Jack's gun. Wimsey's attention was also elsewhere. He paused for a moment, then belted across the grass to the front door of the cottage. Jill wondered why he was so excited. It was Mrs Brunton's day off. There would be nobody at home to make a fuss of him. As they opened the gate, however, she saw Maggie Speed sitting on the bench in the front garden.

'She's dead, isn't she?' said Maggie. She was as pale as distemper.

'Yes,' said Jill. 'I'm so sorry, Maggie.'

Maggie's hand went to her temple, as if she had been struck by a sudden headache.

'I didn't do it,' she exclaimed. 'I'm not a murderer.'

Chapter 27

Wimsey had always liked Maggie Speed, and he was not promiscuous in his affections. Jill could divide Larkwhistle into villagers who enjoyed his favour and those who did not. His approval, unfortunately, was no guarantee of virtue. For him, the butcher was as good as John the Baptist.

'The police will want to take a statement from you,' said Jack, who was tipping tea from the caddy.

'But Len Creech has gone back to Southampton,' added Jill, 'and the chaps he's left here are the sort who get their helmets stolen by kids. So, I'm sure there's time for us to chat first.'

She shook the biscuit tin and popped the lid open. 'Here, have a digestive, take a deep breath and tell us who you didn't kill.'

'Mary Rose Deever, of course,' said Maggie Speed. They were sitting at the kitchen table; the kettle was on. Its sound was soothing. Even more so when Jack lifted it from the hob to fill the teapot.

'I know,' said Jill. 'He didn't scald the pot first. But we'll teach him.' She gave Maggie an encouraging smile. 'How do you know that she's dead, Maggie?'

'Saw her, didn't I? I know that coat. Saw you all. Taking her off on a stretcher. I was on my way to the house. Bringing the paper.'

Jack set the teapot down on the table. 'What makes you think she was murdered?' he asked.

'Because I wanted to kill her. I've wanted to do it for a while. But last night, that was the strongest I'd ever felt it. And I thought you saw it in me.'

'Were you outside the door all that time?' asked Jack.

'Pretty much.'

'How much of it did you hear?'

'From the part about the idiot savant,' said Maggie.

'It was a cruel and stupid thing to say,' said Jill. 'You mustn't pay any heed. She was angry with Patrick and wanted to take it out on someone.'

'She certainly did that,' said Maggie. 'It wasn't much of a surprise, to be honest. Mrs Deever always talked down to me, even when she trying to be nice. *Especially* when she was trying to be nice. She couldn't help that. I think people had done it a lot to her, too, you see. Especially at the beginning. Before she wrote that book.'

Maggie took a biscuit from the tin. 'She's not as posh as she seems, you know, Mary Rose,' she said. 'She grew up in a tobacconist, somewhere in Birmingham, where the men chewed the stuff and spat it on the floor. She used to shudder when she talked about that. That's why she loved her fur and feathers and baubles. Made her forget what she came from. That's what the voice was all about.' The biscuit was dry in Maggie's mouth. She needed tea. Jill began to pour. It wasn't properly brewed, but neither of them cared.

'What voice?' asked Jack.

'Her wireless voice. Like someone on the Home Service. Like she was going to tell you how to make your meat go further.' Maggie blew on her tea. 'She always wanted to be on the wireless.'

'Were there many radio sets in the house?' asked Jack.

Maggie was puzzled by the question. 'Just the one in the living room.'

'You never found another? Hidden, perhaps? While you were cleaning?'

She shook her head.

'And what about Patrick?' asked Jill. 'How do you get on with him?'

'I don't have much to do with him, to be honest. Try to keep out of his way. You know how husbands are.'

299

'Wandering hands?' asked Jill.

'Hand,' corrected Maggie. 'No use touching a girl with the celluloid kind.'

'Just one roving eye too, I suppose,' said Jill.

'Patrick's a snob,' said Maggie, 'but he behaves himself, generally. I'll say that for him. He's not one of those men who presses against you when you're on the mangle. He's an angry person, though.'

'Angry about what?' asked Jack.

'The war. He was angry that it happened at all. Angry that he was called up. Angry that Sam Hill saved him. So very angry about that. He hated being nice to him. Standing him drinks all the time. I once overheard him when he thought he was alone. Cursing Sam Hill. Wishing him dead. Using language I'd never heard before – and I live in a pub.'

'Maggie,' said Jill, gently, 'did you know what was going on between Mary Rose and Peter Brock?'

Maggie was silent. The question was vague. She was trying to work out how much Jill knew.

'He was modelling for her,' said Jack. 'We found a lot of pictures at the house.'

'That's not all he was doing,' said Maggie. She took a noisy sip of tea. 'We might as well use the word, you know. They were having an affair.'

'Are you sure about that?' asked Jack.

Maggie snorted. She took another biscuit from the tin.

'Why do you think I look so sad, Jill?'

'Because you found Peter's body in the woods?'

'Oh yes,' said Maggie, quietly. 'That was horrible. That beautiful boy. Cruel boy, but beautiful. Left as carrion for the crows. It keeps coming back to me, that moment. Walking through the woods. Hoping to see him, I suppose. And then, you know, actually seeing him, broken and bloody, with Patrick hovering over him like a vampire.' She dismissed the image with a shudder. 'But I was sad before then, Jill. As I think you know.'

Jill frowned uncertainly. 'I know you liked him. You stepped out with him.'

'I loved him, Jill. Do you remember the dance at the Memorial Hall in Brockenhurst? You were with that pilot from Beaulieu. The handsome one with the freckles. And I was with Peter. That was the first time I ever danced with him. The only time I kissed him. Properly. I knew he didn't want me. I could tell. I knew his eyes were open when mine were closed.'

'He treated you badly?' asked Jack.

'No,' said Maggie. 'Not quite. And he was very free with his money that night. Bought us a fish supper and a bottle of dandelion and burdock. And I thought: *where's this money come from?* Of course, he was getting it from her. From the same place I got mine.'

'From Mary Rose?' asked Jack.

Maggie nodded.

'For the modelling?' asked Jill.

'Maybe for that,' said Maggie. 'Or maybe to keep him quiet. To stop him telling Patrick about what they were doing. On the divan. With the pencils and the charcoals scattered on the floor.'

She sighed deeply. The cracks in her cynicism were showing.

'You were there in the house?' said Jill. 'While they . . .'

'Work there, don't I?'

'How could you stand to stay, Maggie?' asked Jack. 'Why didn't you quit?'

'Don't know much about love, do you, Captain Strafford?' said Maggie. 'I only took that job because of him. His picture on the walls. The signs of him everywhere. It was like the house loved him like I did. And him coming to see Mary Rose – well, to you that might seem something unbearable or disgusting, but to me it was just another way of keeping him close.'

Her eyes wandered to the middle distance. 'He used to visit her between my shifts,' she said, turning her cup on the saucer. 'When Captain Deever was in the pub with Sam Hill. I got into the habit of pretending to leave, you see, and then going to sit in the next room. I could hear everything they said. Sometimes they talked about me. Some of it was nice. Peter liked me. He defended me when she was rude.'

Jill knitted her brow. 'Oh, Maggie,' she sighed.

'It was better than being at home and just having to imagine it.'

'Weren't you afraid they'd discover you?' asked Jack.

'He knew I was there. He wasn't that sweet little boy from the book, you know.'

Jill let that idea settle. It was true. She had known Peter Brock since childhood, though he had been too young to be her playmate. Had he and Henry possessed more in common, he might have been a stronger presence in the Metcalfes' world. To her, Peter was the boy at the altar, following his father, his surplice dazzlingly white. He was the consummate tree-climber of whom, she knew, her brother had felt mildly jealous. Or he was the young man who fell out with his father and was reconciled. All these versions of him, she now saw, had only a flat two-dimensional quality. They were as much like watercolour plates as the pictures in Mary Rose's book. Maggie Speed had conjured another animal entirely. There was something Pan-like about this being. Mary Rose had captured him, too, in the drawings she hid in the portfolio. The boy on the divan, leering, she now thought, through that mop of fair hair. Kissing Maggie Speed as his eye scanned the Memorial Hall for someone less demanding and less virginal. Jill thought of Maggie herself, leaning against the wall of Woodlander House, with its pretty floral paper, trying to stay silent, listening to the sound of this corporeal, dangerous Peter Brock, performing the offices of a lover while his lover's husband stood at the bar, buying drinks for a man whom he despised. And she thought of Maggie at Peter Brock's funeral, looking as if the tomb were also closing upon her.

Jill reached out for Maggie's hand, and, slightly to her surprise, she gave it to her.

'Do your parents know about this?' asked Jill.

'They don't know much about anything,' said Maggie. She looked in Jack's direction. 'Does your dad know about him?' Jill did not follow her gaze.

Jack, pretending not to hear, looked out of the window.

'The police are here,' he said. The short constable with the tall bicycle was juddering over the green in the direction of the Fleur-de-Lys. 'He'll be coming to talk to you.'

'I suppose I should go,' she said.

'Before you do,' said Jack, 'I'd like you to do something for us.' He laid out a series of pages on the table. 'Read these and tell us what you think.' Unlike Patrick, Maggie's eyes fell hungrily on the paper. 'The first,' said Jack, 'is a letter and, incontrovertibly, the work of Mary Rose. Definitely her handwriting, her signature. The second I found in the portfolio where she kept her drawings of Peter Brock.'

The constable's bike, Jill saw, was now leaning on

the timbered wall of the Fleur-de-Lys. He would soon be moving in their direction. He can wait for a moment, she thought.

'Tender, isn't it?' said Maggie, as she devoured the letter. 'More tender than Patrick ever was to her. When he said "dear" or "darling" he always did it to wound her. Or compete with her. There was always some sharp edge. But there's love in this. Even as she says that her love is gone.' Maggie shook her head. She seemed moved.

Through the window, Jack could see the police constable leaving the Fleur-de-Lys and heading towards the cottage.

'The note,' he said. 'The suicide note, as we should probably call it – is addressed to Patrick. It's an explanation, left on the dining room table, to tell him why his wife didn't come to bed and is never coming to bed again.' He indicated the typed pages in Maggie's hand. 'But this is very different. Patrick's not the intended recipient.'

Maggie sniffed. 'I'll say he isn't. He didn't pay a blind bit of attention to her work.' Her eyes moved over the page. 'Never even asked her what she was doing in her study.'

'You're right,' said Jill. 'When we showed that to Patrick, the most he could say was that it was done on the typing paper that he bought for her.'

'And what do you say about it, Maggie?' asked Jack.

Maggie's eyes stayed on the paper. 'I say she was sadder than anyone knew. Mrs Deever showed me all her stories. She wrote hundreds of them. She'd read them to me from beginning to end, watching me all the time to see how I reacted. I couldn't get it right. If I laughed, she was disappointed. If I said it was good, she was disappointed. If I said I didn't like one – and sometimes I did – she agreed. Whatever I said or didn't say, she'd screw it up and throw it in the wastepaper basket.'

The policeman was at the gate.

'Did you always want to be a writer, Maggie?' asked Jack.

'No,' said Maggie. 'Mrs Deever got me doing it. To get me out of the pub. She thought I was better than that.'

'Do you agree with her?' asked Jack.

'I do when I sit in that back kitchen listening to Sam Hill and the butcher talking about the Maginot Line and whether Pam Sharp wears a suspender belt.'

The policeman knocked at the door. Some version of what Maggie had just said would now be committed to the record.

Chapter 28

Harold Metcalfe had never much liked Patrick Deever. The Captain had a mild contempt for policemen that was common among his class – a tendency to speak to them like tradesmen or railway porters. What made it more galling was that Patrick's claims upon this class were slight. They depended on the wealth conferred by Mary Rose's literary success, which had liberated him from the necessity of work. Most gentlemen of leisure enjoyed that status because an ancestor had done something admirable, like defeating the Armada or inventing a valve. Patrick Deever enjoyed it because his wife had written a very short book and he had lost an arm and an eye in a very short battle.

Now, though, the Captain was suffering a more personal defeat. All his Waterloos had come at once. His wife was lying dead on the tiles at the Southampton morgue, and had been propelled there, it seemed likely, by an act of marital disloyalty. Patrick Deever had been bereaved and cuckolded simultaneously.

The telephone rang. Harold moved to answer it. Patrick surveyed the contents of his dining room – its paintings, photographs, ornaments and books – and could see nothing that pleased him. He imagined an auctioneer taking everything but the divan, which he had already decided to dispatch with an axe and matches.

Harold returned from the hallway.

'Another reporter?' asked Patrick.

'Nobody you'd want to talk to.'

Patrick was looking at the walls. 'I'll sell all this stuff. I don't want to see these pictures anymore. Would you lend me a hand?'

Together, he and Harold moved around the room, turning images of Peter Brock to face the paintwork. The backing boards bore dates and details added by Mary Rose. Harold wondered if Patrick was hoping to find a document concealed behind one of them.

'Do you think people will still buy that book now Mary Rose is gone?' asked Patrick, contemplating the foreign editions of *The Boy Among the Trees*. 'You wouldn't want to give it to kiddies, would you? They'd be afraid it carried a curse.'

'Don't make any hasty decisions, eh?' said Harold. 'Not before the reading of the will.' It had clearly not occurred to Patrick that the objects that surrounded him might not be his to destroy.

'Good of you to stay here, Harold,' said Patrick. 'It's very neighbourly of you.'

Harold picked up the breakfast plates and took them into the kitchen. Patrick followed him like a dog traipsing behind its owner.

'Have you told Sam Hill about what happened?' asked Harold. He had noticed the plate of bird bones from the night before and was scraping them into the kitchen bin.

'Why should I tell him about it?'

Harold sensed that he had touched a nerve. He decided to touch it again.

'I think of him as your batman, I suppose,' he said. 'Since the war you've always come as a pair.'

'I'm no longer obliged to Sam Hill. Nor is he obliged to me.'

'I'm sorry to hear that,' said Harold, scrubbing at the egg pan. 'Man needs his pals at a time like this.'

Patrick Deever bristled. 'He's a damn liar. Made a fool of me. Took me for a ride. All this time I believed he'd saved my life.'

'He didn't?'

'He got me to the pier.'

Harold was well versed in the Dunkirk story. 'And that's not saving your life?'

'I don't recall what happened. I was pretty far gone.

Wounded in the arm, you know?' Harold knew. 'Jerry was an absolute bastard that day. But Sam told me that he'd got me out of the water. Got me onto the little boat. That I'd have drowned without him. And I now know that's a damned lie.'

'Why do you say that?' asked Harold. A stubborn patch of egg was demanding his attention.

'Got a phone call the other night, do you see? From a chap who'd been on that boat. Weekend sailor out of Lymington. Almost a neighbour. Worked out we had a few people in common at the club on the Marina. Alec Thomas. Smutty Thomas's uncle. You know them?'

Harold didn't, but he recognized that even at this desperate moment, Patrick required space to display his social superiority.

'Well,' continued Patrick, 'it was his boat that picked us up. He was one of the volunteers who got us men off the beaches. Chaps with little fishing smacks and herring luggers. Weekend yachtsmen. Alec said that he was the one who dived into the water. Got us both out. Me and Sam. Alec said Sam was floundering. Dragging me down. That if he hadn't seen us then Sam would have drowned us both, which is not how Sam tells it.'

Harold put the pan down on the draining board and began looking for a teacloth. Patrick did not know where they were kept. The task of finding the right drawer gave Harold the means to hide his disapproval.

'But here's the rub,' said Patrick. 'This chap Alec Thomas said he'd been trying to contact me for ages. He wanted to meet up. He was after advice about some sea story he'd written. He wanted to know how to get it published. Ironic, really.'

'Why?' asked Harold.

'Because that's the last thing I'd know how to do. I gave up all that sort of thing long ago.'

'But Mary Rose would know.'

'Of course she would. Which is why he was so keen for me to ask her. Why he'd written to me twice. Well, I know things get lost in the post. I know there's a war on and all that. But twice? And when he has his own printed stationery with the return address on the back?'

Harold leaned against the sink, the teacloth over on his shoulder. 'What's going on, do you think?' he asked, fairly certain of the response.

'Sam Hill's gone on,' said Patrick. 'Sergeant Sam Hill interfering with His Majesty's mail.'

'That's quite an accusation,' said Harold.

'Damn right it is. Do you still hang for it?'

'No, you don't. And you haven't for a hundred years.'

'Maybe I'll report him,' said Patrick.

'With what evidence, Patrick?' asked Harold.

'Maybe the censor stopped his letters. Maybe he didn't send them at all. Maybe your chap Alec Thomas likes to spin a yarn at the yacht club bar, and so what if Sam had help pulling you out of the Channel? He got you that far, didn't he? Still makes him a hero in my book.'

Patrick looked like a man who had just received an unexpected punch. Harold found himself apologizing for inflicting it. 'Sorry, Patrick,' he said. 'I shouldn't be making speeches to you. Not today.'

Patrick met him with a similar sentiment. 'No. You're right. It's a thought for another time. I should be thinking about Mary Rose.'

They stayed in the kitchen, perhaps because it seemed less touched by the presence of Peter Brock. Harold produced his pipe, filled the bowl, teased the flame towards the tobacco. Patrick watched the orange flecks tumble. Perhaps he too was being warmed and coaxed, because he found himself telling Harold about the early days of his courtship. How he first saw Mary Rose at a dance at Birmingham City Hall. How, when the Gaucho Tango Orchestra had struck up 'Peaches Down in Georgia', he was beaten to the mark by the son of a man who owned a thriving bicycle shop in King's Oak, but, undaunted, cut in with a grand gesture and declared: 'Excuse me if you would, that's the girl I'm going to marry.'

The telephone rang again. Harold jumped back

into the hallway to dismiss the caller. Patrick kept on talking. 'I knew she wasn't happy. I knew I bored her. And I suppose she bored me, because she spent all her time banging away at that typewriter, or scribbling away in her drawing book, trying to find another subject like *that* one. She threw them all away, I thought. But maybe there are more around this place. As beastly as the stuff in that portfolio.'

'Drawings, you mean?' asked Harold, returning to the room.

'There was a story, too. Captain Strafford found it. I suppose it must be a picture of what she felt. Depressed. Guilty about that boy's death. And it seems like this was some sort of plan. A pact. Incredible, isn't it?' He shook his head in disbelief. 'I was married to her all this time and I simply never knew.'

'Did you suspect anything?' asked Harold. 'You'd never seen a suspicious letter? Overheard a phone call that you didn't like?'

Patrick frowned. 'Mary Rose got so many letters. Stacks of them. They were all about that book. Never anything else. Fans were always getting in touch. She replied to them all, you know. Every single one. I think that's what mainly came out of her typewriter. That was my job, you see, taking them to the Post Office. Buying the paper, her inks, her pens, her typewriter ribbons. Reams of postage stamps. Gave me something to do. Otherwise, it was the wireless, or the pub, or taking aim at something in the fields. Harold, don't you ever tire of this place?'

'Larkwhistle? It has its faults and petty cruelties, but I can't imagine leaving it. It's *my* place, I suppose.'

'I'm so bloody sick of it,' said Patrick. He was angry and agitated. He looked like he wanted to hit somebody. 'It's killing me. I want to go away. A long way from here. I never want to see these trees again. When I stand under them, when I hear the leaves and branches move in the wind, it sounds like the tide coming in to drown me.'

The telephone rang again. Patrick's patience had run out. He stamped into the hallway and wrenched the cable from the wall.

'Bloody thing,' he breathed. 'Why won't these people leave me alone?'

Another sound now seized their attention. The pebbles squealing beneath the wheels of a black Wolseley police car. Doors yawning and slamming. A sharp rap on the front door.

Len Creech was on the step, flanked by two constables. Patrick recognized one of them. He had given him a ticket for driving with a faulty brake lamp and enjoyed it slightly too much.

Len had a piece of paper in his hand. 'This is a warrant to search this address.' He looked almost embarrassed. Patrick read it and said nothing.

'All right,' said Len. 'Start with the lady's study.'

He handed over the key and the constables walked upstairs. The floorboard creaked.

'Captain Patrick Deever,' said Len Creech. 'I am arresting you in the King's name on suspicion of murder—'

'Oh God,' moaned Patrick. His shoulders sank. His eyes rolled heavenwards. He looked as if he was already stumbling towards the scaffold. 'Oh God.'

'The murder of Peter Brock.'

Patrick flinched as though he too had received a bullet.

'You have the right to remain silent,' said Len, 'but it's my duty to warn you—'

'Peter Brock?' spluttered Patrick. He was reeling. 'That was suicide, surely? The boy took his own life.'

'The coroner has handed down his decision,' said Len. 'I'm quite confident that in the next few hours I will hear enough to bring a charge against you. The car's waiting outside, as you see.'

Boots crunched on the gravel. Patrick seemed dazed. He walked between a second pair of constables like a man being escorted from the scene of an explosion. Len stopped on the threshold and put a hand on Harold's arm.

'Thanks for keeping him here,' he said.

'I'm glad you rang when you did. Patrick tore the phone from the wall. Did Jack Strafford get through to you too? He had something to tell you.'

Len nodded. 'I got his message.'

'Patrick was lying about hearing the gunshot in the woods.'

'Not just the gunshot. I got on to the BBC. Geraldo was delayed on his way to the studio. He never broadcast that day.'

Harold sat on the divan, listening to the sounds from the rooms above. Len Creech's men opened drawers and cupboards, searching for evidence of guilt. The floorboards creaked as one of them crossed the landing and entered the bathroom. Harold heard the lavatory cistern clink. The constable, he surmised, was looking inside it for a hidden object. It was fortunate that Patrick was not present. His heart, thought Harold, would not have survived.

More wheels troubled the driveway. Harold looked out the window to see a thin-faced man in a sports jacket extracting himself from a taxi. He recognized the man's hungry look at once. The notebook in his hand confirmed his identity. This time, thought Harold, claiming to be Betty Grable would not be an option.

Chapter 29

Mrs Brunton was not one of those housekeepers who saw their employers as unfortunate obstacles to a world free of dust and clutter. Jill had heard tales about those from friends who claimed to live in fear of their own servants. All the same, she knew that she had made the right decision to wait until her housekeeper's morning off to turn the kitchen table into a display of evidence.

'They're all paper,' she said. 'When people think of courtroom exhibits, they're thinking of a cosh or a bloodied candlestick. What we have here is material for an anthology. People round here, all betraying themselves with pens and pencils and typewriters.'

The primary sources were laid out in a neat row. The charred diary pages retrieved from the incinerator in the vicarage garden, bearing letters and numbers and little doodles of leaves and flowers.

Maggie Speed's copy of *The Boy Among the Trees*, in which, thanks to Jack, each word of the text had its own allocated number. Jill's transcription of the story in the portfolio, removed from Jack's notebook with the blade of the kitchen scissors. Jill's diligent rendering of Mary Rose's final letter, in which the author confessed her affair and bade her husband goodbye – a document which had seemed to give notice to the end of a marriage, but now read as notice to the end of a life. A pencil sketch of Peter Brock – a three-quarter head-and-shoulders profile, picked out of the portfolio by Jill. The flight log page on which Henry Metcalfe had scribbled three words in the hope that it would lead his comrades to the exposure of a German spy in Larkwhistle. Those three words – 'Whitechapel', 'inscription', 'May' – remained meaningless.

'These are our twisted roots,' said Jack. He was on the phone, waiting to be put through to Woodlander House. His hand was cupped over the receiver; an old habit, but a useful one when Ivy Hill was putting through the call. 'A domestic crime and a crime against the state.'

'All these questions,' said Jill. 'All these people. The trees in the wood. Can we cut any of them out entirely?'

Jack put down the phone. 'Line's dead now. I hope that's not a bad sign.'

Jill circled the names of the Speeds. 'Wally Speed? Can we eliminate him?'

'Effie told me he was a late-night radio listener, but he's gone to bed before eleven every night I've been there.'

'What about Effie? Or Maggie? Maggie can't be a spy, can she?'

'She might be a murderer. She came to tell us about her powerful motives.'

'That would be quite the bluff.'

'But you know,' said Jack. 'I don't think we can even rule out the dead. Mary Rose, for instance, may have been Commoner. She might also have killed Peter Brock. All we know about her whereabouts depends on her husband, and we know his story is weak. Peter could have been blackmailing her about their affair. She kills him, then goes to pieces – which we saw with our own eyes – and then goes off into the woods a few days later and ends her agony.'

'We can rule out Peter Brock. The broadcasts went on after his death.'

Jack shrugged. 'Commoner might be two people. What if Peter was our spy, and then someone else took over, perhaps to save his reputation, prevent his posthumous exposure? His lover might do that for him. Or his father. Or mother. Where is his mother, by the way?'

'Dad went to see them this morning. We thought Mary Rose might have run to Helena.'

Wimsey, in his basket, jumped suddenly to attention. Harold was at the gate. Jack scooped up the flight log page and the marked-up copy of *The Boy Among the Trees*. He had no authority to initiate Harold into the mysteries of Commoner.

Jill opened the door for her father. Wimsey rushed to meet him. Harold's face was clouded. 'Len Creech just arrested Patrick for Peter Brock's murder. He didn't take it very well. He was affronted. Like he was expecting something else.'

'Like what?' asked Jill.

'To be arrested for Mary Rose's murder,' said Harold.

'What swung Len?' asked Jack. 'The lie about the gunshot?'

'And the wireless. All that tosh about Geraldo losing his pep. Southampton put in a call to Broadcasting House. Turns out they put out a different programme, so bang goes Patrick's alibi. And then *they* turned up just a few minutes after they took him away.'

'Who did, Dad?' asked Jill.

'Reporters,' said Harold. 'I recognized the older one. Once tried to pay me for a tip-off about the Sabini brothers, when they were fixing the book at Banister Court dog track. Flashed me his cash as he was getting out his business card. Wouldn't trust him as far as I could spit him.'

'Did you tell them anything?' asked Jack.

'I told them that if they waited an hour, Patrick would come down and give them a statement. I thought it might keep them out of the village for a bit. But I suppose they'll find out soon enough that he's on his way to Southampton.'

Jack looked at the clock.

'So, we've got about half an hour before the pack descends. After that it'll become much harder to ask the people of Larkwhistle a few impertinent questions.'

'Dad, you went to the vicarage this morning, didn't you?' asked Jill. 'Did you see Helena?'

'I only saw Guy,' said Harold. 'Haven't clapped eyes on Helena since the funeral.'

'Well,' said Jack. 'Patrick's arrest might be the catalyst we need. It may loosen tongues. Let's get out there, shall we? Deliver the bad news.'

Jill found Sam Hill behind the counter of the Post Office. This was an unusual sight, except on pension days and during the last week before Christmas. Ivy was in the parlour, trying to amuse Martin with a knitted rabbit that had a squeaker sewn into its belly. She had not taken the morning off: the portable microphone horn remained slung on her chest.

'I see they closed the path through the woods,' said Sam. His face, Jill noticed, was unshaven. Neither he nor Ivy appeared well slept. 'How is he?' he asked. 'The Captain? Captain Deever, I mean.'

'Did you not see the ambulance outside the house, Sam?' asked Jill.

Sam admitted that he had. 'I knocked on the door,' he said. 'But nobody answered.'

Odd, Jill thought, that he had not been sufficiently curious to wait and find out who needed help – or, for that matter, to discover if any of his own was wanted. 'Perhaps you should go and see him yourself,' she said. 'He might appreciate a visit from an old comrade.'

'The police are at the house, aren't they?' said Sam, doubtfully. 'I don't want to get in the way.' He noticed a wedge of letters in her hand. 'First class, is it?' he asked. He opened up the stamp book and began tearing along the perforations.

'They're saying it was a pact,' he continued, placing the stamps on the counter. 'Some kind of suicide pact that went wrong.' He did not sound like a man enquiring after the welfare of a bereaved friend.

'Really?' said Jill.

'Would make sense, wouldn't it?' said Sam. 'The boy and her, meaning to go together, then her bottling it? Makes you wonder how she carried on at that inquest, cool as a cucumber. Giving that picture to the vicars' wife, when all the time—'

'I don't know where you got this idea about a suicide pact, Sam,' said Jill.

'Maggie Speed was in here just now,' said Sam. 'Told us the news. Gave Ivy a terrible shock. Mind you, we already knew someone was dead. We thought it might have been Patrick, not her.'

'Well, I think the important thing is not to theorize with scant evidence. Particularly if it comes from other people's phone conversations.'

'That what they teach you at college?' asked Sam.

'That's the scientific method.'

'I've got my own,' said Ivy, emerging from the parlour, tapping the Bakelite apparatus hanging at her chest. Martin was lying on the rug in front of the fireplace, captivated, apparently, by something on the ceiling. 'Wires have been hot this morning,' Ivy continued. 'Poor Mary Rose. It's so awful. Bad news travels fast.'

'What have you heard?' asked Jill. She was trying not to sound too eager, but not so indifferent as to discourage Ivy's flow of information.

'I put the call through to Southampton,' said Ivy, 'and I couldn't help overhearing that Inspector Creech talk about the mortuary. And a body in the woods. At first, I thought of Patrick. He's been so strange these last few days, like he's sickening with something. And then I heard him talked about, so I knew it couldn't be him, and I thought, it's Mary Rose. Mary Rose Deever, dead under a tree.'

A stranger would have read only horror in Ivy's face,

accompanied by that note of excitement that claims most of us if some outrage occurs in the neighbourhood. Jill, however, thought she detected something more peculiar. Ivy was like someone receiving news of a sporting fixture that had unexpectedly gone her way.

'So shocking to have two suicides in the village, isn't it?' she said.

Jill decided to play dumb. 'Suicide?' she said. 'Really? I didn't know that was official.' Ivy's eavesdropping had not prevented her getting the wrong end of the stick.

'Imagine,' said Ivy. 'Killing yourself over a man. A boy. Bloody fool.'

'You wouldn't do it for me, then?' asked Sam.

'I bloody would not. I'm not bloody Tosca.'

Jill was surprised by the allusion, then admonished herself for her snobbishness. Sam and Ivy had always seemed to her the most unmysterious couple. Ivy had been one of those village girls who wanted to get married as soon as possible. She liked mascara and tight sweaters and might, perhaps, have gone to the bad if she had lived within easy bicycling distance of the port. Instead, she had married Sam, son of the ailing village postmistress, and a man clearly in need of a wife. Sam had buried his mother and married Ivy in the summer of '39. They had not planned it that way, but then they hadn't planned on Germany invading Poland.

A wail came from the parlour. The ceiling had lost its charm and Martin was raising some objection to its existence. Jill expected Ivy to come to his aid, but instead Sam swooped from behind the counter and gathered up the boy from the rug.

'No need for that, is there?' he cooed, engulfing the baby in a tight, pacifying hug. 'Why don't me and you go out on the green for a bit? Get a bit of air?'

Martin accepted the proposal immediately. Jill watched Sam open the Post Office door with a knee and carry the child out into the daylight, talking to him about what birds they might see in the trees.

'That's nice to see,' said Jill.

'He has his moments,' said Ivy. 'I think he's gone off that pub.'

'Perhaps all this death makes us all value life that little bit more.'

'If you say so,' Ivy continued, with the air of someone who considered metaphysical speculation a waste of time.

Sam and Martin settled on the grass. Jill saw Sam raise the baby into the air and blow a raspberry on his bare tummy. Martin giggled.

Jill then noticed another figure. It was the constable who had collected Maggie Speed from the cottage, pushing his bicycle out of the churchyard of St Cedd's. As he arrived at the road he jumped up on the saddle and began pedalling in the direction of Woodlander

House. Sam noticed him too. Jill saw his head move to follow the policeman's progress, then turn back to observe the movement of two new arrivals – Simon Pinn and the Reverend Guy Brock, walking from the church towards the vicarage, grave expressions on their faces. Guy sent the curate onward, while he cut towards Sam Hill and stopped, apparently to admire the baby. It was the first time that Jill had seen Guy interact with Martin since the funeral, and she was mesmerized. She could only see the back of Sam's head, but he was not detectably unhappy. He held Martin up for inspection. But the vicar's face, Jill noticed, was strange and self-conscious, as if he were communicating something he did not wish others to overhear. It seemed quite possible, to Jill, for Ivy to have had an affair with the vicar and passed off his baby as her husband's. It also seemed possible for both men to be ignorant of the fact, or even to have agreed, quite amicably, to say no more about it. Something, however, had shifted. Since death had come to Larkwhistle, Sam Hill appeared to love Martin slightly more than before.

Jill tore her eyes away, sure that her thoughts were an open book to Ivy. Ivy's face, however, betrayed no hint of suspicion. She was as detached as the kid in the Popeye cartoons who wanders from girder to moving girder without noticing that he is hundreds of feet above the ground.

'Did you know about the affair?' asked Ivy.

'I beg your pardon?'

'Did you know? About what was going on between Mary Rose and Peter Brock?'

Jill attempted to recover her equilibrium. 'No,' she said. 'I had no idea.'

'We knew,' said Ivy. 'I don't think it was one of those affairs that was common knowledge. Not like Fanny Henderson and the chimney sweep. Smuts is hard to hide. Especially on a wash day.'

'When did you suspect it?' asked Jill.

'It went on for years,' said Ivy.

'And did you tell Patrick?'

Ivy gave a dry laugh. 'It would have killed him,' she said. 'Sometimes it's best just to stay quiet.'

'Did the Brocks know, do you think?' asked Jill.

'Peter kept a lot of things from his mum and dad.'

'You make me feel very obtuse, Ivy,' said Jill. 'All this going on under my nose.'

'Got your mind on higher things, I dare say,' she said. 'It started in the summer of '40. Dunkirk, when it looked like everything was lost. But it went on after, too. Peter was angry, you see.'

'Angry with his father?'

'Of course with his father. Stopped him fighting, didn't he? Guy told the Medical Board about Peter's weak heart. Wrote them a letter. Had him taken off the list. Guy never admitted it, but Peter knew what

327

had happened. His dad had killed his chance of being a war hero. That made him feel less of a man, so I suppose he had to do it in other ways.'

'With Mary Rose Deever?' said Jill.

The shop bell clattered. 'Ladies,' said a thin-faced man in a sports jacket. 'I wondered if I might have a word?' His voice carried a tubercular crackle. He was already leaning on the counter like one of Ivy's regular confidantes.

'Do you read the *Echo*?' he demanded. 'I do hope so. Why is it so short these days, people ask me? Well, I say, it's those paper regulations. You can't believe how we have to squeeze things down to fit everything in.'

'Do you want stamps?' asked Ivy.

'The post's too slow for me,' said the man. 'I just wanted to negotiate something with you, if that's all right?'

He lowered his voice. 'Now, obviously I won't be the only representative of His Majesty's Press in Larkwhistle today. We'll be here for the inquest on Mrs Deever, naturally. And after that happens, we will of course all be eager to phone our copy through. So, I thought I would call here to just secure my place in the queue.'

He opened his wallet, pulled out a ten-shilling note and placed it on the counter. 'Just a small consideration,' he said.

Ivy took the note, opened the cash drawer and slipped it inside.

'Fine,' she said. 'Who are you, then?'

'I'm the *Echo*,' said the man, rather too grandly. 'Did you know the deceased? The *deceaseds*? Don't worry, I'm aware that's not a proper word.'

'Yes,' said Ivy. 'But I don't want to be interviewed, thanks very much.'

'That's dandy,' said the journalist. 'I just want a bit of background on the situation.' He flipped open his notebook. Ivy had taken the money: she felt a twinge of obligation.

'She's married to an Army Captain, is that right?' said the *Echo*.

'Yes,' said Ivy, blankly.

'And were there any children?'

Ivy baulked at the question. 'If it's all the same to you, we'll leave it there, eh?'

The reporter looked in the direction of the cash drawer with an exaggerated expression of surprise. 'Ten shillings not enough, eh?' he said.

Ivy pulled open the drawer again, ringing its little bell, withdrew the note and handed it back to its previous owner.

'You can use the nearest phone box,' she said.

'That's in Brockenhurst,' said the man from the paper.

'I know.'

The shop bell jangled again. Sam was standing in the doorway with his son in his arms. His face was ashen. For once, Martin was the most carefree person present. The little boy beamed at the man from the *Echo*. Sam did not. His understanding of the scene was far from complete, but he knew that the stranger was on his way out.

Jill was already moving towards the door. Sam did not look at her as she passed.

As Jill emerged from the Post Office and turned towards her own cottage, she realized that the man from the *Echo* was keeping pace with her and moving in the same direction.

'I've just given that lady a bit of time to think it over,' said the *Echo*. 'But what do you think? What did they make of Mrs Deever in the village?'

'She was very well liked,' said Jill, increasing her speed.

'Really?' said the reporter. 'So, when did people first begin to disapprove of her relationship with that young man Peter Brock?'

The question was phrased, Jill noted, to preclude the possibility of a yes or no answer. 'You don't get me like that,' she said, and increased her pace further.

It was then she noticed Jack approaching from the Fleur-de-Lys. He arrived so quickly that Jill felt that she was watching a film projected at twice its normal speed. The man from the *Echo* was silenced mid-sentence. Then he was lying on the grass like an overturned beetle.

'Sorry about that,' said Jack. 'I wasn't looking where I was going.' It was unclear whether he was apologizing to Jill or to the man he had just knocked to the ground.

The man from the *Echo* was moving his tongue around the inside of his mouth. He spat a tooth into the palm of his hand. 'You bloody lunatic,' he gasped.

'Oh dear,' said Jack, genuinely surprised. 'Was it a hollow one?'

'Yes,' the man spluttered. 'But I hardly think that matters.' Others had now joined them. Wimsey and Harold had come to inspect the scene. Wimsey licked the man's face in sympathy. Harold commiserated with a smile slightly less comforting than a lit match in the ear.

'I must have made a mistake about Captain Deever giving a statement,' he said. 'So sorry.'

The man from the *Echo* got to his feet. 'He's been taken off to Southampton, the copper said. Being questioned about that boy.'

'Oh, bad luck,' said Harold. 'I suppose you'll be going back there, then?'

'Not quite yet,' he said. 'I've got my room in the pub. Plenty going on here, I think.' It was hard to disagree.

The journalist walked back in the direction of the Fleur-de-Lys.

'Maggie Speed seems to have got round the whole village,' said Jill. 'The Hills knew about Mary Rose. But not about the coroner's verdict. I think Guy Brock knows that Patrick has been arrested. I think he just told Sam. They were talking out on the green. And when he came back in, Sam looked like he'd just seen a ghost.'

'Let's pay a visit to the vicarage,' said Jack. 'Guy told you to go any time you wanted.'

Chapter 30

Simon Pinn was surprised to see Jack and Jill at the vicarage door. He had seen them walking, arm in arm, and thought at first that they might have been coming to arrange a wedding. He asked how they were, then immediately withdrew the question on the grounds of melancholy absurdity. 'We seem to be on the front line here, don't we?' he said. 'Among the fallen. First poor Henry and then Peter. And now Mary Rose. And with her, it's not just the shock and the awfulness, is it? It's a dreadful diplomatic difficulty for the parish.' This thought appeared to be uppermost in the curate's mind. Would it be right for Guy to take the service, given the revelations about Peter and Mary Rose? 'And how can we make arrangements for Mrs Deever's committal,' he asked, 'when Captain Deever is sitting in Southampton police station?'

Jill might have joined Simon in these reflections,

but there was something in his manner that struck her as insincere. He had not asked them inside. She had the strong impression that he wanted them to go away.

'Do you mind if we come in?' asked Jack, with icebreaker bluntness. Simon said that he didn't. He was almost convincing. He called to Guy. An ambiguous sound of acknowledgement came from the dining room. Jack and Jill found the vicar sitting at the table upon which, a few days previously, he had laid the dead body of his son. The surface was now scattered with Peter's possessions. The wing of a crow. A vole skeleton, carefully preserved. His books about lichens and liverworts. Guy was fiddling with Peter's crystal wireless set. He was clearly listening to something.

'Peter loved this thing,' he said, pulling the little receiver from his ear. 'I can't make head nor tail of it myself. The radiogram's my limit. I dare say you know all about radio, Captain Strafford.'

'A little,' said Jack. 'Do you need it fixed?'

'Perhaps you should ask a child,' said Jill. 'They know about these things.'

Simon fussed for a moment in the doorway, then took his leave. 'I'll be back later,' he said. 'To talk about the Patrick problem.'

'I'll pray for him,' said Guy Brock. 'We all should.'

With a sad frown, Simon left.

'You've heard, then?' asked Jill. 'About Peter and Mary Rose?'

'Len Creech rang me,' said Guy. 'I expect he didn't have time to come round in person, though, to be frank with you, I would have appreciated it. In my line of work, it always seems important to deliver difficult news face to face.'

'How has Mrs Brock taken the news?' asked Jack.

Guy stood up and pushed the door closed. 'It's a delicate matter, Captain. Can I rely on your discretion?'

'Of course,' said Jack. 'Perhaps we can do something to help?'

'After the funeral,' Guy said, lowering his voice, 'she retreated to her room. Wouldn't talk to me. Wouldn't talk to anyone. Wouldn't eat. She just lay there, staring at the wall. Not even crying.' He began to pack away Peter's things in a cardboard box, using the same respectful gentleness with which he handled the chalice on Sunday. 'I think Simon's right about the village,' he said. 'We do feel like the front line.'

'Everywhere is the front line now,' said Jill. 'It's not like the last war. I never saw a Zeppelin as a kid. In those days, war was something adults talked about.'

Guy closed the lid of the box. 'You were at the Deevers' last night, I think?'

'We were,' said Jack.

'Do you think he did it?' asked Guy. 'Do you think

Patrick Deever killed my Peter?' He looked like the most burdened man in the world.

'Oh, Guy,' said Jill. 'Until a few days ago I thought I knew almost everyone in this village. Now they seem like strangers to me. I thought Larkwhistle was a cheerful little place. A bit boring, even. But there's so much sadness here, and anger. All I can say is that when we went to dinner, there was something ferocious going on between Mary Rose and Patrick, and that it had probably been going on for years.'

Guy nodded. 'I think there are New Testament people and Old Testament people. Not everybody's heart is full of mercy and forgiveness. If Mary Rose and Peter were lovers . . .' He paused. 'What a thing to say, but there it is. If they were lovers and Patrick discovered that – well, jealousy and vengeance are powerful motives. Particularly, I think, for a man like Patrick.'

'Why do you say that?' asked Jack.

'We're all sinners,' said Guy. 'But Patrick seems to have more than his fair share of pride and envy. They're a tricky combination.'

'But if Patrick is responsible,' said Jack, 'why would he use Sam Hill's service revolver when he had one of his own?'

'To throw suspicion upon him,' said Guy. 'Make him look bad. The soldier who didn't look after his gun properly. Who allowed a boy to steal it and take it off into the woods. It would suit Patrick, I think, to see Sam in trouble.'

'Could we talk to Helena?' asked Jack.

Guy shook his head. 'I don't think it's a good idea.'

'Why don't you let me try?' said Jill. 'When we brought Peter's body here, I told Helena about Henry's death. And just for a moment, she felt like a sister. We could each do the other some good.'

Guy Brock twisted his mouth into a sceptical expression. 'I don't think so,' he said. He was looking down at the floor.

'Guy,' said Jack. 'Helena *is* here, isn't she?'

He said nothing. His silence expanded to fill the little dining room and the whole house. To Jill, it expressed the idea with which she had begun their conversation; that Larkwhistle and its people had become strange to her – that men and women to whom she had spoken on the street and in church for decades had become silhouettes whose outlines might now encompass anything. An image began to form in her mind. Helena Brock, upstairs, with pills scattered on her eiderdown. Helena Brock in the bath, in cold crimson water. Guy knowing that these scenes were laid out somewhere above his head, but too afraid to go upstairs to discover why the house was so silent.

Jill jumped to her feet, bolted from the dining room and ran up the stairs. Jack realized that his role in this moment was to prevent Guy from impeding her progress. But the Reverend Brock seemed to have no intention of stopping her.

When Jill reached the landing, she pulled open the nearest door. It was Peter's bedroom. The largest wall was dominated by a chart depicting British trees; something acquired by saving the tokens on packets of tea. A small table was home to a pair of field glasses, a bell jar containing a stuffed owl and a sheaf of Peter's own pencil drawings. She recognized the leaves and flowers immediately. Their arrangement on the paper was much fuller and more elaborate than the examples in the diary. It was a beautiful and delicate thing.

Jack and Guy were also on the landing. Guy walked to the far end and opened the door furthest from the stairs.

'This is her room,' said Guy. 'This is Helena's. Look inside if you want. There's really no need to push your way around. I'm not the enemy.'

Jill was ashamed by the extremity of her behaviour, and angry that Guy had given her cause to pursue it. However, having been made the offer of an inspection, it felt impossible to refuse. She withdrew from Peter's room and crossed the threshold of Helena's. Jack stayed with Guy. Jill saw that the bedclothes were smooth and neat. No jewellery hung on the dressing table mirror.

'She's gone, of course,' said Guy. 'Are you married, Captain?'

'No,' said Jack. 'I'm not.'

'Is she coming back?' Jill asked.

'I don't think so.'

'Did she tell you where she was going?'

'No,' said Guy. 'But I think she's with a friend in Southampton. She puts the phone down on me when I ring, anyway. One of her old comrades in the Party.'

'So, she doesn't know about Patrick's arrest?' asked Jack.

'No,' said Guy. He closed the bedroom door. 'I want her to hear that from me. Perhaps it will bring us together again. Sitting in the courtroom. Thinking of our Peter, and what he meant to us. Seeing that man confess to his crimes before God and face his judgement.'

Jill was not listening. She was thinking of the drawings of flowers and leaves she had just seen in Peter's bedroom; how balanced they were in comparison with the irregular formations in the margins of the dead boy's diary. It was not just the topography that preoccupied her, but the species depicted.

As they walked down the vicarage path, she told Jack what she had seen.

The flowers were roses. The leaves were ivy.

Chapter 31

The press had kept away from the inquest on Peter Brock. Had they known about his connection with a certain fictional boy, the circus might have arrived sooner. The deferral, however, brought them several rewards. The chance to enliven a page of newsprint with cameo-framed photos of Peter Brock, young and clean, facing the customary publicity shot of Mary Rose Deever, taken a decade ago. Space to speculate about the relationship between the two main characters. A few days in a quiet English village, the sort in which their readers delighted in seeing blood spilled.

The man from the *Echo* was first, but his colleagues arrived before the sun had dried out the grass, a little retinue of corpse-chasers with winning smiles, unable to believe their luck at being handed a story that had everything. Two deaths under the same tree. The vicar's son and the lady authoress who had turned him into a nursery favourite. It was as if Beatrix Potter had committed hara-kiri after the death of Squirrel Nutkin, unable to face life without him. And with the kind of horrible–delicious coincidence that looked so appealing in a headline and standfirst, the second death occurred on the very morning that the coroner handed down his verdict on the first, and the police made their first arrest.

'They were asking about Mrs Deever,' said Mrs Brunton, unpacking her shopping bag on the kitchen table of the Metcalfe cottage. Wimsey had an ear cocked for the crinkle of greaseproof paper, which, for him, exerted the same power as Pavlov's bell. 'Was she well liked in the village? Had we ever seen her walking out with Peter Brock? Do we think she was giving him money? Disgraceful questions.'

'You've met some of our visitors, then?' asked Jill. She had placed her transcription of *The Pact Beneath the Trees* side by side with Mary Rose Deever's original story, and was hoping for deductive inspiration.

'They had lunch together in the Copper Kettle. One of them said it was quaint and made Pam Sharp an offer for some print on the wall that I know came out of a magazine. He was from the *Daily Express*, I think. The chap from the *Echo* was treating him like royalty.'

The last of the shopping was laid out on the table: Wimsey sank back into his basket, resigned.

'I've had my differences with Pam,' said Mrs Brunton. 'You can't tell her anything unless you want everyone in the village to know it, but with all the facts turned inside out. But she dealt with this lot a treat. Told them Mrs Deever used to be a Gaiety Girl, and that the Captain was her third husband and she'd killed the second with a box of poisoned Turkish delight, but nothing could be proved. It took them ages to realize she was pulling their legs. Maybe it takes an outsider to show what a good liar Pam Sharp is.'

'I think Dad took a similar approach with them,' said Jill.

'Yes,' said Mrs Brunton, with apparent sincerity. 'It's really brought the village together at a difficult time.'

When the evening edition of the *Echo* appeared at the newsagent, another form of Larkwhistle solidarity stirred. The paper sold out almost immediately. And there were some people that night who, having digested an idealized description of their village and an excitable one of a tree fated to gather death beneath its branches, took the kitchen scissors and pasted those paragraphs carefully into their scrapbooks, beside ticket stubs and wedding invitations and coloured plates of the young princesses. Mrs Brunton may have been one of those people. When she left the Metcalfes' cottage after dinner – carrot flan, potato salad with scraps of bacon – Jill noticed a crisp copy of the paper stowed carefully in her bag.

After her departure, the murder talk began. Jack noticed the subtle exigencies of class at work again: killing was not a subject to be discussed in front of the servants. Nor was the infidelity of their neighbours. In the consideration of this matter, the charred pages of Peter's diary were shown to Harold, and, as if doing the crossword together, father and daughter plotted flowers and leaves against days of the week and determined that on one Tuesday in May 1943 – long after Dunkirk – Peter Brock met with Ivy Hill in the morning and Mary Rose Deever in the afternoon.

'Lot here to interest the scholar of rural adultery, Dad,' said Jill.

'More than that, isn't it?' said Harold, sadly. 'It's the primrose path. And it ended in death for two of them.'

'And brought Martin Hill into the world,' said Jack. 'Do you think Helena Brock knows she's a grandmother?'

'No,' said Harold. 'She'd be more tolerant of Martin's moods. But Guy always seems pleased to see him. He never complains when he cries in church.'

'I think Guy just loves kids,' said Jill.

The evening was draining away. Harold went into

the kitchen to do the washing up and would not hear of receiving any help. Jill stared at her map marking the path between the green and Woodlander House. How, she wondered, did Patrick know that Peter was going to be under that tree? And where was Mary Rose? Might she have been there too? She picked up her pencil and doodled an ivy leaf on the margin of the page. Jack was poring over the transcript of *The Pact Beneath the Trees.*

'There's something odd about this,' he said. 'The pact is in the title, but it's not in the actual story.'

Jill shook her head and found the relevant passage. 'I was invited there days ago,' she read, 'and I should have kept the appointment.'

'Is that the same thing?' asked Jack. 'I'm not so sure.'

'I find it so easy to imagine her writing this,' said Jill. 'Saying goodbye to us, then going off into her study while Patrick slept and putting down everything she couldn't say aloud. All these confessions about herself. All her dirty secrets. And she shut them in that portfolio with those drawings.'

Jack switched on the radio. Dance band music flowed from the set and put a curtain of sound between the parlour and the kitchen. 'I wonder,' he said, 'if there'll be anything interesting on the wireless tonight?'

'If there is,' said Jill, 'we can rule Patrick out of

enquiries. We can't listen to it with Dad in the room, though, can we?'

Jill moved into the kitchen. She had never asked her father for privacy before. It was an unusual moment for them both. Harold assumed some romantic motivation, and he was not entirely wrong. Jack pretended not to spot the extravagance of the old man's yawning as he emerged from the kitchen and professed himself too tired to stay up any longer.

'It's been a punishing day,' said Harold.

'And tomorrow won't give us an even break,' said Jack.

Lew Stone was on the wireless. Jack had once heard his band at the Officers' Sunday Club, where, as usual, they had kept on playing through an air raid. Every time an eight-stick incendiary had dropped nearby, they had broken into the Anvil Chorus from *Il trovatore* and let the Luftwaffe look after every other beat. 'Oh,' said Jill, realizing that she had been given a new piece of the jigsaw puzzle of Jack's past. 'You were here during the Blitz?' she said. 'Not all of you Yanks arrived late, then?'

They were sitting together on the sofa. Wimsey had joined them and was resting his head happily against Jack's leg. The room was lit by the dial of the radio. The music was doing its work. It was soft, smoky, insinuating, and made it hard not to fantasize the missing components into place – the light of ballroom chandeliers, the murmur of conversation, the sparkle of glass studs set into mirrored walls, the smell of expensive cigarettes.

'Five more minutes,' said Jack. 'Until they bring on the local act.'

For those five minutes, Jack and Jill listened to the band. Jill was quite certain that if they had been in London, in the rooms where the microphones were placed, she would have been in the arms of Captain Jack Strafford, with her head against the soft serge of his uniform, assessing the clarity of his skin and the recency of his last shave, breathing in the smell of American soap and hair cream and moving over the polished floor, entirely unworried that she would put a foot wrong.

The ether, though, was wailing. Jack's hand was on the dial, negotiating hostile frequencies. It found nothing but the empty howl of the magnetic earth.

'He's late,' said Jill.

'Or retired from broadcasting,' said Jack.

'Or staying with old Party friends.'

'Or in a police cell in Southampton.'

'Or dead,' said Jill. 'You never know.'

Jack saw Jill's eyes flicker sideways.

There was, she realized, someone standing outside the front door of the cottage. A human shape was visible in the glass panel.

Jack's jacket and gun belt were slung over a dining

chair. He skidded across the floor and fished the revolver from its holster.

'We can see you,' he said. He raised the gun. The only sound was the low, uneven whistle of an empty radio bandwidth. The shape in the door altered its position. The letterbox flapped open.

'Would you let me in then?' hissed Len Creech. 'Sorry to call so late. I couldn't tell whether you were still up.'

Jack lowered the gun and replaced it in the holster: he had no wish for their visitor to know that it had been aimed in his direction. When Jill opened the door, Detective Inspector Creech wore such a defeated look that she made him an immediate offer of brandy, which was accepted just as swiftly.

'First of all,' said Len, with policemanly care and attention, 'I just wanted to thank you for doing your bit yesterday. We proved that Patrick didn't hear that gunshot. So that means there's nothing to place him in the house at the moment of Peter Brock's death.'

'Did you find anything else?' asked Jill. 'Those letters?'

'Destroyed, I suspect,' said Len. 'He'd certainly been burning something that night. Ashes in the grate in hot weather.'

'Anything legible?' asked Jack.

'Nothing,' said Len. 'But I did get a trace on George Vatine. I knew I'd heard the name somewhere before.'

'Who is he?' asked Jill.

Len found the relevant page in his notebook. 'George Vatine, also known as Georges de la Vatine, Grisha de la Vatine or Comte de Fossard,' he said. 'Presently a guest of His Majesty at Maidstone Prison, where I'm told the chapel rejoices in the benefit of his rather impressive mural of the Last Supper.'

'And why was he arrested?' asked Jack.

'Because six months ago a young lady died after he'd performed an operation on her. The sort that's expensive, and is usually put down as an appendectomy, if it's put down at all. Mrs Deever, it seems, was one of his luckier clients. He did nose jobs too, apparently.' He drained his glass.

'Mary Rose was pregnant?' said Jill.

'For a while,' said Len. 'This chap has a place in Chelsea. All closed down now, of course. So much more of this kind of thing since the war started. I've sent a few down myself. Abortionists.'

The word, spoken aloud, filled the room with its weight.

'Anyway,' he said, 'the thing I've really come to tell you is that we had to release Captain Deever. He's on bail but we haven't charged him. The case just wasn't strong enough. We found two lies in his testimony, but I'm afraid questioning didn't produce much more. He's pretty good under pressure.'

'Did Patrick know about his wife's trip to Chelsea?' asked Jill.

'Yes,' said Len. 'He said he'd known something was up for a while because he saw the money going out of the bank account. He guessed what it was. You don't get billed for an appendectomy if you had one already when you were a kid. He assumed the child was his, conceived when he was home on leave. But it seems it wasn't. He said he only realized the truth when he found the note she left for him.'

'The crime I committed against him,' quoted Jill. 'That's what she meant. Getting rid of Peter's child.'

'So, we've got no evidence that Captain Deever knew about the affair before Peter's death,' said Len, 'which makes it pretty hard to establish a motive. Which is why he's now sitting at home on his own. Dropped him back there half an hour ago.'

As he said these words, the unobtrusive burble of radio dead air was interrupted by a series of sharp Morse bleeps. Commoner was broadcasting again. For a moment, Jack and Jill stared at each other. Then Jack picked up his notebook and began to transcribe the dots and dashes.

'That one of those code stations?' asked Len.

Jill shushed him with an urgency that took him by surprise. He was even more surprised to be bundled out of the door and told they would see him in the morning. As soon as the door closed, Jack had Maggie Speed's copy of *The Boy Among the Trees* in his hands, matching numbers to words.

'What does it say?' asked Jill.

Jack frowned. The numbers were not working.

'None of this is in the book code,' he said. 'It's indecipherable. It must use the key that we haven't yet found.' He threw down his pencil and notepad. Jill had never seen despair on Jack's face, but she detected it now: a dread shaped by unshareable knowledge gleaned from paper files marked 'for eyes only'.

'Jill,' he said. 'He's stopped taunting us. We can't waste any more time. Tomorrow, we're going to set a trap for this spy. I think it will be extremely dangerous. Is that okay with you?'

'How could it be anything else?' said Jill.

Chapter 32

Although it was further away, Southampton Post Office, they concluded, was a safer proposition than Lymington or Ashurst. Jack would have attracted too much attention at a little branch in a New Forest village. The sub-postmistresses of the district were as thick as thieves with Ivy Hill. As soon as any telegram was sent, they would have been plugging the lines to tell her about the handsome American captain and his funny lists of numbers. The city – and its high Victorian redbrick nerve centre – provided anonymity.

It did not take Jack and Jill very long to construct a message. They were bound by the same limitations that revealed *The Boy Among the Trees* was a decoy, and not the prize. One message would serve for everyone.

84, 15, 800, 350.

As he passed over the telegram form, Jack noticed the clerk behind the window wrinkle her nose at the oddness of the message. His uniform, however, reassured her. Had Jack been a more obviously suspicious character – and her years behind the glass had allowed her to develop a complex taxonomy of such figures – she would have reported him immediately. But his eyes were bright and his teeth were good, neither of which, she felt sure, would be true of a fifth columnist or saboteur.

Jack watched her take down the message, snapped his money on the counter and looked up at the clock on the wall. Half past twelve.

'We don't often see you in here at lunchtime,' said Effie Speed.

Having just taken a bite of cheese roll, Jill found herself unable to respond. 'I just wanted to change my routine a bit,' she said, eventually. 'So easy to get stuck, isn't it?'

Effie cast an eye around the almost empty pub and nodded her agreement. 'I thought you'd just come in to see Captain Strafford,' she said. 'And I said to myself, she's out of luck there, he went off early this morning. Look after the bar for me a moment, would you, Maggie?'

Maggie Speed had walked in through the front door of the pub, holding a magazine with photographs of palm trees on the cover. Her mother kissed her on the cheek and vanished into the back kitchen.

'You should take an outside table, Jill,' said Maggie. 'The summer's almost over.'

It was their first meeting since Maggie's visit to the cottage, and Jill felt burdened by the weight of the girl's confessions. Effie Speed, Jill felt sure, knew nothing of her daughter's complicity in the affair between Peter Brock and Mary Rose Deever. How long, she wondered, would she remain in her sweet state of ignorance?

'I'm fine here,' said Jill. 'I like sitting in the front row.' She hoped that her refusal would not appear strange: it was a gloriously warm late-August day, and the bar was close and stuffy.

'I might join you then,' said Maggie. She grabbed a bottle of lemonade from behind the bar and poured out two glasses. 'Not very cold, I'm afraid,' she said. 'I'd love to go somewhere they put ice in the drinks.'

'They released Captain Deever, you know,' said Jill, taking a glass.

'He's suffered a lot,' said Maggie. She sipped her lemonade. 'But has he suffered enough? That's the question.' Something had changed in her. Her hair was different. She was running her finger around the rim of the glass in a gesture that looked copied from the movies. This, thought Jill, was a young woman in possession of that most exciting form of capital: a heap of dirt on her employers.

Maggie noticed that Jill had a set of papers out on the bar. The transcript of *The Pact Beneath the Trees*.

'She tried so hard, poor Mrs Deever,' said Maggie.

'Why couldn't she get it right, do you think?' asked Jill.

'That first story was a lightning strike,' said Maggie. 'It lit up everything, didn't it? Captured something about the way people felt about the last war, I suppose, and what was lost. But she couldn't make it happen again. I think it was because that first one was about Peter as a child. Then when Peter grew up, her feelings about him changed. And they became something that you couldn't write about. Not in a picture book. It's fine if Mr McGregor wants to put Peter Rabbit in a pie. But you wouldn't want to read about Mrs McGregor getting him into bed, would you? It'd be wrong.'

The pub door rattled open. Sam Hill was standing on the mat holding a small brown envelope.

'It's for your dad,' he said. Maggie snatched the telegram from the postman's hand. Sam complained that he was meant to give it only to the addressee, but Maggie had already been obliged to surrender it to Effie, who, returning from the kitchen, threw her husband's name upstairs. By the time Wally Speed reached the bottom step, however, Effie had already torn open the envelope.

'Is it a bill for something?' she asked, nonplussed. 'I don't like numbers as big as that.'

Wally took it, scanned it and shrugged. 'Means

nothing to me,' he said. 'And I don't know the sender. Must be a crossed wire or something.'

'Any reply?' asked Sam, dutifully, his pencil poised.

'No fear,' said Wally Speed. 'I'm not an abacus.'

Sam took the point, and also his leave.

The bang of the door spurred Jill into action. She gathered up her papers, knocked back her lemonade, climbed off her bar stool, told the Speeds she must be going and picked up the shopping bag she had deposited by the bar.

'Something wrong with that sandwich?' asked Effie. Her tone was not completely friendly.

'No,' said Jill. 'I'm just not that hungry.'

'Wrap it up for you,' said the landlady. It was a statement and not a question.

Jill's eyes moved to the clock on the wall behind the bar. Maggie noticed this impatience but said nothing. A few moments later Effie reappeared with the sandwich cocooned in greaseproof paper.

As she left the Fleur-de-Lys, Jill could see that Maggie Speed was reading the telegram and frowning.

Chapter 33

The midday glare gave Jill a headache. She had slept quite well. Now she felt that she had been up until four drinking gin cocktails. Stress, she supposed; and the next part of the afternoon would be even less relaxing. She looked up at the church clock. She already knew the time, but time was on her mind. She thought of Jack, sitting in Southampton, calculating whether it was the right moment to rejoin the queue for the telegram desk.

Her shopping bag contained the props she needed to modulate a visit to the Larkwhistle branch: a parcel of clothes for Harold's Peterborough cousin; a superfluous telegram message to G.G. Johnston; three brief letters, all quite unnecessary, to staff members at the teacher-training college. She pushed the door and listened to the noise of the bell.

'He's back, I see,' said Ivy as she entered. 'Patrick

Deever. All on his lonesome in that big house. Sam went up there first thing and saw him.'

'Did he speak to him?' asked Jill.

'No, he didn't,' said Sam Hill. He was in the parlour with Martin in his arms.

Jill extracted the parcel from her bag. As she hoped, the process of weighing it was soon interrupted by a flashing light on the switchboard. Ivy plugged in her headset, pulled out a blank telegram form and took dictation from the voice on the other end of the line. Her face twisted like a washcloth. 'Are you sure?' she asked. The voice of a distant GPO colleague gave some unheard reassurance and rang off.

Ivy showed the finished paper slip to Sam.

'It's the same message,' she said.

'Who's it for?' he asked.

'It's for you,' said Ivy.

Sam shifted Martin to his shoulder and peered at the telegram as if it carried a demonic sigil. 'What's this about?' he said. 'Is it a teleprinter fault?' Ivy shook her head. The light on the switchboard flashed again. A moment later Southampton was dictating another message down the line. The same message. This time, however, the sequence of numbers was intended for the eyes of Guy Brock.

Ivy slapped the paper into her husband's hands and took Martin from him. 'Well,' she said, 'don't stand there catching flies – whoever this is, he's paid his sixpence.'

'I'm just on my way to see Guy,' said Jill. 'I could give it to him.'

Sam sucked his teeth in irritation. 'It's not allowed,' he said, without looking at her. 'More than my job's worth.'

Jill concluded her transaction over the parcel as fast as she could and followed Sam through the door. 'Let me walk with you, anyway,' she said. The postman could produce no plausible reason to refuse. Just before the door closed, the light on the switch-board flashed once more. Ivy manoeuvred Martin down to the floor and plugged herself back into the board.

'Message starts,' said the voice on the line from Southampton. '84, 15, 800, 350.'

'I suppose,' said Jill, 'you never know what marriages are until they come undone in public. Most people take their secrets to the grave.' Sam made little attempt to pretend he was interested in her observations. Jill might as well have been a wasp, buzzing at him as he crossed the village green. Even in her excited state, however, she felt faintly aggrieved that he was ignoring her, and yet possessed manners enough to wish good afternoon to the man from the *Echo*, who was sitting outside the Fleur-de-Lys, making notes from a local guidebook.

When they reached the vicarage, Jill knocked on the door.

'He told me one o'clock,' she said, quite untruthfully, 'but he won't mind me being early.'

Guy did not mind because he was not at home. Sam Hill put the telegram back in his satchel.

'Can't you just post it through the door?' asked Jill.

'It's a telegram,' said Sam. 'I hand it to them and then I wait to see if they want to answer.' He tapped the pocket where he kept the paper slips and his pencil, then started to walk back down the path. As he did so, the vicarage door flew open. Simon Pinn was on the other side, looking no happier than when Jill had called the previous day. Helena, she guessed, remained unlocated.

'Sorry about that,' said Simon. 'I was just on the phone.' He noticed the telegram. 'Is it from her?' he asked.

'I've no idea,' said Sam, officiously. 'Private, isn't it? For the Reverend.'

'Then you'd better go to the church,' said the curate.

St Cedd's, however, proved just as silent. For a moment Jill and Sam Hill stood in the nave, observing the light pass through the stained-glass window depicting its dedicated saint. St Cedd was draped in a grass-green chasuble, holding a miniature version of the church in his hands, protecting it from evil.

'If you see the Reverend Brock,' said Sam, 'tell him to come over and collect it.'

Jill nodded. She put down her shopping bag and settled on a pew. The sound of birdsong drifted in through the open door. She thought of all the years that her existence had been entwined with the institution of this church and wondered what it would be like to make a new life somewhere else. She remembered the prayers she had said during the first months of the war, when she had imagined the belltower in ruins and swastika bunting at the village fete. She gazed at Guy Brock's precious hymn board, which he administered so enviously. Envy, she reminded herself, was a sin.

As she looked at the numbers, still on display from Sunday's service, a thought occurred to her. A reckless one.

Jill climbed the steps of the pulpit and rooted in the little box of numeric wooden tiles that was screwed to the wall. If Guy was not going to receive his telegram on time, perhaps the message could be communicated through another medium. She slotted the tiles into their runners and surveyed her work. She did not know the numbers in the English Hymnal off by heart, but fifteen, she recalled from years of Christmas services, was 'O Little Town of Bethlehem'. Even to her, that third line on the board looked out of place; like a reindeer standing on Calvary.

It was at this moment that she heard the sound. It might, she thought, have been made by an animal, or some hunk of Norman timber complaining about a millennium of unacknowledged work. Soon, however, it clarified into a human sob; low, male, drawn deep from the well of suffering. Jill realized that she had heard it before – when the Reverend Guy Brock had cradled the corpse of his son in his arms and cried out to the trees.

He was above her, she reasoned. He was in the belltower.

Chapter 34

Woodlander House had never been quieter. Since being deposited on the doorstep in darkness by Len Creech and his Wolseley, Patrick had spent a lot of his time just listening to the silence. Domestic air untroubled by the *clack-clack-clack* of the Remington. He liked what he heard. He liked what he didn't hear.

The police search had left much of the house in disarray. On his return Patrick had decided to leave the clearing up until the morning. It was now the afternoon. He had discovered some dry crackers in the pantry and, finding no butter or margarine, had spread them with the end of the final jar of last year's plum jam. There was a slightly unpleasant smell in the kitchen. It came from the bones of Sunday dinner that had lain in the bin for two warm days. Patrick tipped them onto the ash heap at the end of the garden. He would have kept the kitchen door open to clear the smell, had there not been so many bluebottles in the air.

He was reading the obituaries in *The Times* when Captain Jack Strafford knocked on the door.

'I hope I'm not disturbing you,' said Jack.

'From what?' asked Patrick. He eyed the jeep parked on his drive. 'Do they really let you gad about the place in that when you're off duty? Very generous.'

They went into the dining room, where both men avoided sitting on the divan. Jack noticed that the pictures of Peter Brock had been turned to the wall.

'Did they treat you well?' asked Jack.

'They didn't charge me, if that's what you mean,' said Patrick. 'They didn't shine a light in my face.'

'Have you heard about an inquest?'

'Monday,' said Patrick. 'Southampton Coroner's Court. Not the Fleur-de-Lys, thank goodness. I should also make some decisions about the funeral. It's hard to hold all these things in your head.'

'Talk to Mr Pinn,' advised Jack. 'He seems a very decent sort of guy.'

'To tell you the truth,' said Patrick, 'I'm a bit worried about how I'm going to pay for it all. Everything is in her name, you see. I'll have to read up on the Married Women's Property Act. I don't think they'll kick me out of here. Depends what the will says, I suppose.' He altered his train of thought. 'Listen, old man, I'm sorry about what I did yesterday. Locking you in. Fighting over that damned portfolio.'

'Really, Patrick, it's fine. You were upset.'

'I damn well was,' said Patrick.

'All that stuff still at the police station, is it?' said Jack.

'I don't want it back,' muttered Patrick.

'I've been thinking about *The Pact Beneath the Trees*,' said Jack. 'It's a good title, but it's a bit of a cheat. There's no pact mentioned in the text. And the style of it worries me. The last page, anyway. Mary Rose didn't like split infinitives, did she?'

'I don't know,' said Patrick, as if this was some impossibly arcane matter.

'Bugbear of hers,' said Jack. 'She told us at dinner. Just before that horribly embarrassing incident with Maggie Speed. You must remember that. I'll certainly never forget it. My toes may never uncurl.'

'Yes,' said Patrick, dully. This was a path he did not wish to follow.

'There are three split infinitives on the last page,' said Jack.

'She wrote it in a great hurry,' said Patrick. 'Late at night.'

'Perhaps she didn't write it,' said Jack, sounding suddenly less convivial. 'Perhaps Maggie wrote it.'

'Maggie most certainly did not write it,' spluttered Patrick. He could hear his own rising panic.

'Has she been here today, Captain Deever?'

'Maggie? No.'

Jack picked up Patrick's copy of *The Times*. 'Anything interesting in the newspaper today, Captain?' he said. 'This is today's edition, isn't it? I suppose you must have bought it from the newsagent by the station.'

Patrick felt the ground of the conversation shift beneath him. He was somewhere in the sand. What else did Jack know? What did he suspect?

'Did you kill Mary Rose, Patrick?' asked Jack.

The question turned Patrick's innards to ice.

'No, I didn't,' he said. 'She did it herself. Over that bloody boy. That's the truth.'

'Is it?' asked Jack.

'It damn well is,' Patrick said. His cigarettes and matches were on the arm of his chair. He lifted the packet, extracted a Capstan Filter with his lips and curled his fingers to take a match and strike it on the sandpaper.

'But you're lying about the story,' said Jack. 'Aren't you?'

Patrick fumbled the match. It jumped from his hand and landed on the carpet. Jack picked it up, took the box from Patrick's hand and struck a little flame.

'Permit me,' he said. Patrick accepted the light.

'Monday, did you say?' asked Jack. 'For the inquest?'

'Yes,' said Patrick, drily.

'Better to tell them the truth,' said Jack, 'because you won't get that lie past the coroner.'

Patrick took a deep breath. Smoke circulated inside him and was then expelled from the corner of his mouth in a long, straight column. He saw the prospect of something before him, like a beach he had to cross to reach a boat that might take him home. But the beach was under fire from the air, and the possibility of taking a bullet was strong. He took a first step.

'I saw the note on the table,' said Patrick, 'and I knew what she'd done. She'd taken herself to that tree. To follow him. I ran out there, down the path. I saw the body in the beam of the torch. She looked odd and unreal, like someone came to the woods to dump a waxwork from a fairground. And I thought: the note isn't good enough. It just sounds like she's leaving me. Not killing herself. And then I thought: has she done this deliberately? To make things difficult?'

'That seems a bit much, Patrick,' said Jack. 'People aren't so malicious.'

'You're young, Captain,' said Patrick. He took another drag. 'I didn't love Rosie anymore and she didn't love me. People don't admit this, but there's a point that comes in a marriage when you just want the other one to die. To have an accident or take some fatal illness and just be gone, without the humiliation of divorce. Or the bother of it all, the dismal bother. So, in a sense I was glad that she'd done it. With her gone, I'd get some sympathy, I'd get silence in the house and maybe even what was left of the estate.'

'But not if you were in jail for her murder,' said Jack. 'And you couldn't destroy that note. Nor could you alter it. So you altered that story instead. It was in the wastepaper basket in the study, I think?'

'Yes,' said Patrick. 'She threw all sorts in there. I used to fish them out and read them sometimes. Her little fantasies and failures. But this one she wrote on the day of Peter Brock's inquest. When I came back from the tree, I realized it was exactly what I needed. Almost exactly. Something that sounded confessional. Something out of her typewriter. That bloody typewriter. So, I sat up for the night. Wrote a new ending. Didn't change too much. And I gave it a title. I was quite pleased with it.'

'If it was in the wastepaper basket,' asked Jack, 'why weren't the pages crumpled?'

'I ironed them,' said Patrick. 'And then I ironed your shirt.'

'Why didn't you give me the story? Like you gave me the shirt?'

'Because I wanted you to find it,' said Patrick. 'I put it in the desk drawer. But then when you opened that awful portfolio, I thought, this is perfect. I'll slip it in there.'

'You tried to destroy that portfolio.'

'I wouldn't have done it. I just needed to get the story inside without you seeing. I thought you'd just kick the door down. You climbing out of the window was a bit of a surprise.'

Jack listened to Patrick take a long, noisy drag from his cigarette.

'Doesn't look great, does it, Patrick?'

'I suppose I'll just have to tell the inquest what I told you. It won't be pleasant, but I won't hang for it, will I? Typing isn't a capital crime.' He looked almost righteous, as if he imagined the coroner would receive this information as a gracious gift.

'Do you think anyone will believe you?' asked Jack. 'Sounds like a lot of bull to me. And if it goes to a jury trial, well. People round here, do they know you used to be a Fascist?'

Patrick had not expected this. 'Well, again, that's not a hanging offence, is it? I had no bother over Regulation 18B. Anyway, if you are called as a witness, Captain Strafford, I'm safe. You're a fine, upstanding chap. And you know what happened. You worked it all out.'

'I have a war to fight,' said Jack. 'I'm supposed to be flying off to Belgium on Monday. I think you're in big trouble.' He paused, giving Patrick the chance to fill the silence with his anxiety. 'Got anything to bargain with?'

Patrick did not reply. He was staring out of the window. Sam Hill was trudging up the drive, his postman's satchel over his shoulder.

'What does *he* want?' said Patrick.

Chapter 35

The tower of St Cedd's was a modest eighteenth-century addition to a church old enough for a listing in the Domesday Book. It did not soar upwards to God in brick, like so many Victorian Gothic spires. The ringers stood on the ground floor, in a wood-panelled space barely big enough to hold the necessary eight. The belfry was reached by an iron ladder bolted to the wall. Jill ascended the ladder.

In the space above, she found a shape on the boards that she quickly recognized as Guy Brock, curled up as if hoping to find himself restored to his mother's womb. His face was turned to the wall; he did not appear to notice her arrival. Her main thought was that she had intruded on something horribly private. Perhaps, she hoped, she might duck down without him ever knowing that she had been there. The notion came too late. Guy sat bolt upright and, seeing Jill, made a slithering retreat into the corner of the belfry, crashing backwards into an old suitcase that had been placed against the wall. Jill noticed ancient dust besmirching his black shirt.

'I'm so sorry, Jill,' he said, tearful and ashamed. His eyes were moving wildly. From his body language, Jill had the sense that there was some object about his person that he did not want her to see. She was struck by the terrible thought that it might be a razor blade; that he might have come to the tower to end his life.

'Guy,' she said, taking the last few rungs of the ladder. 'I do hope you're not thinking of doing anything stupid.'

'I was, actually.' He looked like a small boy who had been detected in a theft.

'Don't you think there's been enough death in Larkwhistle? Enough irreversible decisions? Think of Helena.'

'Helena's gone.'

'This could still kill her.'

'Perhaps I'd like that.'

To Jill's surprise, she found a flame of anger rising in her breast. It was anger about the irrecoverable costs of war; about the time she had lost, the men she had never met, the dinners she had never eaten beside dancefloors upon which she had never danced; about a boy dead in a field in occupied Europe and another on the loam of Hampshire; about the earth scarred and the trees uprooted.

'Pull yourself together, Guy. Remember which side you're on.'

As she said these words, Jill looked towards the bells. They were silent in their wooden frame. Although the wheels that housed them had not turned since the outbreak of war, they stood ready to peal out and declare invasion or victory. There, just a few inches from her face, Jill saw that a word was moulded into the smooth, bronze-alloy body of the tenor bell. It was the name of the foundry in the East End of London from which it had been delivered two hundred years before.

Whitechapel.

Above it, in Gothic script, wrapped like some ancient garland, were lines inspired by Psalm 23 – 'May Peter lead us to the pastures of eternal life.'

It was the key she needed. The key to Commoner's code.

Jill tore her eyes away from the inscription. She thought of Guy's story about his encounter with the Nazi parachutist; his account of the changing phases of deception and pretence. She must not let him see her new knowledge. Commoner would have no have qualms about killing. Murder at the top of a belltower did not seem the hardest job in the world.

'Look,' she said, scrabbling for the appearance of

cheerfulness, 'don't despair. There's a telegram for you at the Post Office. I was there when it arrived. Sam Hill has been looking for you. He wants to put it into your hand. Those are the rules, you see. It might be from Helena.'

Something not entirely unlike hope flickered in Guy Brock's eyes. 'A few days out of the village might be what she needed to clear her head,' continued Jill. 'Perhaps you've been here too long. Perhaps a new parish might do you both good?'

Guy raised himself from the corner of the belfry and made an unfocused attempt to dust himself off. When Jill invited him to descend the ladder, he obeyed. It was like watching a drunk trying to sober up.

'You've been married so long,' she said. 'It's got to be worth trying to save it.'

'Twenty-one years. We met in Trafalgar Square. She was carrying a banner. We went to a Corner House and talked about T. S. Eliot. This was right at the start of the Thirties, of course. One of her cousins was at the International Lenin School in Moscow. We thought she was going to come back and lead the English revolution.' He gave a bitter little smile. 'By 1944, I thought we'd all be lying around in togas quoting Dante, with airships flying overhead. What a joke, eh?'

Jill tried to picture this meeting of young radicals. The mention of Eliot had caused something to click in her head. She recalled the section of *The Waste Land* that retold the story of Philomel, defiled, mutilated, transformed into a nightingale, singing *jug jug jug jug jug jug* in the darkness.

They were back on the ground. Guy opened the door of the church to let Jill pass through. The sunshine was bright. One dragonish cloud rolled in the sky.

'I forgot my shopping bag,' said Jill. 'You go and collect your message. I hope it's good news, Guy. You need some of that.'

Had she persuaded him? Did he know that she had seen the words on the tenor bell, and understood their meaning?

Jill watched him take a few steps towards the lychgate, then turned back towards the church. In the bottom of her shopping bag were her notes of the previous night's radio transmissions. Her heart pounding, she extracted the paper, put her pencil between her teeth and scaled the ladder to the belfry. She had, she reckoned, five minutes to check her theory. She set her paper down on the lid of the old suitcase and wrote out the alphabet in a column. Next, she took the inscription on the bell, and ran it down the page in parallel, missing out the repeated letters. M became A, A became B, Y became C, P became D.

Strings of Morse numbers harvested from the air became coherent and unambiguous messages between a spy and his masters. She scratched away with her pencil.

'Blieu one division. Stny X ten planes on ground.'

She had seen enough. The rest could wait. She shoved the suitcase back into position. As she did so, she heard something metallic rattle inside. When she flipped open the catches, she saw the object for which she and Jack had been searching since his arrival in Larkwhistle. A portable radio set. She recognized the Morse tapper, a midget transmitter with input and output sockets, a blocky grey battery pack. It looked like equipment from the lab at college, except it carried no names or trademarks. Even the valve – clearly not of British design – had been denuded of identifying marks.

Jill closed the lid, pushed the case back against the wall and felt a sick lurch in her stomach as she hurried down the iron ladder back to the ringing chamber at the base of the tower.

The church was silent.

She tried to bring her breathing under control. Anyone walking in now would think she had just run the hundred-yard dash. She slumped down on the pew and pushed the paper into the recesses of her shopping bag, safe from prying eyes.

'It wasn't from Helena,' said Guy Brock.

He was standing in the doorway of the church, the telegram crumpled in his fist.

'Oh,' said Jill, as blithely as she was able. 'Who was it from, then?'

'Nobody I could identify,' said Guy. 'Very strange message, too. Just numbers.'

'Oh,' said Jill, much less convincingly, she felt sure. She got to her feet and hoisted her shopping bag onto her shoulder. Had they, she wondered, now reached the moment when both parties know that the other is dissembling but have yet to reveal it to each other? She moved towards the door.

Guy was looking towards the pulpit. He was reading the numbers on the board. 'The Son of God Goes Forth to War,' he said. 'I can't abide that hymn. "A noble army, men and boys, the matron and the maid, around the Saviour's throne rejoice, in robes of light arrayed." Jingoistic claptrap.'

The change in his eyes told Jill that the moment had come. He had recognized his own code and deciphered it.

'Is this a message for me?' he asked. He was moving towards her with more purpose than she might have wished.

'Guy,' said Jill, her heart in her mouth, 'can I ask you something about the night you met that German parachutist? You were fighting with him, yes? And you called for help, and the gun went off just as people arrived from the village?'

'Yes,' said Guy.

'Dad came running, too. And thinking about it now, I wonder whether you were fighting before you heard those other people getting to the scene? Maybe you shot that parachutist deliberately. Because you didn't want to be exposed. You knew he was going to be captured, and you didn't trust him not to squeal. You killed that man to save yourself.'

Guy nodded, as if he had just been offered a fair account of some contentious academic subject. 'I knew you were up to something, you and Captain Strafford,' he said. 'Fooling about with tombstones. Meeting in corners. I knew you weren't just interested in Peter. One little death isn't enough for your man Jack, is it? He needs a bigger case than a dead boy in the woods.'

The mention of his son's name seemed to exhaust him. Some fire within him seemed to dwindle, as if he realized that he could no longer evade the power of the wartime state. Jill watched him closely. Was this a trick?

'Will they hang me?' he asked.

'I don't think so,' said Jill. 'A double agent might be useful, even at this stage of the war.'

He seemed to mull the idea over, trying to imagine offering himself as a recruit.

'No,' he said. 'They will hang me. Treason. Espionage. Aiding and abetting the enemy.' He heaved a great sigh. 'But they won't hang me before they hang Patrick Deever.'

'Patrick's been released,' said Jill.

The news hit Guy Brock like a comet. They were standing by the font. He reached out his hand to steady himself, almost overturning the Paschal candle mounted beside it.

'But I thought . . .' he stuttered. 'Wasn't he charged?'

'Arrested. Len Creech thought the case was weak.'

'So, he's just back home?' said Guy. 'Sitting in that big house? With Peter's picture on the wall?'

'Yes,' said Jill, quietly.

'Do you think he killed him?'

'We have to let the law take its course.'

Guy Brock looked back at the hymn board.

'What do you think that message means?' he asked.

'You know what it means,' replied Jill.

'Say it,' said Guy. His voice had a dangerous edge.

'It says, "You have been careless,"' said Jill.

'I don't think it was for me after all,' said Guy.

His hand reached for the Paschal candle, which he swung into the air and brought down upon Jill's skull with a *crack*.

Chapter 36

Sam Hill had come to Woodlander House with no intention of crossing the threshold. However, he now found himself standing in the middle of the dining room. He gazed at the bookshelves, the pristine paint-work, the pattern on the expensive Turkey carpet beneath his feet. He wondered why Jack was there, sitting in one of the armchairs, observing the scene with silent keenness.

'Your telephone line's out of order,' said Sam.

'I tore it from the wall,' said Patrick. 'Reporters, you know.'

'You should watch your temper,' said Sam. He offered the envelope.

'What's this?' asked Patrick.

'Open it and look. They've been coming in all morning. For you, for Wally, for Guy Brock. For me. All the same. What's it mean?'

Patrick obeyed. He filleted the envelope and pulled out the paper inside. His eyes moved over the four numbers with an expression of unease. Not, Jack felt sure, the unease of recognition and discovery, but of panic and bafflement.

'Any answer?' asked Sam Hill.

'No,' said Patrick.

'I think I just received one,' said Jack. 'And I can give you one, too. Neither of you know what these numbers mean, do you? Eighty-four. Fifteen. Eight hundred. Three hundred and fifty.' Jack saw both men stiffen slightly. Some instinct from their Army training was reasserting itself. They looked like members of a platoon, responding to a question from a commanding officer. Responding with a negative.

'That's good,' said Jack. 'That clears you of one capital crime. But you're both still in the frame for another. Maybe two. So, let's get through this together, shall we? Like men.'

Sam and Patrick exchanged nervous glances. Jack reached into his jacket pocket and produced a cream-coloured envelope. From this he drew the charred paper with leaves and flowers in the margin.

'This is a little piece of the diary of Peter Brock,' he explained. 'His father burned it because among all the boring village details is an account of his son's sexual life. It's Peter's little system for noting which of your wives he was sleeping with on any given day. As you can see, there's a lot of verdure.'

It was clear that neither Patrick nor Sam had seen the page before. It was equally clear that neither required an explanation of its meaning.

'Peter Brock was having an affair with Rosie,' said Jack. 'Did you know that, Sam?'

'Yes,' said Sam Hill. 'Yes, I did.'

'And Peter Brock was also having an affair with Ivy,' said Jack. 'Did you know that, Patrick?'

'No,' breathed Patrick, staring at the burnt page as if he expected to see the leaves and flowers move over the paper. 'No, I did not.' The answer hung in the air like gun smoke.

'Yes,' said Jack. 'Another thing you might not know. This wasn't a trivial business. It produced a child. Peter Brock was Martin's father. Changes the picture a bit, I think, if you're at the wrong end of a police investigation and you suddenly see that your best friend has just a strong a motive as you.'

'It does,' conceded Patrick. He shifted his eyes to Sam. They did not express comradeship.

'I'm very interested,' said Jack, 'in how knowledge circulates in Larkwhistle. How things get around. Gossip in the Copper Kettle. Remarks passed between the pews in St Cedd's. A GPO telephonist can't help picking up the odd thing, can she, Sam? When she puts you through. When she checks the line. But some things must be written down, mustn't they? Official matters. Personal matters. Some people send their personal communications under plain brown wrap if they don't want to arouse suspicion. Some even enclose pre-addressed envelopes to make the replies look innocuous. So innocuous they could give all this stuff to their husband to put in the mail, and he'd be none the wiser. Unless, of course, he had a friend with access to the contents of the post box, and no qualms about opening the odd envelope or two. Even if he was the sort of friend who doesn't tell you something, if he thinks he can use it to his advantage.'

'That's a very serious accusation, Captain Strafford,' said Sam Hill. He sounded neither angry nor surprised, as if the charge had been levelled against some absent stranger.

'Patrick, did you get an answer about that position in Southampton?' asked Jack.

'No,' said Patrick. 'They haven't replied.'

'What was the position?'

'That doesn't matter.'

'It's not a bad job for an ex-officer. Especially if you like the movies.'

Sam Hill narrowed his eyes. 'Bit of a bastard, really, aren't you, sir?'

'Keep in line, Sergeant Hill,' said Jack. 'Patrick,

Detective Inspector Creech tells me that you knew about Mary Rose's expensive visit to Chelsea to see a man named George Vatine.'

'I didn't know the name,' said Patrick. 'I just knew that she'd gone.'

'How did you know?' pressed Jack.

'Because it cost fifty pounds,' he answered.

'An amazing piece of knowledge,' said Jack, 'given that her financial affairs are a closed book to you, and she hid the letter from the bank in a place you never found it. Not so amazing if you happen to know a crooked postman with a steam kettle who's feeding you all kinds of titbits about your wife's infidelities.'

Patrick was looking at Jack as if he were a bright light that hurt his eyes. Jack did not decrease his glare. 'Maybe he was keeping you in the pub sometimes, knowing that your wife was here with Peter Brock, in this room, on that divan, artist and model. Maybe he was telling you the times and places of assignations so you could be there to spy? Maybe, one morning, he stopped a message from the lover getting through to the wife, so that while she was tapping away on her typewriter upstairs, you were by that tree, the tree on the cover of that book, waiting for that lover to arrive. Did you want to have it out with him, Patrick? Or did you want to kill him?'

Patrick blinked. 'Got there too late, didn't I?' He could feel himself sinking into the sand. 'Got there too late to stop him blowing his own brains out.'

'But he didn't blow his own brains out,' said Jack. 'Did he, Sam?'

Sam Hill did not reply. He was looking around the room; looking from the window to the hallway; looking at the two men beside him; looking at the revolver in Jack's belt. For a moment it appeared that he might make a run for it. His limbs seemed sufficiently tense. But the calculation produced a hopeless answer; one that involved a US Air Force captain firing a shot before he could turn a handle or lift a latch.

'What are you going to do?' asked Sam.

'I'd phone the police if Patrick hadn't ripped that cable out of the wall,' said Jack. 'That being the case, I think we're going to take a walk to the Post Office.'

He removed his gun from its holster and pointed it in the direction of the two men. They walked ahead of him, through the front door, down the path and into the forest. The gun felt like a formality. Neither prisoner seemed inclined to go running off into the bracken. Patrick was mostly silent, Sam content with the occasional burst of sceptical insolence; his rehearsal for the trial.

'You got any evidence for all this?' he said. 'My gun got stolen. What does that prove?'

'It wasn't stolen,' corrected Jack. 'It was reported missing. By you.'

'But nobody saw it for a fortnight,' said Sam. 'Not

till it turned up under that tree. Underneath that dead boy. He killed himself. His parents said he was the type.'

'His parents said he was sad and they didn't know why,' said Jack. 'Maybe he was sad because he knew he had a son that you were bringing up as your own.'

Sam glared at Jack with wounded fury, but circumstance had no use for it.

Guy Brock had appeared.

He was running towards them from the village, and not in an entirely straight line. Jack expected an angry statement; an accusation that he would then be asked to act upon. As Guy came closer, however, it was clear that he had moved far beyond such considerations. His shirt was drenched with sweat. He was desperate and burning with animal rage.

Without any kind of preamble, Guy hurled the weight of his entire body at Patrick Deever and sent him tumbling backwards into the bracken. Patrick did his best to fight back, but Guy's fury was overwhelming. He smashed at one side of Patrick's face with his fist, then punched him in the mouth, cutting his knuckles in the process. Then, placing one hand on Patrick's throat, the vicar of Larkwhistle gave a violent tug to Patrick's artificial arm, wrenching it off at the elbow. For a moment Guy looked at it dumbly, noting its hinges and articulations. He hurled it into the ferns.

A more dreadful idea of revenge suggested itself to him.

'Eye for an eye, Patrick,' rasped Guy. And with a thumb and forefinger, he reached towards Captain Deever's face and plucked his glass eye from its socket. He did not stop to examine it. He threw it into the undergrowth.

Patrick, fearing that Guy might be about to rob him of his remaining eye, began to thrash and kick like an electric eel in a net, and succeeded in unbalancing his attacker. He staggered upwards, then lost his balance and fell again. Guy Brock bellowed at him like a bear, then gasped and snorted, before rolling onto his back and lying among the leaves, gazing upwards. Snot and saliva streamed down his face.

Jack was standing over him, pointing his gun directly at his head.

'No more of that, please, Guy,' he said.

'He killed Peter,' the Reverend gasped.

'I don't think it was him,' said Jack.

'Jill didn't agree with you,' said Guy.

'Where is she?'

'She found me in the church,' Guy continued. 'And then I found her. Found her out, I mean. I realized that she knew. And you know. About the radio. About the messages. About my efforts. My peace efforts. And that's that, isn't it? Played the game and lost, didn't I? That's war, I suppose. So, I smashed her skull with a candlestick and came to find Patrick.'

'You did *what*?' asked Jack. His eyes were glacial.

His finger was on the trigger of the gun. 'I hope she's okay, Guy. I hope you haven't done anything stupid.'

'Oh, I've done lots of stupid things,' said Guy. 'I used to want to stop the war. Did my bit for that. Then I wanted both sides to lose. Tried my best there, too. But now I don't care. It's all the damned same, whether there's a George flag or a swastika flying on my church.'

His eyes moved upwards to look at the light moving in the canopy above. The leaves were threshing and shifting in the summer air. 'The Forest doesn't care,' he said. 'Look at it. The trees get us all in the end. Our blood and our bones. They wrap their roots around us and take everything. All they have to do is wait.'

Guy reached sideways into the bracken. Jack assumed he was trying to get to his feet. He wasn't. The Reverend Brock made a sudden and effortful lunge, and a long pale object came swinging upwards from the ferns, knocking the revolver out of Jack's hand.

The object was Patrick Deever's prosthetic arm.

The gun discharged as it hit the ground, sending it jumping like a cricket and a bullet burrowing hotly into the soil. The blast rang in Guy's ears. The gun had fallen close to him. He clawed it from the ground, dragged himself to his feet and crashed backwards through the undergrowth until his back came into contact with the nearest tree. It was the great fir tree that Mary Rose Deever had captured in pen and ink; the tree under which his son had been robbed of his life.

Guy pressed himself against the bark and took in the sight before him. Jack Strafford, approaching him, saying something that might have been placatory and generous if Guy could have heard him over the ringing in his ears. Patrick Deever, on his knees in the bracken, his face bloody and swollen, one eye socket pink and exposed. Sam Hill, standing like a man caught at a crossroads more profound than a fork in the path between Larkwhistle and Brockenhurst, poised to run, but rooted to the spot. Why was he hesitating?

Then Guy saw them. His parishioners. Forming a human barrier that blocked the path to the village green. *Mob* is not a nice word, but it is the one we use when birds make a temporary alliance against a hawk, and thrushes, crows, sparrows and chaffinches swoop and spit at a common enemy. And it is there, of course, at the start of *mobilize*, a word that, in those days of war, was rarely off people's lips. Larkwhistle had, in some sense, been long prepared for this moment – but it had anticipated a Nazi invasion from the sky, not a hunt for a member of its own community.

Guy knew them all. The Speeds from the Fleur-de-Lys. Pam Sharp, who had once asked his advice after her heart had been broken by a GI from Rochester, NY. Mrs Alder, who was so good and kind to Helena, even when she patronized her unformed thoughts on nineteenth-century fiction. Simon Pinn, that simple man who could see God in the movement of a dragonfly above a ditch on a summer's day. The butcher, whose Fascist tie pin he had noticed during the Munich Crisis. He had felt mild disapproval of that tie pin. The irony did not escape him.

Harold Metcalfe and Mrs Brunton were in the front ranks of the group. Guy thought of the hours he'd spent in their comfortable little sitting room, exchanging parish gossip or gloomy views on the state of English cricket; saying prayers in the hope that Michael Brunton would be found safe and well in a POW camp somewhere in Axis territory. Beside them was Ivy Hill, with Martin in her arms. The boy was looking at the faces of the people, the restless leaves and branches and the endless headland of clouds and sky and air. And he was smiling.

Guy tried to focus on the boy; the son of his son. Beads of sweat, however, were stinging his eyes. He wiped a hand across his face and peered again, but someone was standing in the way.

He was looking into the eyes of Jill Metcalfe, whom he had left for dead. The mark of his violence was livid and purplish on her temple. She was shaky, dizzy, disorientated, bloodied, utterly determined.

Guy raised his gun.

Jill moved forwards, into its range and towards Jack, holding herself with a startling air of defiance, staring down the barrel of the revolver.

'He's Commoner,' said Jill. She winced with pain. Her skull was throbbing. 'It's him. Those words. They were the beginning of an inscription on a bell. From the Whitechapel foundry. I cracked the code. It all works out. Then he tried to crack me. You couldn't do it though, could you, Guy?'

Jack absorbed the information as calmly as he could. 'You can't shoot your way out of this, Guy,' he said. 'I only put in two rounds. You've got one left.'

The shriek of the bullet had not quite vanished from Guy's ears, but Jack's words were perfectly clear to him. It was time to ask the most important question. The last question. He raised the gun and pointed it at Sam Hill.

'Did you do it, Sam?' he asked. 'Did you kill Peter?'

From the distance came the wail of sirens. Ivy Hill had done her work: women on switchboards in Sub-Post Offices across the New Forest were tracking the progress of ambulances and police cars over the hills and B roads.

'Sam?' she said, her voice low and sonorous. '*Sam?*'

Her husband said nothing; did nothing. He did not shake his head. He did not nod. He did not protest. He did not deny the charge. Ivy began to weep. It was all the answer that Guy Brock needed.

'I hope you hang for it,' said Guy.

He levelled the gun at Sam, then turned it, placing the barrel against the side of his own head. His finger trembled on the trigger. He imagined the villagers would recoil. Some, he thought, might even urge him to do the deed and get it over with. He did not expect Jill Metcalfe to move towards him; to sit down beside him on the moss and leaf mould at the foot of the old fir.

'Don't do it, Guy.' Jill leant back against the dark body of the tree. 'You've blessed me. You've ministered to me. You've said so many prayers for me. You buried my brother. You've done so much for this village. You could still do more.'

'She's right,' said Jack. 'The bombs that are coming here, you could help to frustrate them. Put things right. It's not too late.'

'It's never too late,' said Jill. 'Help your country. Help this village. Help *us*.'

For a moment, she thought she had persuaded him.

Then he closed his eyes and pulled the trigger.

Jill's ears rang with the shot, like the bells of St Cedd's.

As the gun discharged, a shout of shock and alarm went up among her neighbours. Harold and Mrs Brunton ran to the body to administer first aid, though they knew it was pointless. Jill thought she would feel compelled to turn away from the sight of Guy Brock's lifeless body, but squeamishness eluded her. The impact of the bullet had thrown him backwards into the bracken, and his blood had gone with him. When Jack rushed to her side, he saw there was scarcely a mark on her. He wrapped her up in his jacket. He spoke to her, but the song of the bullet drowned out everything.

Effie Speed ushered her family and the book club ladies back down the path towards the green, out of the way of the police officers and stretcher-bearers. Simon Pinn sat down and wept. Ivy wept too, and when Sam held out his arms to embrace her and their son, she did not resist. Sam pressed his face against Martin's head and inhaled deeply. Patrick Deever stood to attention, his shoulders uneven and his raw and empty eye socket closed, as if awaiting orders from a superior.

Len Creech, when he arrived, was senior enough.

'The last march, Sam?' said Patrick.

'I'm done marching,' said Sam Hill.

'Do you wish you'd let me drown?'

'No, sir,' said Sam. 'Because I'd have drowned too. And then I would never have met my son.'

The cuffs clicked around their wrists, and Len Creech and a pair of constables escorted them down the track.

Jill watched the ambulance crew carrying Guy Brock's covered body down the path. The howl in her ears was beginning to recede. 'He nearly killed me,' she said. 'When he knew that I knew who he was. *What* he was.'

'He was a spy,' said Jack.

'I know,' said Jill. 'And who knows how many deaths he caused. Ones we don't even know about. But he's been part of my life for twenty years. It just makes me feel I can't be certain of anything.'

'Yes, you can,' said Jack. He threw his arms around her. She rested her head on the soft serge of his jacket and closed her eyes. She had seen enough. Now she wanted to hear the singing of the birds, the music of the trees. She wanted Jack. Her hands searched out his shoulders, the warmth of his throat, the line of his neck.

The end of Jill's meeting with Guy in St Cedd's would always remain unclear to her, as if the important details had been padlocked inside some obscure part of her head. She remembered steeling herself for an outburst of violence, but not quite believing that Guy would go through with it: this was a man in whom she had observed selflessness, sensitivity, the tenderest pastoral care. She remembered the cold flagstones beneath her cheek and the view, from that position, towards the presbytery, and feeling that she was lucky to be alive. She remembered the strong conviction that she must get to Woodlander House as soon as possible, knowing that Guy was on his way there with fury in his heart, and that Jack would be there to receive him. There was nothing, however, to help her connect these impressions with what followed. Others did that for her, through observation, deduction and a fair amount of guesswork.

She knew that when she had turned her head, she had seen the body of a man splayed on the floor nearby; that his jaw was broken and that he appeared to have fallen and hit his head on the font; that he was dead. In the months to come, the rest of the story would be presented to her in a series of testimonies, a drawing made by the police pathologist and a number of lengthy newspaper articles. They told of Guy Brock being interrupted by the arrival of a third party, who tackled him in order to prevent further injury to Jill; a man who took a heavy blow to the chin from the candlestick, which had the effect of pitching him backwards towards the hard, unyielding marble of the seventeenth-century font. He was killed instantly.

The details were reported in vivid prose – most vividly, perhaps, on the pages of the *Echo*, which saluted the courage of its chief reporter across several pages of the Saturday edition and ended its appreciation with a substantial quote from Jill:

'I did not know the name of Mr Meredith Evans when he saved my life in the church at Larkwhistle. My gratitude to him is profound. As profound as my regret that he lost his life in the commission of this selfless act, and that his was not the only death on that dark day in the history of our village.'

Chapter 37

Early the next morning a man arrived in Larkwhistle who might have been taken for an emissary of Death, had Death been the sort to send his representatives out by bicycle. He came bearing news for Maggie Speed, with a raven-wing flap of his frock coat tails and a stack of legal documents, in the event that she or her parents refused to believe that news without written evidence.

'Copyright is a phantom commodity,' he explained, as Maggie sat on a stool in the Fleur-de-Lys, hoping that the visitor would not register the sticky line of yeast that ran beneath the lip of the bar.

'Australia?' she questioned. 'And India? And America?'

The solicitor nodded. 'Mrs Deever's book sells well in these territories,' he said. 'It remains to be seen, of course, whether the sad end of her life will depress those sales or amplify them. The reading public can be fickle.'

Some of these words were directed at Jack, who realized that he had been assumed to be a member of the family. He was eating his porridge at a table in the public bar, his kit bag leaning against the table leg.

'The details are here,' said the solicitor, passing Maggie a pair of letters fixed with a paper clip. 'If you would like any further explanation or clarification then please don't hesitate to call on the office in Brockenhurst. Though of course you may also ask your own legal advisors to contact us on your behalf. I imagine they may want to do that.'

'I imagine they may,' said Maggie, imagining that such people existed.

'You will see that Mrs Deever has also assigned you the rights to any unpublished work by her. I'm sorry to say that this seems to be a worthless codicil, as no unpublished work has been discovered and she certainly did not file any manuscript material with us. But I suppose if any turns up one day, then that might provide you with further sums.' He smiled. 'Bit of a one-trick pony, wasn't she?'

'I suppose so,' said Maggie.

'Well,' he said, 'just sign those two documents in the presence of two witness – *not* your parents, I hasten to add – and bring them to the office at your earliest convenience.' He folded up his reading glasses and slipped them back into his pocket.

'We can ask Jill, can't we?' said Maggie.

'I'm sure she'd be happy to oblige,' said Jack. 'I'm going over there in a moment. To say goodbye.'

'And I must also take my leave,' said the solicitor.

'Would you like a pint before you go, sir?' asked Wally Speed. His hand was already on one of the better glasses.

'No, thank you very much,' said the solicitor. 'I must convey some sad news to a gentleman in Sway, who, it seems, is not in fact the inheritor of a Malaysian rubber plantation.'

As the door banged shut, the Speeds began to celebrate. Wally Speed wrapped his wife up in his arms and danced around the saloon. It was only when they stopped that they realized their daughter had gone back upstairs.

Maggie was kneeling next to her bed. She reached underneath and dragged out a scuffed suitcase that had belonged to her maternal grandmother. It bore luggage transfer stickers from places that Maggie had never visited. Some old linen was stored inside. She decanted this onto the bed. Underneath was a foolscap file. She lifted it out in triumph. It contained a thick typescript bearing the name Mary Rose Deever.

'All right, madam,' said Maggie. 'We'll see if lightning doesn't strike twice.'

Harold Metcalfe had tact. He also had a dog that needed its morning walk. Knowing the hour of Jack's departure, he and Wimsey made a diplomatic withdrawal. Harold climbed over the stile into the woods with self-conscious certitude: murder would not colonize his pleasures. Wimsey skittered ahead down the path. That, thought Harold, was the right attitude.

Jill was disappointed, therefore, when she saw Jack walking down the path accompanied. She'd expected him to be carrying his kit bag, but not for Maggie Speed to be beside him. She put the kettle on for three.

'I talked to Ivy Hill this morning,' said Maggie.

'Oh yes,' said Jill. 'How is she doing?'

'Seemed fine to me. She's like nylon. Stuff rolls off her. You know what she said about Mrs Deever: "I kept mine and she killed hers, so I won."'

'Good grief,' said Jill.

'She'd never say that to you,' said Maggie. 'You're too refined.'

Jill's refinement, Maggie explained, was the reason for her presence in the kitchen. She pulled the documents from her case and placed them on the table. 'I was hoping you'd oblige,' she said.

'Maggie,' said Jack, 'you went to see Patrick Deever the morning after he was released from police custody, didn't you?'

Maggie looked shifty. 'To take him his newspaper.'

'Anything else?'

'To tell him that the end of that story wasn't by Mrs Deever,' she said.

'Was he surprised to hear that?' asked Jack.

'He was surprised that I knew,' she said.

'Split infinitives?' asked Jill, looking up from the letter.

'Oh yes,' said Maggie. 'It was also her reading it to me a couple of days before. A different version. Somebody beat me to the bin, you see.'

'Why didn't you say so?' asked Jill. 'We could have gone to Patrick together. Or sent the police to sort him out.'

'I was just thinking about what Mrs Deever used to say. About me being better than Larkwhistle. So, I went to him. To do a deal, you might say.'

'To blackmail him,' said Jack.

Maggie shook her head. 'I just wanted some money to go away.'

'Well,' said Jill, putting down the document. 'You've got it now.'

She signed the paper and passed it to Jack.

'What about your parents?' she asked.

'What about them?'

'I'm sure they care about you,' said Jill. 'I'm sure they love you.'

'Maybe,' said Maggie. 'But they can't see further than the end of the bar. They'll die behind it. And Dad will go first. He's had a few near misses. He goes grey and palpitates. I used to think, *Good, let him go, this'll free me from this place.* And I felt bad about that, wishing him dead so I might inherit a bit of money to get out.'

Maggie took the signed document and returned it to her case. She was ready to leave. 'I used to dream of running away with Peter,' she said. 'But when he died that put paid to that. Then when Mrs Deever died and you showed me that story, I thought, *I don't have to wish death on my dad anymore.* So that's good, isn't it?'

Jill did not know what to say, so she said, 'Send us a postcard.'

'I'm only going to Southampton. Mrs Brock got in touch. I'm going to stay with her for a few days. She's living in the Elmfield Flats by the P&O landing. But when peace comes, who knows?'

Jack and Jill watched the gate close behind Maggie. They stood together at the kitchen window, following her progress across the green towards the railway station.

'She's at the start of her story,' said Jack. 'Leaving this village. Going out into the world. What's going to happen to her?'

'I think she'll be all right,' said Jill. 'Possibly too all right.'

'What about you, Jill?' A soft, serious note had entered his voice. 'What's your story? Where are you going? Are you going to pack a case and say goodbye to this place?'

'I love it here, Jack. This is my place.'

'Oh,' said Jack. 'I was going to suggest a dramatic

exit. There are trials to come. The war's not done with us. More bombs will fall, but Guy won't be helping to target them. And one day soon, they'll stop. Paris will be free in days. The rest of Europe must follow. When that happens, Jill, would you come home with me? Would you come with me to America?'

It was a beautiful offer, but it felt like an act of cruelty. 'I can't do that,' she said. 'Pull me up by the roots, and you'll kill me.'

'Well,' he said, with a sigh. 'That's that, I suppose.'

'I suppose,' said Jill. She stared straight across the green. She was willing herself not to cry. Jack was standing behind her. He was so close she could smell his hair cream. She imagined herself on her own, remembering its perfume.

'What's the soil like round here?' he asked. 'I hear it's terrible.'

'Pretty terrible,' said Jill. 'Gravelly. Too dry in summer. Too wet in winter. But we thrive.'

What would happen, she thought, if she turned to face him?

'Shall I tell you my story?' asked Jack.

'Please do,' she said. Her heart was racing.

'Well,' said Jack. 'I suppose it's about a simple American farm boy . . .'

'From the Philadelphia Main Line?'

'A simple farm boy from the Philadelphia Main Line,' he continued, 'who came across the sea to fight.

He made a friend and lost him, then met his sister. And something happened.'

'What happened?'

'Oh,' he said, 'he fell in love with her. But it was difficult. They had a job to do. A dangerous job. There was another boy who died, you see. And they had to find out what happened.'

'Sounds a bit sad,' she said. 'There's so much death in it.'

'It happened during the war. There's a lot of death in wars.'

'Is it a war story?'

'I don't think so. Some other kind.'

'Which kind?'

'It's a romance.'

'The kind that ends with a kiss?' asked Jill. 'And a glowing mist, and two hearts entwined under the heavens and an embrace that takes the breath of their souls and sends it dancing?'

'Sounds a bit over the top,' said Jack. 'Have you read it?'

'No.'

'I thought not, because that's not how it ends. That's how it begins.'

She turned round to face him. They gazed at each other, poised in the moment before a great event.

'Is it a long story?' she asked.

'I see no reason,' said Jack, 'why it should ever end.'

Acknowledgements

Jack and Jill went up the hill from the offices of Eagle Eye Drama, where Walter Iuzzolino and Jo McGrath are my closest partners in crime. It was a pleasure to be guided through the woods by Katherine Armstrong at Simon & Schuster – and to have the details of the journey checked so carefully by Georgie Leighton and Charley Chapman.

Tig Finch, New Forest native, and Luke Mulhall, New Forest explorer, were my guides to the territory and marked my homework. (Remaining errors are of course mine.) John Leete's *The New Forest at War* (revised and updated, 2014), the New Forest Heritage Centre in Lyndhurst and St Nicholas Church, Brockenhurst were invaluable sources of information. My agent Simon Trewin provided the support and reassurance he has given me for twenty-five years. But my deepest thanks are for Nicola, Freddie and Connie, who are always in the woods with me.